Pumpkin Spice Peril

Jenn McKinlay

BERKLEY PRIME CRIME
New York

BERKLEY PRIME CRIME
Published by Berkley
An imprint of Penguin Random House LLC
penguinrandomhouse.com

ISBN: 9780451492654

First Edition: April 2020

Printed in the United States of America
1   3   5   7   9   10   8   6   4   2

Cover art by Jeff Fitz-Maurice
Book design by Laura K. Corless

For two of the best readers
a writer could ever ask for:
Kelly Vaiman and Risa Lindquist

ACKNOWLEDGMENTS

Thanks to my team for making my books sparkle and shine: Kate Seaver and Christina Hogrebe for their invaluable input and editorial acumen, as well as Jessica Mangicaro and Brittanie Black for their genius with marketing and publicity. As always, things would fall apart without Stacy Edwards, and there's always a gasp of delighted gratitude for Jeff Fitz-Maurice for his fabulous covers.

Many thanks to my family and friends for their years of support and encouragement. I am so very lucky to have you all in my life, especially as I plunder your lives for material. Because . . . writer!

One

"Hi, how can I help you?" Angie Harper asked the customer across the bakery counter. She had her lips pulled back in what should have been a smile but looked like a grimace instead.

Melanie Cooper glanced at her partner. Angie sounded odd, as if she were forcing herself to be friendly when what she really wanted to do was reach across the counter and rip the person's head off. Judging by the wary gaze of the customer, they weren't buying the show of teeth, either.

"You okay there, Ange?" Mel asked.

"Yes, of course, why wouldn't I be?" Angie frowned. Her long curly dark hair was pulled back in a knot at the nape of her neck. She was dressed in her usual bright pink apron over a tank top and jeans, and she plopped her hands on her hips as if spoiling for a fight.

Mel raised her hands in the air. "Just getting a vibe, an unhappy vibe, and I'm willing to step in if you need a sec."

"Why would I need a sec? I'm fine, totally fine!" Angie insisted.

"Then why are you yelling?" Mel asked.

"This isn't yelling!"

"Not for nothing, but over on this side of the counter it sounds like yelling," said the customer, a thirty-something man in khaki slacks, sandals, and a festive Hawaiian shirt that was a rowdy repeating pattern of orange hibiscus blossoms and blue macaws. In other words, loud.

"I'm *so* sorry," Angie said. It would have worked as an apology, except she said it in an exaggerated voice that made it clear she wasn't sorry at all.

The customer glanced from her to Mel. "Maybe you can help me. I'd like some red velvet cupcakes, please."

"Oh, sure, get someone else to help you," Angie said. "Because I'm incompetent, is that it? Is that what you're trying to say?"

The man pursed his lips and raised his eyebrows. He was obviously a smart guy, realizing there was no winning here.

"He might not say it, but I will." A woman spoke up from the back of the line of people. She had gray hair, twisted into a topknot of corkscrew curls, and she wore a chef's coat in a bright shade of blue. Olivia Puckett.

"Oh, crud," Mel said. Owner of a rival bakery, but also dating Marty Zelaznik, one of Mel's employees, Olivia was the last person Angie needed to tussle with right now, as the two women rubbed together about as well as static and hair. "Olivia, don't poke the bear."

Angie swiveled her head slowly in Mel's direction. Her

voice when she spoke was filled with disbelief. "Did you just call me a bear?"

"Um . . . well . . . affectionately," Mel explained. "You know, like a teddy bear, all cute and cuddly and squishy."

"Right, or, more accurately, like a ginormous grizzly bear," Angie said. "Admit it, you think I'm fat!"

"Oh my god." Mel pressed the heels of her hands against her forehead as if it would keep her head from exploding. "You're not fat, you're not chubby, you're not even pleasantly plump, and I'm an expert as I cycled through all of those stages on repeat for most of my life, as you well know. Honestly, what is going on with you today?"

"She looks hormonal to me," Hawaiian Shirt Guy said.

"Ah!" Angie sucked in a gasp and glared at him. "I. Am. Not. Hormonal."

"Nailed it," Olivia chimed in.

Angie whipped around with a glower. "You hush."

"Angie!" Mel hissed. They might not like Olivia, but it wouldn't do to verbally abuse her in front of a customer.

Olivia laughed and nudged the guy with her elbow. "If you want cupcakes without the drama, you can hit up my bakery, Confections. It's just down the street, and we have red velvets to die for."

"Thanks, it's tempting, but I'm already here and I've got my eye on those beauties right there," he said. He tapped the glass case, which displayed a shelf full of red velvet cupcakes. "I can wait out the pregger rage."

Angie blinked. "What did you say?"

The man turned to look at her. "Pregger rage, you know, the unreasonable fury that comes with being pregnant. My wife was exactly like that when she was expecting our kids.

We have four, so I've been at this rodeo before. Yee-haw and congratulations!"

"But I'm not . . ." Angie's voice trailed off. Her eyes went wide, and then she clapped a hand over her mouth and ran back into the kitchen.

"Vomiting," the man called after her. "That's another symptom."

Mel glanced from him to the swinging door, behind which came the unmistakable sound of someone retching. Should she follow, or would Angie punch her in the throat? It was clearly a toss-up.

As if they'd been shot out of a cannon, Mel's two bakery workers, Marty Zelaznik and Oz Ruiz, blasted out of the kitchen.

"Don't go back there!" Marty said. His eyes were round in his bald head. "It's bad."

"Really bad!" Oz confirmed. Standing well over six feet tall and almost as wide, he looked visibly shaken by a tiny woman heaving her guts out.

Mel stared at the door. Could Angie really be pregnant? She and her husband Tate had been trying for months. Did it finally take? She needed to call Tate for backup, but she didn't want to blow it if it wasn't true or if Angie wasn't ready to tell him. *Dilemma!*

"Hi, handsome," Olivia called to Marty.

"Liv, what are you doing here?" he asked. He beamed at her.

"I locked myself out of the house and I need your key," she said. She was staring at the display case full of cupcakes. She pointed to a section of cupcakes that sported festive cherries and striped straws. "Who made those?"

"I did," Oz said. "Root beer float cupcakes."

Olivia raised one eyebrow. "If they taste as good as they look, you've got some skills."

Oz looked pleased. "They do, and I do."

While Mel loved seeing his confidence, she wasn't sure she liked the covetous gleam in Olivia's eyes. She knew her rival wouldn't hesitate to sink her hooks into Oz.

"You could be doing great things in the culinary world," Olivia said. "And staying in one place of employment for a long time doesn't fill out a chef's résumé or round out their skills."

And there she went, trying to poach. Now Mel's internal alarm system was clanging like a fire truck on a call.

"Do not even think about trying to pinch my staff for your bakery, Olivia," Mel said. She lowered her voice, hoping she sounded zero tolerance enough.

Olivia blinked at her, the picture of innocence. Marty handed her his keys, and Olivia glanced back at Oz and made a call-me gesture with her free hand. With a wink and an air-kiss at Marty, she turned and left the bakery.

"Marty, you need to rein her in. I won't have her coming in here trying to take my customers or my assistant chef," Mel said. She glanced at Hawaiian Shirt Guy, who'd been patiently waiting. "Red velvet, did you say?"

"Yes," he said. "Two, please, one for now and one for later."

Mel smiled at him. She took a two-pack box out from under the counter and folded it into shape before putting two red velvets inside. She passed it off to Marty, who was already ringing up the man's order.

The sound of a curse and a door slamming from the kitchen brought her attention back to Angie. She gestured for Oz to take her spot behind the counter as she popped back into the kitchen to check on her best friend. There was no sign of the petite brunette. On the upside, there was no sound of upchucking, either.

Mel noticed the door to the employee bathroom was closed, and she crossed the kitchen and knocked.

"Angie, are you all right?" she called through the door.

"I'm fine," she said. "I just need a minute."

Mel stood by the door, debating what to do. She didn't hear any noise, so that was good, but Angie didn't open the door, which seemed bad. Did she force Angie to open the door and prove that she was okay, or did she give her a minute? She tried to decide what she would want if the situation were reversed, and went with giving Angie a minute, but just a minute and no more.

"All right," Mel said. "I'm going out front to see if things are under control, but I'm coming back."

"Whatever," Angie called.

Okay, safe to say Angie was still feeling salty then.

"Hey, Mel." Oz stuck his head around the door. "Peter Klein is here."

"Oh, right, it's Friday," she said. "Tell him I'll be right there."

Oz disappeared, and Mel went to retrieve Peter's cupcakes from the cooler. A regular, Peter had stopped in every week for as long as Mel could remember to buy his wife, Rene Fischer-Klein, a four pack of her favorite cupcakes. The flavor changed every few months, but lately her favorite had been the pumpkin spice cupcakes. Peter absolutely doted on his wife, and he never missed a Friday.

Rene was a glass artist at the art gallery, Desert Winds, down the street. This was one of the things Mel loved about the location of Fairy Tale Cupcakes. There was always something happening in Old Town Scottsdale. It was packed with art galleries, jewelry stores, restaurants, and bars. All of which made the place a happening spot year after year for tourists and locals alike.

Shortly after Mel and Angie had opened the bakery, Peter and Rene had dropped by to welcome them to the neighborhood. Rene had even brought them a small handblown glass cupcake that Mel kept on display in the front of the shop. They had become friends with the couple over the years, and both Mel and Angie agreed that Peter and Rene most definitely represented their marriage goals, as they seemed to be the perfect combination of business partners who were very much in love.

Desert Winds housed several artists and their studios, one of which was Rene, and Mel and Angie often popped in on art walk nights to see what Rene had going. The last time Mel visited, Rene had made the cake topper for Mel's wedding cake as her gift, and Mel was just thrilled. Rene's career had taken off in the past couple of years, and her work was in high demand all over the country. To have a Rene Fischer-Klein original glass sculpture on her cake was almost too much.

Mel pushed through the swinging door into the bright and happy pink bakery. Red Velvet Hawaiian Shirt Guy was gone, but a new line had formed at the counter. Not bad for the middle of the morning, which was usually their slow time. Oz and Marty had it under control. She spotted Peter waiting in the corner and crossed the bakery to greet him.

He was on the tall side, built lean, with a thick thatch of rust-colored hair that stuck up in the back no matter how often he smoothed it with his hand. Mel had noticed the gesture over the years, particularly when he was talking about art. A painter himself, Peter loved everything about art and the artist's life. When he saw Mel, he broke into a grin that was reflected in the blue eyes behind his wire-framed glasses. Mel had always thought he looked more like an accountant than an artist, but she had the good sense not to say so.

"Hi, Peter." She waved with her free hand. "Happy Friday!"

"Hi, Mel," he said. "How're things?"

Mel glanced back at the kitchen with concern but forced a smile and said, "Good, really good."

"Who are you trying to convince?" he asked. "Me or you?"

His eyes were kind, and Mel found herself confiding in him when she handed him his box of cupcakes. "Truthfully, Angie doesn't seem to be herself today. She's a bit moody, and by that I mean super surly and stomach sick."

"Oh, no," Peter said. "I hope she doesn't have the same ailment as Rene."

Mel looked at him in surprise. "Rene is sick?"

Peter nodded. "She's been suffering for a while now. She can't sleep. She can't eat, unless it's your cupcakes."

Mel smiled. "We do try to bake some magic in them."

"Thank goodness, or I'm sure she'd starve," he said. Mel thought he was joking, but the look of concern in his eyes and the anxiety in the tight lines on his face made her pause.

"Has she seen a doctor?" she asked.

Peter shook his head. "She refuses. Even when I found a clump of her hair in the bathroom, which was not a normal amount of hair loss, she brushed it off as nothing. She's got that big installation over the city canal coming up that has consumed her for the better part of the year. She keeps saying she'll go to the doctor when it's done, but I feel like she's taking a dangerous risk by putting it off. It would destroy me if anything happened to her, but I just can't make her see sense."

"Some people are stubborn about these things. Do you want me to talk to her?" Mel asked. "We have a meeting set up tonight to discuss the cupcakes that we're baking for the opening of her show. Maybe if I express concern, it will back you up and get her motivated."

"Would you?" he asked. "I'd so appreciate that. I've had a few people at the art studio talk to her, but she won't listen. She seems to think everyone is out to ruin her big career moment. It's as if she's forgotten that we've been the ones cheering her on all along."

"That doesn't sound like her." Mel frowned. "She's always been so gracious."

"I know," he said. "Sometimes I feel as if I'm dealing with her evil twin and the real Rene is locked up in a tower somewhere. There are days where I don't even recognize her."

"So, I'm betting our meeting tonight will be interesting," she said. "Any advice for me?"

"Do whatever she wants," he said.

Mel laughed. He didn't. "I'm serious. Whatever her vision is, just say okay even if she gets a wild hair for kale cupcakes."

Mel blanched. "I'm sorry, but that's a line I just can't cross."

He laughed, and she felt her tension ease, realizing he'd been kidding.

"You're one of Rene's favorite people," he said. "If anyone can ease her stress, it's you. Plus, I'll deliver these, and she'll already be mellowed. I just hope she's feeling well enough to discuss her ideas. Maybe if you mention to her that Angie's ailing, too, she'll realize that it could be something serious and get checked out."

"Sounds like a plan," Mel agreed. She didn't tell him that what Angie had would likely be over in about nine months. The Kleins were well into their fifties, so she was pretty sure that Rene wasn't pregnant.

She watched him leave and decided that she'd given Angie enough time to get it together. She pushed through the swinging door to the kitchen to see how her bestie was doing. She found Angie sitting on a stool at the steel worktable, staring off into the distance as if pondering the meaning of the universe.

"Hey, Angie, how are you feeling?" Mel asked. She spoke softly so as not to startle or annoy her, whichever way it was going to go at the moment.

Angie held up a plastic stick. She was pasty pale and her dark eyes were huge. "There are two lines."

"Come again?" Mel asked.

"There are *two* lines," Angie said. "One line is not pregnant. Two lines is pregnant. I have two. Like I peed on the stick I bought this morning on my way into work and blamo, those two lines appeared like that." She snapped the fingers on her free hand. "Mel, I *was* hormonal because I *am* pregnant!"

"Ah!" Even though Mel had suspected as much, it was still a surprise to hear it confirmed. Pregnant? Angie? Whoa. "Have you told Tate?"

"No," Angie said. "I think I might be in shock. I mean, a gal spends years, and I mean years, actively trying not to be pregnant. Even though we're trying to have a baby, it's kind of huge. You know what I mean?"

Mel tried to imagine being pregnant. Morning sickness, bloating, backaches, endless pelvic exams, and then the big moment. "Oh, man, you're going to have to push it *out* of *there*!"

They stared at each other, eyes wide.

Angie turned her head and gave Mel a side eye. "'Is it cool if maybe I just spray a little PAM down in that area right before the baby comes out?'"

"*Baby Mama*," Mel identified the movie quote with a half laugh. Hard-core movie buffs along with Angie's husband, Tate, they had been playing this game since they were in middle school.

"I'm kind of freaking out," Angie said. She swallowed, looked at the test in her hand, and let out a shaky breath.

"Of course you are, Ange," Mel said. She shook her head and hurried over to her friend and hugged her tight. "Even though you and Tate have been trying for months, it's got to be hard to take it all in. I mean, a baby, that's life changing!"

"Ugh," Angie moaned. "I think I might throw up again."

Mel quickly let her go. She stared at the woman who'd been her best friend for almost as long as she could remember. "Angie, you're going to be someone's *mom*."

Angie blanched. "Oh, god, I can't do this. I'm not qualified to have a fish, never mind a kid," she said. She crossed her arms on the table and put her head down. "I'm definitely going to throw up again."

"Not in my kitchen!" Oz cried as he came in through the swinging doors with Marty on his heels.

"*Your* kitchen?" Mel asked. He ignored her and grabbed a large trash can and placed it beside Angie.

"Aim for the trash can," he said. He glanced at Mel. "Shouldn't she leave if she's sick? She might be contagious and contaminate the cupcakes."

"She's not contagious," Mel said.

"How do you know?" Marty asked. "The stomach flu is not something to mess around with. I once had it so bad, I was leaking out both ends and—"

"Oh, no." Angie lurched off the table and put her head over the trash can. She began to dry heave, and Mel felt her own stomach stage a revolt.

"Nice work," Oz said. He glared at Marty. "You made her puke again."

"Hey, squad, what's the haps?" Tate Harper, Angie's husband of less than a year, asked as he stepped through the back door into the kitchen. As the corporate arm of their baking franchise, he wore his usual trousers and dress shirt, looking like the lone professional in a business of friends. His wavy brown hair flopped over his forehead, and his eyes narrowed as he took in the scene at a glance. "Angie, sweetheart, are you all right?"

For an answer, Angie held up the stick while keeping her head in the trash can. Tate glanced at the stick and then at her and then back at the stick.

"Is that what I think it is?" he asked. His voice was strangled, and his face went pale as he staggered a bit.

"Uh-oh, he's going down, too," Marty said. "Oz, grab another trash can. Looks like there's going to be an up-chuck party in here."

"Me?" Oz asked. "Why do I have to do it?"

"I'm sorry, did you want puke all over *your* kitchen?" Marty asked.

Angie's head popped up. "Stop talking about it."

She looked fierce and they all took a step back.

"Oz, Marty," Mel cut in. "I think we need to leave them alone for a little while."

"Like quarantine them?" Oz asked. "In our kitchen? I'm sorry, but I really feel like they need to be elsewhere. Maybe out in the alley, or here's a thought, they could go home and take their germs with them."

Everyone ignored him as Tate crouched beside Angie.

"Angie, are you—does this mean—are we?" Tate couldn't seem to find the words as he studied his wife's pale profile as she gagged into the large trash can.

"What's he talking about?" Marty asked. "Are they what? Down with the plague?"

Mel put her finger over her lips. Since she couldn't get them to leave, she needed to at least keep them quiet.

A shudder rippled through Angie, and she popped her head up and turned to look at her husband. Her brown eyes were soft and nervous, and her voice was barely above a whisper when she spoke. "Yes," she said. "We're going to be parents."

Two

"Oh, sweetheart," Tate said as he scooped her into a hug. "Are you sure?"

"Two lines," she said. "It's ninety-nine percent accurate. We're having a baby."

"What?" Marty clapped his hands to his bald head. "A baby? Here?"

"Now?" Oz looked aghast.

"More like in forty weeks, give or take," Mel said with a laugh. Okay, she was getting used to the idea. Plus, Tate was here and he could talk Angie down better than Mel. She looped one arm through Marty's and one through Oz's and said, "Let's give them some privacy, okay?"

As she pushed them through the door to the front of the bakery, she glanced back over her shoulder.

14

Angie was looking up at Tate. Her eyes were worried. "Are you happy?"

"Oh, Ange," he said. He hugged her close, then cupped her face and kissed her forehead. His voice cracked when he spoke. "I'm thrilled, aren't you?"

A tear streaked down his cheek, and Angie caught it in the palm of her hand. "I am. I really am."

She laughed and then hugged him. Mel let the door close behind her as a grin of her own spread across her face. This was turning into the best day ever.

"Oz, we're going to be uncles," Marty said. He held up his fist for a knuckle bump, and a shaky Oz returned it.

"A baby," Oz said. He shook his head. "That's, like, huge news. Everything is going to change now, isn't it?"

Mel shook her head but then she paused. Actually, he was right. Everything was going to change. Babies were helpless little blobs. Adorbs, but utterly useless, and Angie and Tate were going to be responsible for it for the rest of their lives. Oz was right. Nothing would be the same after this.

"Relax," Marty said. "Babies are not as hard as they seem. Sure, they need to be fed constantly and they poop their pants a lot, but really, once they outgrow that, it's not so bad. They can be super entertaining, when they're not screaming their heads off."

Oz looked at Mel. "Why am I not feeling better?"

"It's going to be fine," Mel said. "We have many months to get used to the idea that there's going to be a mini Harper running around." She took a deep breath, trying to sound calmer than she felt. She wanted to call Joe, her fiancé, but it was complicated since he was Angie's older brother and Angie would probably want to tell him herself.

Oz blew the fringe of bangs that perpetually drooped over his eyes, and met Mel's gaze. "I need a cupcake."

She nodded. "Good plan."

"You?" he asked Marty.

"Nah, I'm trying to watch my girlish figure."

Oz rolled his eyes. He went to the display case and grabbed two of his root beer float cupcakes and handed one to Mel. Marty glanced between the two of them and shook his head. "Why are you being so weird about this? They're having a baby, not adopting an elephant."

Mel could tell by the expression on Oz's face that he'd prefer the elephant. There was a teeny tiny part of her that agreed. Babies were something grown-ups did, and she hadn't even managed to get married yet, not for lack of trying, but a baby? That was next-level adulting. She bit into the cupcake and let the buttercream ease her anxiety. Truly, was there anything better than a mouthful of buttery, sugary goodness to make the world okay again? No, there wasn't.

Two customers entered the shop and Marty went to help them. Over his shoulder, he said, "We need to have a baby shower. I'll be in charge. There are some hilarious games we can play like Baby Bump or Beer Belly, Diaper Pong, or My Water Broke. So fun!"

Oz plowed through the rest of his cupcake and reached for another. He glanced at Mel and she gave him a frantic nod. With every word Marty uttered, she felt her panic surge.

"Do you think it's a boy or a girl?" Marty continued, seemingly unaware of the anxiety his monologue was creating. He snapped his fingers. "We need to have a betting pool. We could get the customers in on it. Winner gets a month of free cupcakes."

Mel and Oz said nothing while they demolished their

second round of cupcakes. When there was nothing left but wrappers and the sticky residue of cupcake on their fingers, Mel felt her stress level drop a smidge. Perhaps it was the sugar coursing through her veins, but she felt as if everything was going to be all right. Probably because Marty had stopped talking.

Despite Oz's worry that everything would change, she knew Fairy Tale Cupcakes would take it in stride. It was just expanding into the next generation. Huh. The thought was not as reassuring as she would have supposed.

"Another one?" Oz asked.

"Yes, please," she said. She hated herself a little bit, but stressful times called for extreme measures.

⋎⌣⌣⋏

The baby news, like most events in the DeLaura family, leaked out pretty quickly. The first of Angie's seven brothers to arrive at the bakery was Ray DeLaura. This was not a surprise, as Ray was the brother who was the most dialed in, meaning he had a lot of time on his hands as he didn't seem to have a regular job since retiring from the postal service several years ago and yet always had plenty of money. He was the brother Joe worried about the most, and he worried about them all.

"All right, where is she?" Ray asked as he banged through the front door in the middle of the evening rush.

"She who?" Marty asked. He and Ray had a love-hate relationship on account of Marty's ability to pick winners at the racetrack and Ray being jealous.

"She, Angie, that's who," Ray said. "Who'd you think I meant?"

Marty waved his hands around the bakery to indicate the females in line and Mel. "Could have been anyone, but thanks for clarifying. Angie is in the back." He narrowed his gaze at Ray. "Wait, why do you want to see her?"

"Can't a big brother check on his baby sister?" Ray asked.

Marty gave him a hard stare.

"All right, all right, so I heard from Sonya, a checkout girl at the pharmacy, that Angie was in there this morning and bought a pregnancy test," he said. "Naturally, as a concerned big brother, I felt it my duty to come by and check up on her."

The bells on the front door chimed, and two more DeLaura males, Tony and Al, the youngest of the brothers, entered the bakery.

Mel's eyes went wide. "Did you call everyone?"

"No," Ray said. He looked peeved.

The bells chimed again, and the brothers Dom, Sal, and Paulie joined the unofficial DeLaura brother meeting now happening in the bakery.

"Why do I feel like there's going to be a scene?" Oz asked. "And quite possibly not a pleasant one. Should we sneak Tate out the back door?"

"Damage control," Mel said. She looked at Marty. "We need to contain the situation until I can warn Angie. Set up a line of cupcakes. No one gets to Angie until they've had a cupcake or two."

"Roger dodger," he said. He turned to the wall of brothers and rubbed his hands together. "What'll it be, gentlemen? Any cupcake you want."

"We're here to see our sister," Dom said. He was the oldest and subsequently the most serious of the brothers.

"Absolutely," Marty said. "Mel is going to go get her,

and while you all patiently wait"—he paused to give them a pointed look—"you can have a cupcake."

"This is not going to help my diet," Al said. Then he shrugged. "I'll have a Cinnamon Sinner, eh, make it two." His brothers looked at him, and he shrugged. "What?"

"I'll just go let Angie know you're here," Mel said. When Dom made to follow her, she held up her hand in a stop gesture. "Sorry, no one in the kitchen except staff. We can't risk germs and such."

Dom frowned but gave her a tight nod. Mel pulled her phone out of her pocket and called Joe as she walked into the kitchen. He was the middle of the seven brothers and as such was generally the voice of reason. She had no idea how the brothers were going to process the news about their baby sister's pregnancy, but given that they tended to be an overprotective, reactionary bunch, she knew there would be drama.

"Hey, cupcake, what's happening?" Joe answered on the first ring.

"An impromptu DeLaura family meeting," she said. She pushed through the kitchen door and came to a sudden stop. Sitting at the steel worktable next to his sister was Joe, and he had a plate of Dreamsicle cupcakes—orange cake with vanilla frosting—sitting in front of him.

"You're here," she said, lowering her phone.

"DeLaura brother group text," Joe said. He was in a suit and tie, obviously having just come from his district attorney position. His thick dark hair was mussed as if he'd run his fingers through it, and his deep brown eyes sparkled at the sight of her, which always made Mel's heart flip over in her chest.

Angie, however, was looking green around the gills and

staring at the cupcakes in alarm. "I think the smell of the cake is making me sick. That can't be good."

Tate, who was sitting on her other side, jumped to his feet. "What can I do? How can I help? Ice chips? Back massage?"

"Outside," Angie said. She pointed to the door. "I need to be outside."

Tate took her hand and walked her out the back door to the alley. Mel watched with concern as they left. "I don't think the smell out in the alley is going to help. It's all sour milk and rotten garbage."

Joe shrugged. "Tate's got the situation under control." Then he bit into his cupcake. A look of sublime satisfaction crossed his face, and Mel smiled. Her man did love his sweets.

She'd had a crush on Joe since she was twelve and he was sixteen, but they hadn't gotten together until after she opened the bakery with Tate and Angie. Joe's sweet tooth was legendary in the DeLaura family, and she wondered whether he ever would have noticed her if she'd stayed on the corporate path. She supposed she'd never know, but it was one more reason that she was so grateful she had walked away from the corporate life to become a cupcake baker.

"I appreciate your love of my cupcakes, I do," she said. "But we have six brothers in the bakery that Marty is trying to divert with buttercream frosting. Maybe you should talk them all down before they pile on Angie with the big brother stuff."

"I'm on it," he said. He polished off his cupcake in one big bite, wiped his fingers on a napkin, and kissed her quick before rising from his seat and heading out to the front of the bakery.

Mel dashed across the kitchen and glanced outside to see

Tate and Angie walking by the Dumpster. Angie was looking better. No more green tinge to her face, and she wasn't sweaty or pasty. Huh. Seriously? A Dumpster smelled better than cupcakes? Mel wasn't sure how she felt about that.

A commotion sounded from the bakery, and she spun on her heel and headed back into the fray. Joe managed the brothers very well, but given the circumstances, he might need backup.

"I can probably make a gizmo to monitor her vitals," Tony said. "She can wear it like a watch."

"Excellent." Dom nodded. "We'll need to make up a schedule of her doctor appointments, so we can take turns going with her, and of course she needs to get on prenatal vitamins right away. She'll have to start taking naps. It would be bad for the baby if she's exhausted and even worse for her as the pregnancy progresses."

The brothers had taken over the center of the bakery as if it were a command post. Marty and Oz were standing behind the counter, with slack-jawed expressions, as if they were watching a meeting of the dumbest men who ever drew breath.

"Do they not even know her?" Oz asked. "I mean, she's their sister. You'd think they'd have caught on by now."

"Right?" Marty agreed. "Given the mood she's been in, if she overhears this, she'll murder them with her bare hands."

Joe sighed. Mel glanced at him and said, "Go get 'em, tiger, before Angie does."

He stepped out from behind the counter, loosening his collar as he went. "Now, hold on, Brothers—"

"Listen, we need to plan for more than the pregnancy," Ray said. "If baby Ray is going to live up to his full potential, I think we need to start a college fund, get some of those music programs to listen to in utero."

"Baby Ray?" Al looked at him like he was cracked. "How do you figure she's going to name the baby after you?"

"Because I'm her favorite brother, *duh*," Ray said.

"What?" Paulie cried. "I'm the one who taught her to tie her shoes. I'm her favorite."

"No, no, no, I was the one who played dress up with her," Al said. "I'm totally her favorite because I looked almost as good in her frilly dresses as she did."

The brothers all turned to stare at him.

"What?" he cried. "I can't help it if I'm pretty in pink."

"Excuse me," Dom said. "I'm her oldest brother. Of course she'll name the baby after me."

"But I'm the smartest," Tony argued. "Clearly, she'll go for brains, plus, Tony can be for a girl, too, if you spell it with an *i*."

"So could Sal, as in short for Sally," Sal argued. "I'm the one who taught her to drive. She owes me—big-time."

Of course, this started an argument about who had done the most for Angie and whom she favored. It got ugly, and insults began to fly. Joe glanced back at Mel with a pained expression on his face. If this was any indicator of how the next forty weeks were going to go, this was going to be the longest pregnancy in the reproductive history of humankind.

"What the hell is going on in here?"

The DeLaura brothers stopped yelling and they all turned to face the swinging door, where Angie had just entered the bakery. Her color was high, her hair was loose, and the fire in her eyes could have detonated a dynamite stick at a glance.

"They all want naming rights," Marty whispered out of

the side of his mouth. One problem, Marty didn't know how to whisper.

"Naming of what?" Angie asked. "A cupcake?"

"More like your cupcake," Mel said, and she pointed to Angie's belly.

"You all *know*?" Angie cried in outrage. "How?" She turned and glared at Tony, the inventor of the family. "Did you bug my phone again?" It had happened before.

"Nope," he said and raised his hands in innocence. "We all got a text from Ray."

"What did you do? How did you know?" Angie turned a fierce look on Ray. He just kept eating his peanut butter and chocolate cupcake, clearly not fazed by her ire.

"I'm dialed in, you know, connected. I know people," he said with a shrug. Then his eyes softened, and his look became tender. "How are you feeling, kid? More importantly, how is baby Ray?"

"*Baby Ray?* You have got to be kidding me," she said.

Tate blanched but was wise enough not to say anything, being outnumbered by the DeLauras and all.

"But I'm your favorite," Ray said. "We all agreed—"

A mass brother explosion of protests erupted, cutting off his words, and Angie held up her hands to silence them.

"You are not my favorite," she said to Ray. When the brothers looked cheered, she scowled. "I don't have a favorite. I dislike you all equally most of the time."

"Ouch," Al said. His tone was reproving, but Angie didn't look sorry in the least. She ignored his disgruntled look and addressed the group. "Did any of you tell Mom and Dad, because I will murder you if you did. This is my news to share. I'm the one who gets to make Mom cry the happy tears, understood?"

Furious nodding ensued, and Mel was relieved that the brothers hadn't blown that moment for Angie. As Angie was the only daughter to the DeLauras, her entrance into motherhood was going to be very special for them.

"Good," she said. "Tate and I are headed over there right now, and you will all stay away, far, far away, am I clear?"

As one, the DeLaura men answered in the affirmative. Angie made a shooing motion with her hands and gestured for them to leave. They each paused by their sister to hug her, kiss her head, and give Tate a considering look. This was their baby sister, after all, and he was the one that had gotten her in the family way, never mind that he was her husband. The idea that their baby sister was pregnant was still going to take some getting used to.

When the bakery was blissfully quiet again, Angie grabbed Tate's hand and looked up at him. "Let's go tell our parents. I don't trust those numbskulls not to blab."

"Hey!" Joe protested. "I'm a brother."

"Yes, but you really are my favorite," Angie said. Then she winked and added, "Don't tell the others."

Tate and Angie left, leaving Mel, Oz, and Marty to finish the day. Mel glanced at the clock. Oz was baking tomorrow's special tonight, and Marty was manning the front of the bakery until they closed at eight. Mel needed to leave soon to get to her meeting with Rene. She hadn't forgotten Peter's concerns about his wife, and she wanted to see Rene for herself.

"What's going on in there?" Joe asked. He gently tapped her temple with his index finger. "You look like you're worried. Is it Angie? Do you know something about the baby?"

"No." Mel shook her head. "Nothing like that." Then she

grinned. "You hide your worry better than your brothers, but you're just as freaked out as they are that your baby sister is having a baby, aren't you?"

Joe shrugged. "Maybe. A little."

Mel hugged him. "Don't worry, I won't tell."

They left Marty and Oz in the front of the bakery, and Joe sat back down to finish his remaining cupcakes. While he ate, Mel told him about her visit with Peter Klein. Joe frowned when she got to the part about Rene being sick. He was fond of the couple as well.

"Aren't you baking the cupcakes for her big opening next week?" he asked.

"Yes, and we have a meeting tonight to discuss what she wants them to look like," Mel said. "I'm going to try and see if I can work in a little self-care advice while we're talking. From what Peter said, she needs someone to tell her to take it easy as she's not listening to anyone in the studio. I have a nagging feeling that she needs me as an outside person looking in, objectively, of course."

"Of course," he agreed with a grin. "A visit from a friend will cheer her up, and you'll be reassured to see her for yourself. I have to swing by the police station to pick up a report, otherwise I'd offer to go with you."

"No problem. The meeting is pretty straightforward— flavors, colors, that sort of thing—and I'll keep my mother hen routine short. I've heard people can only listen to about twelve minutes of badgering before they check out. Meet you at home for a late dinner?" she asked.

"Unless you need to stay with her longer," he said.

Mel shook her head. "Nah, it's just a pop in. Easy peasy, I promise."

Three

Desert Winds Gallery was located in the heart of Old Town Scottsdale. Not far from the bakery, it was situated in the middle of a street full of shops and stores that catered to the single-digit percentage of the population who had money to burn on aesthetics and preferred to get their art from real artists instead of mass-produced products from home-goods stores.

Mel loved the gallery. It always smelled of eucalyptus and mint with the faint whiff of fire. The potter, Byron James, had kilns in the stone courtyard at the back of the building next to Rene's furnace, where she heated her glass sculptures. The two of them frequently worked side by side, putting on a show of sorts as they crafted their works of art.

The front of the shop was an enormous room with highly

polished wood floors and stark cream-colored walls that were the backdrop for the current artwork for sale. Sunny Davidson, the gallery owner, interspersed the pieces so that the artists' creations complemented one another. Rene's glass art displayed very well beside Bernadette Ortega's life-size wire sculptures. And Byron James's kiln-fired clay pieces grounded their more whimsical styles with his earthier tone.

Rene's work was the showstopper, however. Hers was the sort of art that punched the viewer right in the chest with its bold colors and creative lines. She somehow managed to twist her towering sculptures of glass into waves and spires of brilliant color. Angie always called it eye candy as it was so pleasing to look at, although the price tags were enough to cause a mild case of sticker shock.

In contrast, Bernadette's work was contained artistry, the wires so tightly coiled that it seemed inconceivable that a person had managed to twist and bend and solder them all together. Byron's work was big and blunt, giving no quarter to any other pieces in their vicinity. His thick clay sculptures were reminiscent of rust-colored desert mesas and boulder-strewn landscapes. The three artists were perfectly matched in this space, and it was a treat to be surrounded by their work.

Mel paused to appreciate the precisely placed, enormous glass sculpture just inside the doorway. She admired how the overhead light lit up Rene's glass as if the pale blue piece, which appeared to explode up from its round steel base, were actually a wave shot through with sunlight just before it crashed onto a rocky shore. Brilliant.

Adjacent to it was one of Bernadette's wire sculptures of

a jaguar about to pounce. Bernadette favored pieces of animals and people, from birds in flight to couples strolling hand in hand, all of which had an ethereal charm as if they weren't really of this time and space, which captivated Mel. And Byron's pottery, meticulously shaped, engraved, and glazed, held it all together with its blunt edges and unusual shapes, and its deep colors that could only be found in nature, all wrestled forth from his imagination and skill on the potter's wheel.

"Can I help you?" Sunny appeared in the doorway of her office at the back of the gallery. It took her a moment to recognize Mel, and the corners of her mouth turned down. "Oh, it's you."

Months ago, when Rene had first approached Mel with the job, Sunny had made it clear she was not a fan of having Fairy Tale Cupcakes provide the refreshments for Rene's big show. She had caustically said that she felt cupcakes were too pedestrian. Rene had laughed and ignored her, but Mel had remembered the comment, suspecting that it wasn't the end of the argument.

"Hi, Sunny," Mel said. "I just popped in to see Rene to finalize the details of the cupcakes for her art exhibit."

The corners of Sunny's mouth drooped even lower. She was in her seventies but easily looked twenty years younger. Tall and thin with a dancer's build, Sunny favored flowing dresses—today's was bright yellow—and accessorized her outfits with big chunky jewelry, such as the Wilma Flintstone turquoise necklace she presently wore around her throat. It was a statement piece, no doubt, but it drew the eye to the sagging skin of her neck, revealing her true age more than her eyes, which had been surgically smoothed around the edges.

Sunny had a heavy hand with the eye makeup and dyed her hair a streaky shade of honey blond, which hid the gray that was longing to be free. Mel always wondered about women who were clinging to their youth with such a tight grip. Was their life currency really their looks? Sunny owned a world-famous art gallery. Did she really have to be forever young as well? Mel hoped the cupcake industry was not so exacting. When she was seventy, she wanted to embrace it, not fight it to the death.

"I'm afraid Rene is busy," Sunny said. She crossed her arms over her chest. Mel got the feeling that Sunny was planning to turn her away. As if!

"Yes, with the canal installation," Mel said. "I know. I'm just here to take her order for the cupcakes. I won't linger."

"No, you won't," Sunny said. "Because Rene has asked not to be disturbed, and you need to respect her wishes."

"But we had a meeting set up," Mel said. "I'm sure Rene is expecting me."

"No, she isn't. I told you, she's working. You know how temperamental artists can be. When the muse calls, they must answer. But don't worry, I'll be sure to tell her you stopped by. Perhaps she can text you her ideas for the cupcakes."

Sunny didn't wait for Mel to respond but instead swept past her to the door, which she pushed open. She stared at Mel expectantly. For a nanosecond, Mel debated ignoring her and trotting up the staircase at the back of the gallery that led to the second floor where the artists' studios were. Would Sunny tackle her? Yell at her? Call the police? She studied Sunny's narrowed eyes and the slight curl of her ruby red upper lip. Yes, she probably would do all three, in fact.

29

"Well, okay then," Mel said. She moved toward the open door, not bothering to hide her irritation. "Good-bye—"

Sunny shut the door in her face and locked it. Mel stepped out onto the sidewalk. It was September in Old Town Scottsdale, and the tourist season was just beginning to pick up as the heat of the summer was finally fading. The temps were still high, but the nights were cooler, making the district the happening spot for locals trying to enjoy the last few days of summer before the winter visitors arrived and clogged up the restaurants, shops, and galleries.

Mel considered heeding Sunny's words to leave Rene be. If Rene didn't want to be disturbed, Mel certainly wanted to respect that, but it just didn't feel right. Instead, she strode down the sidewalk and slipped down the narrow alley that separated the gallery from the jewelry store next door. She moved swiftly and silently, scooting around the back of the building until she was at the wooden gate framed with decorative wrought iron that opened into the courtyard where Byron and Rene frequently worked outside.

She stood on her tiptoes and peered over the gate, hoping to see Rene. No such luck, but Byron was there. He was shirtless with his long black hair twisted up into a knot on top of his head and his robust beard looking as if it was growing wild. The manual labor of shaping lumps of clay into delicately beautiful works of art had given him quite the physique. Bulging pecs, forearms, biceps, and triceps, the man was all muscle.

Mel closed her eyes for a moment. She might have been distracted by the perfect specimen of manliness in front of her if she didn't already have a perfect guy. Ji . . . Ja . . . Joe. That was it. Joe. Joe was her guy. She was not all impressed by Byron. She shook her head, firmly dislodging his image. Nope, not even a little wowed by him. Honestly.

She knocked on the wood part of gate, hoping he could hear her, as she didn't want to make too much noise and risk having Sunny catch her. It took just a few seconds, but the gate was pulled open and there stood Byron, framed perfectly in the iron doorway, because of course he was. He stared at her for a moment, and then recognition kicked in and he grinned. The man had a lethal smile. It was the sort that made a woman forget her name, her address, or the fact that she was engaged—momentarily.

"Melanie Cooper, of cupcake bakery fame," he said. His voice was deep, and it echoed off the brick wall enclosing the courtyard. "What are you doing here?"

He remembered her. Well, wasn't that flattering. Mel stared up at him. Being tall herself, there weren't many men she had to look up to. A light sheen of perspiration covered his torso, and she was riveted by the sight of one bead of sweat running down his right pectoral. By god, he was something.

"I . . . um . . . the thing is . . ." she stammered. This was not working. She closed her eyes. *Focus, Cooper!* She opened her eyes, setting them on the rack of pottery behind him. "I'm here to see Rene about cupcakes for her art opening."

"Ah, the snake wouldn't let you in the front," he said. He stepped back and gestured for her to follow. "Poor Rene, she's practically a hostage. Sunny's been running her ragged about her *Seasons* installation for months."

"I thought the installation was for the city," Mel said. "Why does Sunny care, I mean, how does the gallery gain anything from it?"

"Exposure," he said. "Sunny is hoping that Rene's success will bring the buyers into Desert Winds in droves. Come to think of it, so am I." He laughed, and Mel felt herself chuckle in response. On top of being hot, the man was pure charm. Oh, dear.

"That makes sense," Mel said. She supposed she could understand it in a high-tide-raises-all-ships sort of way.

"Go ahead. Sneak up the back stairs. I won't tell, assuming of course that the next time you visit you bring some of those amazing lemon cupcakes of yours," he said.

"Sure," she agreed. "Anything you want, uh, I mean any flavor . . . of cupcake." She looked away from him. *Gah*, this was embarrassing. She hiked her thumb over her shoulder and said, "I'm going to go now."

He nodded as if he was used to women becoming completely brain dead around him and found nothing out of the ordinary about it, which meant on top of all his irresistible good looks and charm, he was a nice guy, too. Then again, maybe it was easier to be kind when you were good looking, because the world went out of its way to accommodate the pretty people.

Then Mel thought of some of the pretty people she knew who were not so nice, and there went that theory. No, she suspected that Byron simply had no idea how good looking he was. How was that even possible?

A staircase along one side of the courtyard led to the studios upstairs. Mel was halfway up when she couldn't resist glancing back over her shoulder. Byron had returned to unloading his kiln. He was humming something that sounded like a Michael Franti song with a hippie surfer vibe that was cheerful and upbeat. She wondered if Byron ever had a bad day. It seemed doubtful.

Turning back, she ran up the steps to the landing above. She didn't want to linger and have Sunny catch her. She knew, without question, there would be hell to pay. She pulled open the door and stepped into the hallway, smacking into another person as she went.

"Sorry!" she cried. "So sorry."

Mel rocked back on her heels and grabbed the person by the arms to keep them from toppling over backwards. It was a young woman who appeared to be in her early twenties. Mel's first thought was, *Thank goodness it wasn't Sunny.* Then she felt bad for ramming the poor kid so hard. She let go of the woman's arms and steadied herself against the wall with one hand.

"Are you all right?" she asked.

"Sure, yes, I'm fine. Just startled," the woman said. Up close, she appeared even younger, probably a college student. She had long brunette hair, round eyeglasses, and a wide smile. She put her hand over her heart as if checking to make sure it was still beating. "It was my fault. I didn't hear you coming up the stairs."

"I should have knocked," Mel said. "I was just coming up to see my friend Rene."

"Oh, I'm Rene's assistant." The young woman held out her hand. "Emersyn Allen."

"Melanie Cooper. I own the cupcake bakery down the street." Mel shook her hand. She was pleased that Emersyn had a firm grip. There was nothing worse than a cold limp handshake.

"Oh, you're the cupcake baker? Rene raves about your cupcakes," Emersyn said. "She always puts one aside for me and I have to say, they're fantastic. It's like there's a whole stick of butter in the frosting."

Mel grinned. The girl had good taste. "Thank you. I'm glad you enjoy them. Is Rene in? We're supposed to discuss the flavors she wants us to bake for her art opening."

Emersyn's smile faded. Tension made her shoulders creep up a bit, and Mel sensed the young woman was anxious. She glanced over her shoulder and said, "I'm not sure if this is the best time."

"With the opening happening next week, I'm afraid we're out of time," Mel said. "This is going to be a huge order and I need to get my people moving on it."

"Of course, right," Emersyn said. She looked worried.

"Listen, Peter told me Rene hasn't been feeling well," Mel said. "I promise I won't take much time at all. It'll just be a pop in, confirm the flavors and the overall look of things, and I'm out."

Emersyn looked relieved. "Oh, okay, I didn't want to say anything and have it look like I was gossiping, but the truth is she has been . . . unwell."

"What do you think is wrong?" Mel asked. "Peter said something about work stress over the installation."

Emersyn frowned. "I suppose that could be it."

Mel tipped her head to the side as she considered her words. "But you don't think so."

Emersyn's eyes were huge behind her glasses. "I don't know what to think. *Seasons* is her largest installation to date. It's going to be suspended over the canal for months. There are so many people involved and the media scrutiny is huge, but . . ."

Mel waited. She didn't want to say the wrong thing and shut Emersyn down, so she said nothing, a technique she'd picked up from her uncle Stan, who worked for the Scottsdale PD as a homicide detective. He managed to get more information out of people by not saying anything at all than he did by battering them with questions. Mel had a million questions at the moment, but she held them in through sheer force of will.

Emersyn glanced at Mel and her expression was one of confusion. "I don't think it's just nerves. There's something really wrong with her. She's not the same woman who hired me a year ago, and I don't know how to help her."

Mel nodded in understanding, hoping to encourage more confidences. It worked.

"I mean, she used to be so vibrant. She'd arrive at the studio crackling with energy, joy, and ideas, but over the past few months, she's become tired all the time, and moody, and a little, well, not a little, a lot paranoid."

"Paranoid?" Mel blinked.

"She seems to think everyone is out to get her, and there's one artist in particular that she is obsessed with—"

"Emersyn!" a shout sounded from Rene's studio, and Emersyn flinched.

The door to Rene's studio slammed open.

"What are you doing out here? Do I pay you to just stand there and ogle Byron when I've sent you to fetch me coffee? Where is my coffee? You know I have to have my coffee in exactly the same way at the same time every day if I'm going to push through and get my work done. You have literally one job to do, how can this be so hard for you?"

Rene stood in the doorway, wearing her usual studio clothes: ripped jeans, a form-fitting purple tank top, and a ratty pair of classic Vans slip-ons. Her hair was white and cut short in choppy spikes that shot out from her head, contained only by the vibrant aqua scarf she wore as a wide headband. She was glaring at Emersyn, who began to stammer.

"Sorry . . . I . . . uh . . ."

"It's my fault," Mel interrupted. "I bumped into her in the doorway and almost knocked her flat. I was just checking her for injury."

Rene's gaze moved from Emersyn to Mel. She stared at her for a moment, still caught up in her aggravation, before recognition kicked in. It had only been a few months since Mel had seen her, and she was startled by the difference in her friend. Rene looked gaunt, her skin ashen, her eyes sunken, and her clothes hung on her thin frame as if she'd shrunk over the past few months. Mel felt the first real stirrings of alarm.

"Mel?" Rene blinked. She stepped forward with her arms wide and a smile on her face. "It's so good to see you."

"You, too," Mel said. She had to hunker down a bit, as Rene was almost a foot shorter than her. When she patted Rene's back, she could feel her shoulder blades jutting through her skin. She wished she had brought more cupcakes. The woman desperately needed to eat a dozen or more.

When she let her go, Rene smiled at her, and Mel saw her friend's hazel eyes sparkle with their usual warmth, reassuring her that perhaps Rene was just overdoing it. Rene then turned to Emersyn and snapped her fingers twice. "Coffee?"

"Oh, right, sorry, on my way!" Emersyn said. She stumbled through the doors and down the stairs at a jog.

"Honestly," Rene said with an eye roll. "I did that child a favor, hiring her as a paid intern, but I swear she's useless."

"She seems friendly," Mel said.

"Friendly with the men, for sure," Rene said. Her expression was dark. "Enough." She shook her head. "Come into the studio. You've caught me at a good time. I was just putting some pieces up so I'm doing cleanup. Of course, if I could trust Emersyn, I'd have her do it, but . . ."

Her voice trailed off as she turned and went into her studio. It was a large room with big windows and ventilation. A drafting table was off to the side, shelves of materials lined the walls, and a worktable was in the center of the room. Several finished pieces were laid out on it, and Mel marveled at the shape and color Rene had managed to achieve.

"Are these for your installation?" Mel asked. "They're beautiful."

"Thank you," Rene said. She had a tattoo of the small black silhouettes of a flock of birds spiraling up her left arm. Mel had always thought the tattoo was perfect for Rene, as her career had always seemed to be on an upward spiral. She watched as Rene lifted one of the heavier pieces, what looked like an enormous pale blue flower, and put it on a shelf near the window. She stared out the window for a long moment and then said, "I feel as if I might actually pull this thing off."

"I have no doubt of it," Mel said. She saw the box of cupcakes that Peter had picked up earlier. It was empty, and Mel hoped that meant that Rene had eaten them. "Peter told me when he stopped by the bakery today that you've been working extra hard lately. He's worried about you."

Rene slowly turned to face Mel. She tossed the trailing ends of her aqua headscarf over her shoulder and asked, "You talked to Peter? About me?"

"Uh-huh," Mel said. She studied more of the pieces on the table before her, wondering if there was a way to incorporate them into the cupcakes she was planning for the event. The one closest to her was thick and round and resembled an enormous desert poppy. There were several others similar to it, but not exactly. Because of the nature of glass art, every piece was a little bit different. "I talk to him every week when he picks up your cupcakes."

"You do?" Rene sounded surprised.

"Of course, you're our friends," Mel said. She glanced up from the table to find Rene watching her with a fierce expression. She assumed Rene was concerned about her opinion of the artwork. Mel was, of course, completely in awe. "I know you're nervous, but you're brilliant and your show will be, too."

Rene stared at Mel. Her eyes narrowed, and she asked, "What do you know?"

"Excuse me?" Mel asked. She blinked at the sudden look of rage on Rene's face. Had she said something out of order? She'd called her brilliant. Was that a bad thing?

"You bake cupcakes for a living," Rene scoffed. "Just because they're pretty and tasty, that hardly makes you an expert on the arts."

Mel frowned. It felt as if Rene was insulting her. Was she insulting her? And why? The Rene she knew raved about Mel's cupcakes, was always kind to other artists, and was humble about her own work. She was beginning to feel as if Emersyn had been right in warning her that this Rene was not the Rene she once knew.

"No, I'm not an expert," Mel said, trying to defuse the sudden tension. "I've just always admired your work."

"Really?" Rene snapped. "Is it my work or my husband you admire?"

Mel felt her eyes go wide. She had an urge to check the

room for a hidden camera. Surely this was some sort of sick prank. Rene could not be serious.

"What are you talking about?" she asked.

"Aw, come on," Rene said. "Stop pretending. You've been trying to steal my husband for years. I know it. He knows it. Everyone knows it. Just admit it."

Four

"Rene, if you're making a joke, it's not funny," Mel said. She had a bad feeling in the pit of her stomach. It reminded her of being bullied as a kid. What Rene was saying was crazy and not true and made Mel feel as if she was being gaslighted. She really hoped Rene was teasing her, but judging by the furious expression on Rene's face, she wasn't.

"Oh, I assure you, I'm not," Rene said. "But I'm betting this whole thing is just a big joke to you, isn't it?"

"I just came here to talk about the cupcakes for your art opening," Mel said. "We had an appointment, remember? You wanted to give me some ideas so that the cupcakes would complement the art."

"Is that how you woo him?" Rene asked. "With baked goods?"

Mel shook her head. Rene took a combative step towards her.

"Is that what you and Peter do? Laugh at poor stupid Rene behind my back? I bet it's just hilarious, sleeping with him and mocking me, isn't it? Isn't it?!"

Mel held up her hands in a defensive move. She was half afraid that Rene was going to charge her. She swallowed. She didn't know what to say. There was a mad light in her friend's eyes that made her think, *Crazy eyes.*

Her silence was clearly the wrong answer, as Rene picked up one of her recently finished pieces of glass and pointed it at Mel. Her chest was heaving, and her nostrils flared. She waved the pretty glass, which was in the shape of a red maple leaf, like she was wielding a weapon. Mel wondered if she was fast enough to duck an incoming glass projectile. Suddenly, the simple job of baking cupcakes for Rene's art opening looked like it should come with hazard pay.

Since silence wasn't working, she decided to go on the offensive. She hardened her face and made her voice firm and in control.

"Stop it, Rene," she snapped. "You know that isn't true."

"No, I don't," Rene hissed. "You think I don't know how everyone wants him. You think I don't know that everyone is trying to steal my man. That slut Bernadette, and that bitch Willa Kincaid. They're both trying to take him from me, but they can't have him. He's mine. Mine!"

"I don't know about those other women," Mel said. "But I know about me and I have no interest in Peter as anything other than the husband of my friend Rene."

"Liar," Rene hissed.

Even though she knew something was terribly wrong

41

with her friend, Mel could feel her temper starting to heat. She didn't lie. She didn't want Rene's husband. And she was getting fed up with feeling stressed out and afraid.

"Enough," she said. "I'm not going to listen to this."

"Yes, you will!"

The chunk of glass in Rene's hand flew past Mel's head and crashed against the wall with an explosion of glass shards. Mel ducked and covered her face. She waited a bit to make certain nothing else was getting thrown at her before she glanced up and saw Rene, standing frozen and looking at the shards that littered the floor. She jumped forward and grabbed Rene's hands, making certain she didn't grab another piece of glass.

"Rene, look at me," Mel ordered. She shook her. "Look at me."

Rene lifted her gaze from the floor to Mel's face and then down at her hands and back up at her face. She looked dazed and confused, completely bewildered, and Mel could see that she was utterly lost inside her own mind. She wanted to hug Rene and tell her it was going to be okay, but she suspected that unless Rene got some professional help immediately, it wasn't going to be okay anytime soon.

"I'm sorry, I don't . . ." Rene paused. She swallowed and held Mel's gaze as tears formed in her eyes. "What's happening to me? Who am I? Why am I doing these crazy things?"

"I don't know," Mel said. "But you're not yourself."

"It's like I'm possessed," Rene sobbed. "One minute I'm fine and the next, it's like there's this demon inside of me and I'm saying the most hateful things. Things I don't even believe."

"Then you remember that I'm engaged to Joe, right? Joe DeLaura? Hot county attorney with a sweet tooth? We bought a house together. You made a beautiful glass sculpture for the top of our wedding cake."

Rene blinked at her. She looked confused. Then she frowned. "That's right, you're going to marry Joe. You love Joe, not Peter, Joe."

"Yes, I love Joe. Very much," Mel said. She felt her chest loosen as her adrenaline slowed and she downshifted out of high anxiety into a state of deep concern. This was all so weird and so wrong. Even now that she was calm, whoever this person was in front of her, it was not her normally ebullient friend Rene with the twinkle in her eye and a ready laugh.

"I'm sorry." Rene closed her eyes, looking like she might cry. "I'm just so tired."

"It's all right." Mel gave in to the urge and hugged her friend, alarmed again by how frail she felt. "Here. I'll help you clean this up."

Mel crossed the room and grabbed a broom and a dustpan. As she swept up the shards of glass, Rene collapsed onto the love seat against the far wall. She reclined, resting her head on the armrest while she stared up at the ceiling.

Mel dumped the glass into a nearby trash can as quietly as she could before sitting in the chair nearby.

"Talk to me," Mel said. "Tell me what's going on."

"Work," Rene said. "Work, work, and more work."

Mel was silent, waiting. Unlike with Emersyn, not talking did not open Rene up. Her hands moved restlessly over her abdomen as if being still was impossible.

"So, what were you thinking for the cupcakes for the art show?" Mel asked. She sensed Rene needed to think about something, and cupcake flavors would be a nice neutral topic.

Rene turned her head towards Mel. "*Seasons*, that's the name of my show. Maybe you could bake cupcakes that represented all four seasons, like gingerbread for winter, lemon for summer, and I don't know."

"Pumpkin spice for autumn?" Mel asked with a smile.

"Oh, yes, my favorite," Rene said. She relaxed into the love seat with a sigh. "Those really are the best cupcakes . . ." Her voice faded, and her eyes drooped shut.

Mel wondered if Rene had fallen asleep. She leaned closer to her. Rene's chest was barely moving. She gently put her fingers on Rene's exposed wrist, feeling for her pulse. It was sluggish and faint. She frowned in concern. The erratic behavior, Rene's haggard appearance, and now her weak pulse and faint breathing, when put together, were all rather alarming.

Mel pulled a violet chenille throw over her friend to keep her warm. Rene didn't flicker an eyelid at the contact. She was in an exhausted slumber that Mel hoped gave her some peace. In all the years she'd known Rene, she'd never seen her angry or frustrated or even sad. What could have happened in the past few months that could have caused such a drastic change? It had to be more than work stress.

The door opened, and Emersyn reappeared, carrying a huge paper cup of coffee. Mel put her finger to her lips and Emersyn nodded. She put the cup down on the worktable and gestured for Mel to follow her outside. Mel closed the door softly behind her as they huddled in the hallway that led to the other artists' studios.

"She's going to kill me for letting her fall asleep," Emersyn said. "That's why she wanted the coffee, so she could pull another all-nighter."

"Technically, I'm the one who let her nod off," Mel said.

"I'll take the blame. The absolute last thing she needs is an all-nighter. She looks like she's on the brink of a collapse."

"Are you going to be here when she wakes up?" Emersyn asked. She sounded hopeful, as if she couldn't bear to face Rene alone.

"No, and neither are you," Mel said. "I don't care how important this installation is, you were right, she is not herself. I'm not sure you should be working alone in there with her."

Emersyn studied Mel's face, her own very solemn for one so young. "Did she have a freak-out on you?"

Mel thought about not answering. She hated that they were talking about Rene behind her back, but good grief, the woman was unraveling.

"A bit of one, yes," she said.

"Did she accuse you of trying to steal Peter?"

Mel glanced at the closed door. "Yes, me, Bernadette and someone named Willa Kincaid. I don't even know who that is."

"She's an up-and-coming glass artist that Rene is obsessed with," Emersyn said. "Willa is in Phoenix and she's been gaining traction in the art scene in the Roosevelt district. She does some amazing work, not nearly as good as Rene's, but she's got potential. She's also twenty years younger and the media loves her. Rene has been tracking her on social media and going to her gallery in disguise to see what she's working on. When Willa did a piece that was just a little similar to Rene's, she contemplated suing her for stealing her designs. She was out for blood and wanted to ruin her. It took Peter weeks to talk her down from that."

"Oh, wow."

"Yeah," Emersyn said. "Honestly, I'm at my breaking

point. I've wanted to quit for months, but I hate to leave her like this. I told myself I would stay through the canal installation and then I'm done."

"It's good of you to stay through her biggest show. She needs help," Mel said. "Does Peter realize how serious this is? Has he considered having her see someone?"

"The only person she yells at louder than me is Peter," Emersyn said. "He used to be here all the time, but I think she's forbidden him from coming to the studio. She calls him all day long, however, and always wants to know where he is and what he's doing. She has him run errands, like bringing your cupcakes to her, but when he arrives, he meets him outside. It's like he's banned from the studio. I think he thinks everything will go back to normal once she finishes the canal installation."

"But you don't think so?"

"I don't know what to think," Emersyn said. Her shoulders slumped, and Mel thought that this was much too heavy a load for an intern to be carrying.

"Tell you what," Mel said. "I'll have a talk with Peter and tell him that I think Rene needs help, and if it means hiring more people to help with the show, so be it. Her health is more important than this art installation."

"She'll be furious with you," Emersyn said. She pushed her glasses up on her nose. "She's scary when she's angry."

"So I noticed," Mel said. "Which is one more reason she needs help, before she hurts someone or herself."

Emersyn nodded. "What should I do now?"

"Go home," Mel said. "Call it a day. I'll call Peter and have him come and watch over her. If she wakes up, I'll take the blame for your departure by telling her I sent you home."

"Are you sure?" Emersyn looked awed.

"What's she going to do?" Mel asked. "Fire me from making cupcakes for her opening? It's in a week. No one else will be able to pick that up on the fly."

"Thank you," Emersyn said. She looked so relieved, Mel knew that the tension she'd been operating under had to be unbearable. Impulsively, she hugged Mel. "Thank you."

And then she was gone. She slipped out the door and down the steps without a backward glance. Mel took out her phone and opened up her contacts. She had Peter and Rene listed under regular customers and she scrolled through to the name Klein. When Peter's name popped up, she pressed call.

The phone rang three times before he picked up.

"Hello?" he answered.

"Hi, Peter, it's Mel," she said.

"Mel? Hi, what's up?"

"Not Rene," she said.

"What? What do you mean?"

"I'm at Rene's gallery with her," Mel said. "Peter, she's more than not well, and this isn't something that's just going to pass when she finishes this installation."

He was silent for a moment. His voice was unsteady when he said, "I know."

"We need to talk about that later," she said. "At the moment, she's asleep and I'm keeping watch over her until you come and collect her. She needs to rest, Peter. She looks beyond exhausted."

"I'll be right there," he said.

He disconnected the call, and Mel leaned against the wall, relieved that he was on his way. The window across the hall looked down into the courtyard but Byron was no longer there, so she didn't even have man candy to entertain her while she waited.

She opened her phone and thumbed through the bakery's social media pages. Tate had hired a young whiz kid, Mikayla, to curate their pages, and she did an amazing job, putting up pics of their products, locations, and funny cupcake memes. Mel went on a liking spree, chuckling at some of the pics and impressed with how good the daily specials looked. Her thumb was just getting tired when a door opened at the opposite end of the hallway. She tensed, bracing for the appearance of Sunny, who would not be thrilled to find Mel there. It wasn't Sunny.

A curvy woman, who looked to be somewhere in her thirties, strode out of her studio in a clingy red dress that looked more appropriate in a night club than an art gallery. Mel had never met her, but she recognized Bernadette Ortega from her artist's portrait in the gallery downstairs.

Bernadette was the sort of woman who intimidated the bejeezus out of Mel. She was an exotic beauty who knew exactly how hot she was and how to use it to her best advantage. Her curly black hair hung to the middle of her back, while her dark brown eyes, framed by long thick lashes, tipped up in the corners, giving her a sly come-hither look. Her lips were full and rich and painted a deep cherry red. The woman had taken her own sex appeal and weaponized it.

As Bernadette's long stride, made even longer by the stilettos she wore, devoured the floor between them, Mel wanted to tell her the rolling hips and thrust-out bosom were wasted on her, but of course it wasn't. It did exactly what it was supposed to do by making Mel overly aware of her denim capri pants with frosting splotches, her beat-up white Converse sneakers, and an old, well-loved Slim Shady T-shirt. Mel could kick herself. Why hadn't she at least fluffed her short blond hair so she could really embrace her rebellious look?

Bernadette paused beside her. She glanced from Mel to Rene's studio and back. When she looked as if she was going to enter, Mel jumped in front of her.

"Don't go in there!"

"Excuse me?" One perfectly sculpted black eyebrow rose.

"I'm sorry," Mel said. "Rene is resting."

Bernadette looked her over from head to foot. It was not a warm look. Mel got the feeling a wad of gum on the bottom of her shoe would receive less disdain than Mel. "You're not her mousy little intern. Who are you?"

"A friend," Mel said. She didn't feel the need to explain it any more than that.

Bernadette tipped her head back and studied her through narrowed eyes. "Whose friend exactly? Rene's or Peter's?"

Mel sensed it wasn't an idle question. She thought about telling the woman to mind her own business, but that seemed unduly harsh and aggressively unfriendly.

"Both," she said. "I own a bakery in the neighborhood, and we've been friends since we opened."

"Oh! You're the little cupcake baker?" Bernadette tipped her head to the side and considered Mel. "You're not what I expected."

Knowing better than to ask, she did anyway. "What did you expect?"

"I thought you'd have a little more heft," she said. "You know what they say: Never trust a skinny cook."

Mel could have told her that she'd once had weight issues, but why would she? What purpose would it serve? Instead, she went with the truth. "I'm not exactly a twig."

Bernadette looked her over and shrugged, the physical representation of *meh*, which Mel took to mean she was bored by the subject already. Fine.

"Did you have a message to leave for Rene?" Mel asked. She was pretty over this conversation herself. "I'd be happy to send it along when she wakes up."

"Nothing that can't wait," Bernadette said. She studied the door behind Mel. "You know she's in over her head with this installation."

"I have no information about that," Mel said. That was the straight-up truth. But she also felt the need to defend her friend, crazy behavior or not. "Rene is one of the most talented artists I've ever known. If anyone can pull it off, she can."

"It's killing her, the stress," Bernadette said. "It happens to some artists. Their big break comes, and they're not prepared for all it entails. She's going to fail, and her career is going to plummet into the canal, just like her work."

Mel could feel her back tighten, and her chin jutted out. She really did not like this woman. "Sounds like you're jealous."

"Jealous? Don't be stupid." Bernadette tossed her head back and laughed.

There was no mirth in it. She was trying too hard. Mel had clearly scored a point. Bernadette was very jealous of Rene. Mel didn't say a word. She just raised her eyebrows in a look of disbelief. It was enough. Bernadette's laugh rolled right into a sneer. "As if I could ever be envious of that used-up no-talent troll."

"And yet, she has a huge installation going up in a prominent location for the city and you don't. Huh," Mel said.

Bernadette looked like she wanted to slap her. Mel rocked back on her heels, preparing to duck for the second time that evening. Honestly, if this sort of thing kept up, she was going to have to take up kickboxing.

"Mel!" Peter's voice broke the stalemate as he pushed through the door and joined them in the hallway. "Is Rene okay? Where is she? I called her cell phone, but she didn't answer."

"She's fine," Mel said. Relief pumped through her at his well-timed arrival, but she refused to let it show. "Ms. Ortega and I were just getting acquainted."

"Peter." Bernadette ignored Mel and turned to him. "Rene isn't well. She is working too hard. You have to get her to quit the installation."

"You know that's never going to happen," Peter said. "She's worked her whole life for this."

"She can't handle it. It's beyond her capability and we both know it," Bernadette warned. "It's going to be the death of her."

"You'd like that, wouldn't you?" a voice hissed. They all turned to see Rene standing in the open door of her studio. She swung her arm wide, encompassing the three of them. "You'd all be happier if I were dead."

"No," Peter said. "Sweetheart, you know that isn't true."

Rene glared at him. "Sweetheart? Really? Who are you talking to, me or her?"

She jabbed a finger in Bernadette's direction.

"You know I'm talking to you," he said.

"You're not supposed to be here," Rene said. "And

you're never supposed to be around her." She gestured between Bernadette and Peter. "We had an agreement."

It appeared Bernadette was the focal point of Rene's
rage. Mel was okay with that, relieved that it wasn't her this
time. She glanced from Bernadette to Peter to see how they
reacted. Bernadette looked unfazed, as if being accused of
being the other woman was an everyday occurrence for her.
It probably was. Peter, however, turned beet red. A vein
throbbed in his neck, and he looked as if he was trying to
keep a lid on his own temper.

"Rene, you have to stop," he said. "I'm tired of your
temper and your rages and your accusations. We've talked
and talked and talked about this. I thought we'd come to an
agreement. You have nothing to worry about with me. I am
yours, completely and totally yours."

"Liar," Rene snapped.

Mel really didn't want to be here for round two. She was
hungry and tired and upset, and it felt as if this drama was
never going to have an intermission.

"Well, I'm going to leave you two lovebirds to sort this
out," Bernadette said. She stepped forward and before Peter
could move out of the way, she draped her arms around his
neck and kissed him right on the mouth. "Bye, lover."

Peter shoved her off him, sending her staggering back a
few paces. Bernadette tossed her hair and glanced at Rene.
It was a look of pure malice that made the hair on the back
of Mel's neck stand on end.

Giving them all a condescending finger wave, Bernadette cackled as she strode back to her own studio. Mel
glanced at Rene in alarm. Her friend was so angry, she was
practically vibrating.

"I will kill her," Rene hissed. "I swear I will."

Five

"You know she's just trying to hurt you," Peter said. "Come on, Rene, you know this. Don't let her do this to you—to us."

Rene turned to look at him. Her eyes were haunted. Without a word, she retreated into her studio and slammed the door.

Peter removed his glasses and ran a hand over his eyes. Mel felt for him, she did. In other circumstances, she might even have hugged him to bolster him, but not right now. She wasn't going anywhere near him today.

"I'm sorry," she said. She glanced at her phone. "I think she only got about a half hour of sleep. She clearly needs more."

"Yeah," he agreed. He gave her a sad smile. "I'll see

what I can do. Were you able to talk about the cupcakes that she wanted at the opening?"

"A little bit," Mel said. "She mentioned something about cupcakes that would represent each season."

"Like pumpkin spice for autumn?" he asked. He looked sad when he said it, as if something that used to be joyful wasn't anymore.

"Exactly."

Mel wondered about what Emersyn had told her, how Rene wouldn't let Peter be at the studio anymore. It was shocking to her that things seemed so strained between the couple that she had always thought of as perfect.

"I'm sure they'll be wonderful," he said. "And Rene will be so pleased."

Mel thought of the horrific moment when Rene had thrown the red leaf at her head. Would she be thrilled? Or would this exhibit break her? She didn't know what to say.

"If there's anything I can do—" she began, but Peter interrupted.

"I'll let you know," he said gently. "Thank you for calling me tonight, Mel. You're a good friend."

"I just wish . . ." Her voice trailed off. There were many things she wished, mostly that tonight hadn't happened the way that it had and that her illusions about her friends and their marriage hadn't been shattered like that glass piece.

As she passed Peter, she gave in and squeezed his arm before she headed to the stairs. She paused before she pushed through the door and glanced back. Peter straightened his shoulders and stepped into the studio. Mel was half afraid of the sound of shattering glass, but there was nothing. And in its own way, the silence was even more chilling. She pushed through the doors and escaped.

"Ange, wake up." Mel gently nudged her friend's arm. "Come on, you can nap in the office, not on the worktable."

"Huh? What?" Angie blinked. Her long dark hair was piled up on her head, making her look much younger than her early thirties, but she also looked so pasty and drawn that Mel wanted to tuck her into bed for a week with nothing to do but binge-watch *Gilmore Girls*.

"Did you take your prenatal vitamins today?" she asked.

"Are you kidding?" Angie replied. "Tate has an alarm on his phone that goes off every morning to remind him to remind me."

"Aw, that's sweet."

"Or annoying, it can go either way depending on the day."

"You look exhausted. Why don't you go sack out in the office for a while," Mel said. She brushed her blond bangs out of her eyes with her forearm and gestured to the steel worktable in the bakery that was covered in chocolate cheesecake cupcakes. "I've got this."

"Mel." Oz poked his head around the swinging kitchen door. "I need to duck out today for a little while."

"Sure," she said. "For how long?"

"Just for an hour or so in the middle of the afternoon," he said.

"That should be no problem." Mel glanced at him, then did a double take. She blinked. "Oz?"

"Yeah?" He looked away as if embarrassed.

"What happened to your hair?" Angie asked. Mel glanced at her friend to see her staring at their protégé with the same wide-eyed shock she felt.

"Nothing." Oz shrugged.

"I can see your eyeballs," Angie said. "That's not nothing."

"It's no big deal," he said. He looked annoyed.

On the contrary, it was a very big deal, Mel thought. In addition to his many piercings and tattoos, Oz had worn his shaggy black mop over his eyes, making it impossible to meet his gaze, from the very first day Mel had hired him. Oh, sure, sometimes he'd brush it to the side or hold it back from his face with his chef's toque for formal occasions, but mostly, his fringe was his buffer between him and the world, and now it was gone. Like lopped off, sheared, buzz cut—gone, baby, gone.

In front of them stood a grown man, with a haircut that was high and tight and looked like it came right off the cover of *Esquire*. The punk teen was suddenly a handsome and mature young man, ready to be way more than Mel's sous chef. She felt her heart hammer in panic at the thought, but she forced herself to breathe through it. He could have just decided to update his look. No need to overreact.

"You look good, Oz, really good," she said. "So, why'd you need the time off?"

He looked at her fleetingly as if he couldn't bear to hold her gaze. "It's just an appointment. Routine stuff."

"Appointment with whom?" Angie asked. "Your doctor? Dentist? Chiropractor?"

"Something like that," he said.

"Which?" Angie persisted.

"Which what?"

"Which something like that?"

"You look pale," Oz said. "Shouldn't you be resting?"

"Don't change the subject," Angie said. "You can't distract me."

Mel could see Oz was uncomfortable. She knew that they really had no right to demand he tell them where he was going. Personal time was personal time for a reason. Still, her curiosity was twisting inside of her like buttercream frosting in a mixer.

"It's okay, Oz," she said. "It's none of our business."

Angie's head whipped in her direction, but Mel held up a hand to ward off her protest.

"Pfff." Angie expelled a breath, but Oz looked relieved.

"Let me know when you leave, so I can make sure the front is covered," Mel said.

"Sure thing, boss," he said. His concerned gaze lingered on Angie. "My mom says naps are key when you're expecting."

"Wise woman," she said. Then she yawned.

Oz disappeared behind the door. Mel watched it slowly swing to a stop. Something was up with her sous chef, and she had a feeling she wasn't going to like it.

"Maybe it's about a girl," Angie said.

"Maybe."

"You don't believe that."

"Doesn't matter what I believe," Mel said. "It's none of my business."

"How can you say that?" Angie asked. "Oz is as much a part of this bakery as Marty or Captain Jack."

"Marty works here for something to do," Mel said. "Captain Jack is a kitten we found in the Dumpster and

57

rescued. Oz is neither of those things. He's a chef, a graduate of culinary school, and eventually he's going to want to make his own way in the food world."

"But . . . but . . ." Angie protested, but there was no argument to be made. What Mel said was true and they both knew it.

"Whatever happens," Mel said, "I will support Oz to the fullest of my capabilities. He's going to make an amazing chef."

"All right, if you're determined to be big about it, I can do the same, unless . . ."

"Unless?"

"He goes to work for Olivia," Angie said. "Then I will kick him in the behind so hard, he'll walk with a hitch in his get-along for a month."

"Kind of think threatening an employee with bodily harm is a hard no in our policy manual."

"It's not a threat, it's a promise."

Mel shook her head. "You're so cranky."

Angie frowned. "I am, aren't I? It's the hormone roller coaster I'm on, I swear. Today I burst into tears because Tate didn't replace the toilet paper roll in our bathroom. And not piddly annoyed tears of frustration, but big, wrenching, the-world-is-ending tears of despair over toilet paper."

"Well, that seems entirely reasonable to me," Mel said. Angie smiled as she intended. "Now go take a nap in the office or I'm telling Tate you fell asleep on the table."

"I don't nee—" Angie broke off in another yawn. "Fine, I'll go close my eyes for a few minutes, but just a few minutes." She shuffled into Mel's office, closing the door behind her.

Mel took up her pastry bag with the cream cheese frosting. She squeezed a thick swirl of frosting on top of the chocolate cupcake and then sprinkled tiny chocolate chips all over it. Given her sudden stress about Oz, she wanted to power eat the whole thing. She resisted. This was tomorrow's special and she had several batches to go until she was done.

Instead, she forcibly stopped thinking about Oz and focused on the other concern that had been dogging her since the week before: Rene. She hadn't heard from Peter, and likely wouldn't until he stopped in later that day to check on the progress they'd made on the cupcakes for tomorrow's exhibit opening when he picked up his usual four pack of pumpkin spice for Rene.

Mel and Oz had decided to keep the cupcakes simple in style, not wanting to compete with the art. Instead, they'd gone all out on the flavors. Gingerbread cupcakes with vanilla buttercream frosting for winter, pumpkin spice with cream cheese frosting for autumn, strawberry rhubarb cupcakes with whipped cream frosting for summer, and crème de menthe cupcakes with mascarpone icing for spring. She hoped the variety would entice any palate just as the uniform look of the cupcakes would appeal to the eye.

Maybe once the exhibit was finished and open to the public, then Rene could finally relax and get back to being her old self. Mel had told Joe about the altercation last week when she met him at home for dinner after leaving the gallery. Both Captain Jack, their cat, and Peanut, their dog, had demanded all of her attention when she got home, so she waited, trying to think of what to say. Joe had whipped up his mother's fettuccini Alfredo, and they'd enjoyed their food at the table on the back patio with wine and a partial view of Camelback Mountain.

Joe had listened intently to her description of Rene's behavior and advised her to steer clear until after the art show was open. He thought Rene might be having a creative meltdown or perhaps it was something else, such as trouble in the marriage, but either way, Mel was better off not being in the thick of it. She didn't need to be told twice.

Mel glanced at the clock. Despite distancing herself from the situation, she would be eager to hear what Peter had to say about Rene's state of mind now that the show was about to open. She hoped, for both of their sakes, that Rene had leveled out.

Midday passed with no sign of Peter. Oz went on his mysterious errand—in a dress shirt and tie!—and returned, and still Peter didn't show. As far back as Mel could remember, not a Friday had passed that Peter didn't stop in for cupcakes. The only times he'd missed, he and Rene had been on vacation or traveling for work.

She knew that with the installation happening locally, this wasn't the case. She started to worry. Rene had been so weird when she accused Mel of having a thing for Peter. Could she have circled back to that and decided that they could no longer be friends? That would be crazy, and hurtful, but Mel couldn't think of any other reason why Peter wouldn't be here.

Perhaps it was because of the art show launching tomorrow. Maybe they were pressed for time. She imagined they were in a mad scramble at the canal, putting the final touches on the exhibit. But they'd had big shows before and he'd never missed his Friday pickup. Mel started to get a bad feeling in her gut. She grabbed her phone, thinking she'd call Rene. She paused.

The woman was busy. Mel didn't want to be a pest. After all, it was just a four pack of cupcakes. No need to freak out. She'd see Rene at the exhibit's unveiling tomorrow when they delivered the cupcakes. Invitations to the exclusive opening had been sent months ago, and Mel and Angie were attending as guests with Joe and Tate as their plus-ones, while Oz and Marty would manage the cupcake tiers during the event.

She put down her phone. She wouldn't call. She would trust that the universe had everything in hand and that all would be well. Using her work to channel her worry, she kept her head down and worked on tomorrow's cupcakes while Angie, who had woken up from her nap a much less cranky person, went out front with Marty and Oz. As much as she loved her people, Mel was grateful for the alone time in her kitchen.

Stock was running low, so Mel whipped up the usual suspects: Blonde Bombshells, Death by Chocolates, and Tinkerbells. Keeping busy kept her mind off Angie and her pregnancy, Oz and his secrets, and Rene and her crazy. It worked, right up until the last batch of cupcakes was put into the walk-in cooler. As she scoured the kitchen, she felt all of her worries creep back.

Crowding out Angie and Oz was Rene, since her situation seemed more worrisome at the moment. Mel checked her phone again. Maybe Peter had asked for a delivery. She checked the app where they managed their special orders. There was nothing. It was almost dinnertime. Peter always came at mid-afternoon at the latest. Mel retrieved the four pack of pumpkin spice cupcakes from the cooler. It wouldn't hurt Mel to stop by the canal, the location of the art exhibit, on her way home. It wasn't even out of her way.

She wondered whether this was too intrusive. Maybe Rene was furious with her for sending Emersyn home last week. Well, Mel could take her lumps if Rene wanted to yell at her. She put the box aside and went to take off her apron. She would let the others know that she was popping out for a while. Surely it wouldn't take that long to drive by, see if the exhibit was ready for its unveiling, check that Rene was doing better this week, drop off the cupcakes, and head back. She knew it would bug her if she didn't at least check.

She was about to step out front when the door slammed open and Angie strode into the kitchen, carrying her phone. Her eyes were wide, and her face looked horrified. There was a news story blaring out of her phone, and she turned it towards Mel.

"You have to see this," she said.

Mel glanced at the phone. Had there been a robbery in Old Town? A drug bust? What?

"It's the gallery," Angie said. "Desert Winds."

"What?" Mel grabbed the phone. A local news anchor, dressed all in pink with her long hair flowing in the breeze, was pressing on her earpiece while she spoke into her microphone. An ambulance parked in front of the gallery filled the screen behind her.

"No word on who has died, but police did confirm that a death has been reported at the famed Desert Winds Gallery."

Mel shoved the phone back at Angie. She remembered the look of cold fury on Rene's face when she stared down Bernadette Ortega. She had said she was going to kill her, and having almost had her own head split open by Rene's flying glass, Mel didn't think it would be too far out there to assume Rene had snapped, especially after Bernadette had planted that kiss on Peter. Oh, god!

"I'm going over," she said.

"Of course," Angie said. "I'm coming with you."

"No, you're not," Mel said. "You're pregnant."

Angie looked at her. "Good thing there's an ambulance on the scene then, you know, in case I go into labor." Then she raised her hands in the air in exasperation.

"That's not what I meant," Mel said. "We have no idea what happened. Whatever we find could be very upsetting for you."

"No worse than standing around here wondering what happened," she countered.

Mel had to concede the point. She'd go slowly mad if she were told to wait.

"All right, but you stay in the car," Mel said.

"Whatever, let's go!" Angie strode back through the door, leaving Mel to follow.

She sincerely hoped the brothers did not get wind of this or they were going to be so unhappy. She hurried to the front of the bakery to tell Marty they were leaving, and then grabbed the four pack of cupcakes she'd put aside for Peter. If nothing else, they were a great excuse to stop by. When she got outside, Angie was already behind the wheel of her car, revving the engine and looking determined. Oh, boy.

❜⸜•⸝❜

The street in front of the gallery was cordoned off with yellow tape and officers in uniform turning everyone away. An ambulance, two police cars, an unmarked police car, and a crime scene unit van were parked in the street, blocking off any access. Parking in Old Town was always a challenge, but this made it even worse. Angie drove to the next street over and found a space to wedge in her SUV.

"I'll be right back," Mel said.

"You didn't really think I was going to let you go in there alone, did you?" Angie asked.

Mel looked at her friend. Her chin was thrust out at her most obstinate angle. There was no winning this argument. "Fine. You can carry the cupcakes."

They climbed out of the car and walked back to the gallery. "This is good," Angie said. "We can say we were just in the neighborhood and are checking on our friends."

"I doubt they're going to let us in," Mel said. "In fact, I'm sure they won't. We're not family, and we don't know who is dead. I mean, it might have nothing to do with Rene and Peter at all. It could be a customer, Sunny, or Byron, although it's hard to imagine someone as fit as Byron passing away."

"Agreed." Angie nodded. "Maybe it was Sunny. She's well preserved but definitely getting up there in years. Possibly, she just died of natural causes."

"Maybe," Mel said.

"You don't believe that."

"No, I don't think the local news media would be on the scene reporting a natural death. She'd have been a belated mention in tomorrow's news, at best, unless the cause of death was something salacious. Besides, I wish you'd seen Rene when I did. She was . . ."

"Scary?" Angie filled in the blank. They walked along the sidewalk towards the gallery.

"That, but even more," Mel said. She had told Angie some of what had happened the night she stopped by, but not all of it. Partly, it was because she felt weird about the incident, but also because she hadn't wanted to taint Angie's feelings about their friend. Angie was fiercely loyal, and Mel hadn't wanted her to feel as if she had to take Mel's side against Rene, hoping that Rene would come back to her senses and their friendship would be restored.

"Honestly, there were moments where I didn't even recognize her," Mel continued, feeling the need to brace Angie for whatever they might find. "She was so angry and paranoid and volatile. I hate to even say it, but she looked like she could do a person harm and not even feel bad about it."

"But none of that makes sense. That's not the Rene we know. She was always happy and sparkly. Besides, her biggest career achievement, the canal installation, opens tomorrow night," Angie said. "Surely, even if she was having a mental episode, as you said, and hates Bernadette Ortega and every other woman who comes into contact with Peter with everything in her soul, she wouldn't have done something crazy on the eve of her biggest show, would she?"

"If she was derailed by stress and exhaustion," Mel said. "Who knows? I mean, I know what I get like when I'm hungry."

"You get hangry," Angie said with a nod. "An ugly combo of angry and hungry, and while it's super unpleasant, you don't turn into a homicidal maniac."

"I think Rene was more than hangry," Mel said. "I'm telling you, she was positively unhinged. She even lashed out at me and accused me of chasing after Peter. Angie, in her rage, she actually threw one of her glass pieces at me. And I have to say, I really thought she was trying to do me in."

"She what?! Wait, why didn't you tell me about this?"

Angie stopped walking and stared at her with her mouth slightly open.

"I felt bad about it," Mel said. "It was so out of character, I just wanted to forget it."

"Why do I have the feeling there's more to the story?"

"There is," Mel sighed. "It's not just me she lashed out at. I talked to her assistant, Emersyn, and she confirmed that Rene has been unwell. I even saw how Rene spoke to Emersyn, and she was nothing like the calm, gentle, loving Rene we know. She was actually mean and a bit verbally abusive."

"Why hasn't anyone called her on this behavior?" Angie asked. They resumed walking. "I can't believe Peter or one of the other artists hasn't said anything."

"My sense is that they're ignoring her behavior, blaming it on her artistic temperament, until after the show opens. Sunny, the gallery owner, tried to stop me from going to meet with Rene about the cupcakes for tomorrow. At the time, I thought it was because she'd been against cupcakes from the beginning."

"Too pedestrian," Angie said, remembering the insult.

"Right," Mel said. She shrugged in a *whatever* gesture. "Sunny wouldn't let me in the front to see Rene, so I snuck up the back stairs. I think we should do that again, as I doubt the police are going to let us through."

"Sounds like a plan," Angie agreed. "Do you think Uncle Stan is here?"

"I don't know. I guess it depends upon whether the death is suspicious or not," Mel said. "Which is another reason to try the back."

"We'll just pop in and make sure Rene and Peter are all right. We don't have to stay long. We can pretend we're just finalizing everything for the exhibit tomorrow," Angie said. "If we're lucky, Uncle Stan might never know we were here."

As they approached the gallery, they saw several news vans parked in front along with the emergency vehicles and police cars. The hair on the back of Mel's neck prickled. She'd seen this setup too many times before. This was exactly how a homicide investigation looked from the outside.

She and Angie slipped down the narrow alley that ran alongside the building, and turned the corner. Mel glanced back to make certain there were no police stationed at the entrance to the courtyard behind the gallery. There was no one. She crept up to the wooden gate and peered through the wrought iron detailing along the top.

"What do you see?" Angie asked.

"No one," Mel said. She reached over the gate and tried the handle. It unlatched. The sound of voices growing louder made her snatch her hand back. "Spoke too soon. Someone's coming."

She and Angie scuttled away from the gate and pressed themselves against the thick brick wall.

"What should we do?" Angie whispered.

"Wait to see who it is," Mel said. "If it's Rene, we can get a look at her, see how she's doing, and then bail. Maybe we don't even have to talk to her."

Angie nodded. The voice they heard was deep, like gravel deep. Mel knew without looking that it belonged to Byron. But who was he talking to? Rene? Emersyn? His voice was so low, she couldn't make out the words. Being tall, she rose up on her toes, hoping to get a glimpse into the courtyard from where she was standing.

Byron had his back to her. His man bun was perched on top of his head, but he was wearing a shirt today. The person he was speaking to was blocked from view by his wide shoulders. Whatever he was saying, he was upset, as he was gesturing around the courtyard to emphasize his point. Stretched as high as she could go, Mel wobbled on her tiptoes as her legs started to cramp.

"Who is it?" Angie whispered.

"Byron," she said out of the corner of her mouth.

"Oh, the hot potter." Angie nodded. "I remember him from an opening a few months back. He's the one with the muscles and that amazing head of hair, right?"

"Yup. I can't hear what he's saying but he's gesturing pretty wildly, so I'm assuming he's upset," Mel said. "I don't know how well he knew Bernadette but if she's the one who . . . oh, wait."

Mel dropped back down on her heels. She looked at Angie in alarm.

"What is it?"

"The person Byron is talking to *is* Bernadette."

"That's good, right?" Angie asked. "I mean, at least we know Rene didn't kill her like she threatened to."

"Yes, but if the deceased isn't Bernadette, then who is it?" Mel asked.

Angie frowned. "There's only one way to find out."

Angie pushed off the wall and strode to the gate. She tried to reach up and unlatch it while holding the cupcakes in her other hand, but she was just a few inches too short.

"Here, let me," Mel said. She reached over Angie, who looked annoyed, and unhooked the gate. She opened it and they both stepped inside. Byron and Bernadette spun to face them, and Mel forced her face to remain blank. She didn't want to give anything away. She glanced at Angie, who had a similar smooth expression on her face.

"Mel, and . . . Angie, right?" Byron asked. When they nodded, he added, "What are you doing here?"

"Delivering Rene's cupcakes," Mel said. "Peter never arrived to pick them up today, so we thought we'd deliver them. Is Rene up in her studio?"

Byron and Bernadette exchanged a look. It wasn't a good one, and Mel felt the hair on the back of her neck start to prickle again. All of her instincts were telling her that something was wrong—very, very wrong.

"The thing is . . ." Byron stalled and then huffed out a breath. "Rene is dead."

Six

"Ah!" Angie and Mel gasped in unison.

"I'm sorry," Byron said. "We don't know what happened. They arrived back from setting up her installation over the canal and she was so happy. Peter brought out champagne to toast her success, and the next thing we knew she clutched her chest and collapsed."

A tear slid out of his eye and he brushed it away with the backs of his fingers. He looked genuinely devastated. Mel felt her own throat close up. She shook her head. This couldn't be right. She didn't want to believe it. Not Rene. Not now. Not on the eve of her greatest success.

Mel felt gutted, and when she glanced at Angie, she knew she felt the same.

"I can't accept this," Angie said. "She's our friend. We've known her for years. How could she be . . . ?" She staggered on her feet. Byron jumped forward and scooped her up into his arms.

"Whoa," he said. He lifted her as easily as if she weighed no more than a bouquet of flowers. "You all right?"

Angie looked up at him in alarm. Her face was pale and faintly green. Mel stepped close.

"You may want to put her down," she said. "She's pregnant and—"

"Going to throw up," Angie interrupted on a hard swallow.

"Oh, gotcha." Byron carried her across the courtyard to a bench in the corner. He gently set her down and then grabbed a huge ceramic pot and placed it before her. "Puke into that if you need to."

Bernadette vibrated with outrage. "Byron, that's one of your most valuable pieces."

"Totally washable." He shrugged. "In the wake of today's tragedy, who cares?" He crouched down beside Angie and asked, "Can I get you anything?"

Angie shook her head and held on to the urn, her rebelling stomach overriding any other feelings besides shock and grief. There just wasn't room for embarrassment at a moment like this.

"You let me know, okay?" he said. Angie nodded. Tears coursed down her cheeks, and she wiped them away with her sleeve. Mel put down the cupcakes and went over to Angie. She ignored her own tears and the burning knot in her throat. With shaking hands, she pulled Angie's hair back and fastened it into a quick braid to keep it from falling into the urn if Angie got sick.

"What about you, Mel, can I get you anything?" Byron asked. Mel shook her head. She had always liked the ridiculously good-looking ceramicist, but now she positively adored him for his compassion and care. He didn't even flinch when Angie dry heaved into the large green glazed urn.

"Revolting," Bernadette said with a lip curl.

Mel ignored her and turned back to Byron. "Do you know what's happening now?"

"The paramedics came immediately and tried to revive her. She . . ." He paused, looking stricken. He took a deep breath, held it, and then let it out slowly. His gaze met hers when he said, "She came and went three times before she didn't come back at all. One of them noted the time of death and then the police were called."

"Why the police?" Mel asked.

"Because Rene was only in her early fifties and had no known health issues," Bernadette said. "There was definitely something wrong with her. She's looked like garbage for weeks, and she's been acting bizarre. We think she might have been self-medicating and overdosed."

"No, that can't be right," Angie protested, her voice rough. "She wasn't the sort who would do that." She blanched and stuck her head back in the urn.

Bernadette ignored her and turned to Mel. "You saw her last week. She was clearly losing her mind."

Mel's dislike for this woman, who had taken such pleasure in torturing Rene last week, burned like acid in her gut. She didn't want to agree with her on anything and certainly not on the mental fitness of her friend.

"Maybe," Mel said. There was no doubt Rene had been suffering, but she didn't like the way Bernadette was talking about her, reducing Rene's life to the chaotic weeks before she . . . died. Rene was dead. Mel's heart clutched at the thought as if it could tighten up and reject the horrible news, making it not so. She took a steadying breath and focused on the conversation. "But an overdose? I just can't see it."

"None of us could. She's been working so hard," Byron said. "She might have been on some powerful uppers to maintain her output. I've known other artists who've done the same. The stress on her heart might have been too much for her."

Mel frowned. It all seemed so neat and tidy and not at all like the sort of thing that would happen to the kind, generous, big-hearted woman she once knew. She glanced at the three of them.

"I'm going upstairs," she said.

Angie's head popped up even though she still clutched the edge of the urn with white knuckles. "I'll come with you."

"No, you're in no shape."

Angie closed her eyes and swallowed. "Do you think you should? Uncle Stan may be up there."

"All the better," Mel said. "I might be able to get some information out of him."

She turned around and crossed the courtyard to the stairs. She was on the first step before she was busted.

"Hold up there, Cooper. Where do you think you're going?"

Mel stopped and turned around to see her childhood nemesis turned friend—sort of—Dwight Pickard, walking through the back gate. He was big and built, a lot like Byron, except he wore his hair in a military buzz cut that emphasized his big blocky head. She blinked.

"Dwight, what are you doing here?" she asked.

"I stopped by the bakery, and the guys told me where you were and why," he said. "I called Joe and asked him if he wanted me to do a little cupcake baker recon and he said yes."

"So, you're spying on me?"

"More like tailing you."

"That's supposed to be better?"

Dwight shrugged. He'd served several tours of duty in the Middle East, which had left him hardened in ways only deployment could. Despite their childhood animosity, Dwight had saved Mel's life a few months prior and she knew it was a debt that could never be repaid, so she had offered him forgiveness and friendship. To her surprise, he'd accepted both and even taken a job working security at the courthouse in Phoenix where Joe had put in a good word for him. It was the first job he'd managed to hold on to for more than a few months, and she and Joe had high hopes for him.

"Not better so much as more accurate," he said. He didn't look as if he found anything wrong with the situation.

"I appreciate the good intentions," Mel said. "But tailing me is not necessary, and Joe and I will be having a conversation about that later."

He ignored her. "The dead artist is a friend of yours?"

His words hit like a blunt-force trauma. Not unexpectedly, a lump formed in Mel's throat and she choked. "Yes."

He nodded, studying her with a considering look. He'd lost a close friend recently and Mel knew he was still grieving. "Come on then. Let's go see what we can find out."

Mel would not have been surprised to have Dwight

throw her and Angie over his shoulders and forcibly remove them from the gallery. His unexpected cooperation made her suspicious.

It must have shown on her face because he said, "Please, I know you. You're not leaving until you get some answers. Am I right?"

"You're right."

"So let's get it done." He gestured to the staircase, signaling for her to lead. "Standing here being a sad sack isn't helping anyone."

She should have bristled at his callousness, but instead it gave her the kick in the pants she needed, which she suspected he knew. She cleared her throat and nodded.

Mel glanced back in concern at Angie. Byron interpreted the look and said, "I'll keep an eye on her."

"Thanks," she said. "I'll be right back, Ange."

"I'll be here," she sighed. She swallowed hard and hugged the urn tighter. She glanced at Dwight and said, "Watch her back."

"Don't worry about it, short stack," he said. Angie glowered. While Mel and Dwight had buried the hatchet, Angie was still working on not burying it in Dwight's skull. Grudges were a way of being for the DeLaura family, and Mel knew it would take time before Angie managed to let go of her animosity toward Dwight completely.

Bernadette watched Dwight with keen interest but to Mel's surprise, he didn't appear to notice her at all. Interesting, since Bernadette was not a woman to be ignored. Mel led the way up the stairs.

"Who's the Mary with the girly hairdo?" Dwight asked as he stepped up behind her.

Given that Dwight didn't come with a whisper, Mel

75

shushed him and then hissed, "He's an artist and a friend. Be nice."

"Joe know you're friends with him?"

"Yes," Mel said. "Do *not* go all Neanderthal on me." Dwight's eyebrows lifted as if to argue with this assessment, but Mel cut him off. "Don't bother. We both know you're seventy-five percent knuckle dragger."

He shrugged, then heaved a put-upon sigh as he followed her up the stairs. She could hear him muttering, but she refused to try to decipher what he was complaining about. Truthfully, she was ridiculously grateful that he was here. If nothing else, Dwight was a solid buffer against the wall of grief that felt as if it was going to come crashing down on her at any second. For that alone, she'd put up with an awful lot right now, even muttering, which she detested.

Like pressing on a bruise to see if it still hurt, she kept replaying in her mind the fact that Rene was dead, and every time she felt the same cocktail of disbelief, denial, and grief swirl through her gut. She just couldn't believe that Rene was dead.

Mel didn't get far in her quest for information. The door at the top of the stairs was open, but it was marked off by yellow police tape. She stuck her head over the top and scanned the hallway. There were clusters of police personnel and crime scene investigators milling around the hallway as well as several reporters on the far side, also peering over the yellow tape on their end as they tried to get the story.

"What are *you* doing here?" a voice snapped, and Mel turned to see detective Tara Martinez striding toward her.

This was not good, as in it was very, very bad. Tara had disliked Mel from the very first day they'd met. Tara said it was because Mel had broken her cousin Manny's heart, and he had moved to Las Vegas to get over her, but Mel didn't believe it since she knew he was very happy with his new girlfriend Holly Hartzmark, a former Vegas showgirl who had opened the bakery's very first franchise, just off the Strip.

No, Mel suspected, from the longing looks Tara cast at Joe whenever he was around, that Tara's real beef with her was that she wanted Joe and Mel got him. So high school.

"I'm looking for my uncle," Mel said. "Seen him?"

Tara glared. "He's busy."

"Yup, and I still need to see him."

"Why is he with you?" Tara jutted her chin at Dwight.

He raised an eyebrow and leaned against the doorjamb. "I'm her backup. Nice seeing you, too, Detective."

Tara ignored him. The one time they had met, the same night he'd saved Mel's life, it hadn't gone well. Probably because he'd saved Mel's life and Tara would have preferred he hadn't. Mel frowned. Did the woman really hate her that much?

"I'm not disturbing him for you," Tara said. "And if you don't leave right now, I'll have you arrested." So, that was a yes on the hatred.

"For what?" Mel asked. "Breathing?"

Dwight laughed, which gave Mel just enough encouragement to stand her ground. "I want to see my uncle."

"What do you not understand about the word 'no'?" Tara snapped. She planted her hands on her hips. She was wearing heels, for real, like a television detective. Mel always expected the female cops to break a leg or a heel on those shows, and felt it unrealistic when they didn't. Oh, and they managed to chase down the bad guy. Ridiculous.

Objectively speaking, Tara looked pretty in a slim skirt and pale blouse, her dark hair meticulously curled and her makeup on point. Why, it was almost as if Tara was dressed for a date.

"Did you have court today?" Mel asked.

"How is that any of your business?"

"It's not," Mel said. "You're just a bit dolled up for a regular day at the office."

"She was probably on her way to a date," Dwight said. "It is Friday night after all."

"I was not . . ." Tara began, then she held up her hands in a stop gesture. "I am not talking to you people about my personal life."

"Totally a date," Mel said to Dwight, ignoring Tara's huff of outrage. She surreptitiously glanced past Tara and saw Uncle Stan. He had just stepped out of Rene's studio and was talking to a crime scene tech. She knew if they could stall Tara long enough, Stan would see her standing here without her having to shout down the hallway.

"It's not—"

"No?" Dwight interrupted Tara. He cast Mel a side eye, and she knew he'd seen Uncle Stan, too. "Then you should let me take you out for a steak after you're done here. It'd be a shame to waste all of that"—he made a circular gesture with his index finger to indicate her look—"on just going home to eat over the sink with only your cat for company."

"I would never ever go out with you." Tara's lips compressed into a thin line. "And I don't have a cat."

"Dog," he said.

"That either."

Dwight looked at Mel and asked, "What's it say about a person who doesn't have any pets?"

"Nothing good," Mel said.

"I have a pet," Tara snapped. Dwight looked at her expectantly and she added, "A fish, okay?"

"What kind of fish?" he asked, still stalling. Mel could have hugged him.

"I am not talking to you anymore!" Tara snapped. Her voice echoed in the hallway. Mel saw Uncle Stan's head turn their way. Perfect.

"Saltwater or fresh?" he persisted. "Does it have a name? I mean, if it's really a pet it should have a name."

Uncle Stan started walking toward them. He didn't look happy to see Mel. Shocker, not really. Nor did he look surprised. Also, not a shocker.

"Raymond, all right?" Tara cried. "The fish's name is Raymond."

"Raymond?" Dwight asked. He made a face like he tasted something bad. "For a fish?"

"It was a gift," she said. "It came named."

"Raymond?" Dwight asked again as if he just couldn't wrap his head around such a thing.

"Are you talking about the fish Ray DeLaura gave you?" Uncle Stan asked.

Tara's spine went rigid, and her eyes widened as Uncle Stan joined them.

Mel studied the woman in front of her. "Ray gave you a fish named after himself?"

Well, well, well, wasn't this an interesting turn of events? Tara's face went pale, then red, and then back to pasty. Mel tried not to enjoy her mortification too much, but it was a

struggle. Her amusement must have shown on her face because Tara gave her a scathing look.

Tara stepped back from the doorway and looked at Uncle Stan. "These people are your problem. I don't have time
for this." She tossed her hair, turned on her heel, and
stomped away.

"She's feisty," Dwight said. "I like feisty."

"Stop," Mel said. "If she's dating Ray—" She paused
and turned to Uncle Stan and asked, "Is she dating Ray?"

"I don't know," he said. "And I don't care, and neither
should you."

"But Ray is my fav—" she began, but Uncle Stan cut
her off.

"Mel, what are you doing here?" he asked. He gestured
to the scene behind him. "I'm in the middle of an investigation."

She blinked. Just like that the reality of why she was
here came roaring back. Rene. Her grief over the death of
her friend came back around and sucker punched her right
in the chest.

"I know," she said. She sniffed. "Rene was my friend."

"Aw, crap." Uncle Stan lifted the yellow tape with one
hand and held out his other arm, offering the solace she so
desperately needed.

Mel stepped into his big bear hug and let her tears, the
first since learning about Rene's death, pour out to get ab-
sorbed into his cotton dress shirt. He smelled of bay rum
and breath mints just like her dad, his older brother Charlie,
and he hugged just like him, too. Mel's father had moved
on to the nineteenth hole in the sky over a decade ago, and
Uncle Stan had stepped up to fill the void. He'd even re-

cently begun dating Mel's mother, a fact she was still processing.

Uncle Stan patted her back with his big square hand and made soft soothing noises, letting her know that he was there and everything would be okay. It helped, even though she knew it wasn't true. No one could make this situation okay.

The Cooper men were good huggers. They used both arms and squeezed good and tight, letting the recipient know without words how much they cared even if they couldn't really make it better.

Mel pulled in some of his strength. A homicide detective for many years, he'd seen it all. He was in his element at a crime scene, able to process the event without getting sucked into all of the emotion and yet still able to be empathetic to those who suffered from the loss. In some policemen, the job made them cold and hard, but in Uncle Stan's case it allowed him to connect as someone who had known great loss himself. Mel's father, Charlie, had been his best friend, and when he died, Stan had grieved as much as any of them.

The loss of a loved one whether by natural causes or homicide was devastating, but homicide was so much worse, because the victim's life had been taken from them, not by accident, but with intent. Wait. If Uncle Stan was here, did he think Rene's death was a homicide?

She jerked back and looked up at Uncle Stan's face. "Why are you here? Is it just a formality or has Rene's death been ruled a homicide?"

Uncle Stan shook his head. "I'm not talking about this with you. It's an ongoing investigation."

"So, it *is* a homicide."

"No." Stan shook his head. "Not yet, but given Mrs. Klein's relative youth and the lack of any preexisting conditions, we're taking the situation very seriously."

Mel stepped back and wiped the residual tears off her face with the palms of her hands. "Okay, that makes sense."

"Listen, kid, I know she was your friend but there's nothing you can do here," Stan said. He glanced past her at Dwight. He gave him a speculative look. "Or you, either."

Dwight raised his hands. "I'm just keeping an eye on her for Joe."

"Ah." Uncle Stan nodded as if it all made sense now.

"Can I see her, Uncle Stan?" Mel asked. "I . . . It's just that the last time I saw her . . ."

Mel didn't want to explain. It hurt too much. She didn't want to remember Rene the way she'd last seen her. She wanted to remember her the way she'd been before. Happy, smiling, and full of vision for her art.

"I'm sorry," he said. "She's already been taken to the medical examiner's office. We're in her studio, trying to piece together her last few days."

"Oh." It hit Mel hard, the finality of never seeing Rene in her studio ever again. She supposed it was ghoulish, but there was a part of her that just wouldn't believe Rene was dead until she saw her for herself.

"From what I understand, it was quick," Uncle Stan said.

"Except for the three times the paramedics almost brought her back," Mel said.

"Who told you that?"

"Byron," she said.

"The Mary with the hair," Dwight added helpfully.

Uncle Stan's lips twitched but he ironed out his features

by coughing into his fist. "Yes, we interviewed him already. He was working in the courtyard at the time. He didn't know what was happening until the ambulance arrived."

"I don't understand," Mel said. "I was just here last week—"

"Last week? You were here?" Uncle Stan glanced over his shoulder as if to see if they'd been overheard. "Are you saying you saw her recently?"

"Yes, I told you she was my friend," Mel said. She didn't usually get impatient with Uncle Stan, but he was acting weird and a little slow on the uptake. "We're providing the cupcakes for her art opening tomorrow night. Oh, I wonder what they'll do. Her art installation *Seasons* was supposed to open tomorrow. It's a huge event."

"I imagine they'll cancel or postpone," Uncle Stan said. He stared hard at Mel. "When was the last time you spoke to her exactly?"

"Last Friday when I stopped by to discuss the flavors for the cupcakes."

"It was a work-related meeting?" he asked. His phone chimed, and he pulled it out of his pocket and checked his messages. Whatever he read made him frown.

"Yes, Peter and I talked about it earlier in the day, and I told him I was going to stop by and finalize the flavors with Rene."

Uncle Stan nodded. "Good, that's good." He glanced over his shoulder at the door to Rene's studio. "Listen, I want to talk more about this but not here and not now." He shooed them with his hands out the door to the stairs. "I'm going to be here for a while. Can you come over to the house for a late supper? I'll tell your mom to make one of your favorites."

"Sure," Mel said. She tipped her head as she considered him. Uncle Stan was definitely acting strange. She was about to ask what was going on, when Uncle Stan turned to Dwight.

"Do me a favor, get her out of here without anyone else seeing her."

"What's going on, Uncle Stan?" she asked.

"Trust me. Just go."

Seven

Dwight didn't have to be told twice. He hooked Mel by the elbow and half carried, half dragged her down the stairs to the courtyard below.

"Wait," Mel protested. "You don't have to be so pushy. I'm going. I'm going."

"Not fast enough," Dwight said. "Your uncle wants you out of here for a reason, and I'm not going to second-guess his orders. Something is going down around here and we're going to git while the gittin' is good."

"Fine, whatever, but we have to collect Angie," Mel protested.

"Tate already scooped her up," Dwight said.

"What? When?"

"He was right behind me when I arrived," Dwight said.

"And he was very unhappy that she'd come here, and in her condition, too."

"Oh, boy."

"Or girl, I hear it hasn't been determined yet," he said.

"I tried to leave the bakery without her, but she insisted," Mel said. Dwight hustled her across the courtyard, not listening to her justification. "We had no idea that Rene was the one who died, we thought—"

She stopped talking as they passed Byron and Bernadette, who were still standing in the courtyard, although they'd been joined by some other artsy-looking people. Mel waved, and Byron waved back, kissing the tips of his fingers and blowing the kiss in her direction.

"I am seriously going to vomit harder than Angie," Dwight said in disgust. "Does Joe know about that guy?"

Mel felt her face get warm. "Byron's like that with everyone. It doesn't mean anything."

"That makes him a jerk, right? I mean, women don't really like that flirty guy stuff, do they?"

Mel shrugged. She had no idea. Her brain felt like pudding and her heart hurt. Beyond that it was all she could do to put one foot in front of the other.

Dwight opened the gate and pushed Mel through, missing the fact that there was another person coming through the gate at the same time. Mel bounced off a hard chest encased in black leather.

"Hey, watch it!" a voice chastised. "You crushed my tea roses."

"I'm sorry—wait." Mel would know that New York accent anywhere. "Ray, what are you doing here?"

"Mel?" His eyes went wide, and he glanced around to see if there was anyone else he recognized. "Sorry. Didn't mean to bark at you. It's just." He ran out of words and gestured to the flowers.

Mel blinked. Flowers? "Did you know Rene?"

"Rene?" he asked. "Who's that?"

"The artist who died," she said. "She was a friend of mine and Angie's."

"Oh, hey, kid, I'm sorry," Ray said. He gave her a one-armed hug. "That's rough. You gonna be okay?"

"Yeah, I'm here, and I'll take care of her," Dwight said.

Ray shot him a dark look. The brothers were very turfy about who looked after Angie and Mel.

"Joe know you're here?" Ray asked.

"He sent me," Dwight said.

"Well, all right then." The matter seemed resolved to Ray's satisfaction. Mel wanted to point out to him that he was the least evolved man she'd ever met, but what was the point? Ray was never going to change. He went to move past her to go up the stairs, but that couldn't be right. The police were up there. Who could he possibly . . . The fish!

It hit her like a dart right between the eyes. Holy bananas! Ray was here for Detective Martinez, which explained why she was so dressed up in the middle of an investigation. She must have been planning to punch out for her date, not knowing she'd be called to investigate. Ray and Tara? It was so unexpected, and yet the few times they'd crossed paths, there had definitely been something between them. Mel had thought it was contempt and disdain, but maybe it was pure animal attraction. Oh, *ew*. She shook her head.

"You're here for Tara, aren't you?" she asked.

"What?" Ray looked shocked. "How . . . I don't see how this is your business."

And now Mel was sure of it. Although she would never admit it, even under threat of torture, of all the DeLaura brothers, Ray was her favorite, which was not overly surprising given that they'd once been shot at together. He was the unabashed black sheep. He dressed in black leather even in the heat of the Arizona summer. He drove sports cars of dubious origins, wore a gold chain around his neck, and talked in a thick New York accent even though he hadn't lived there in over twenty years. He was also the brother who'd gotten her in and out of more mischief than all of the DeLaura brothers combined, including Joe.

To put it simply, despite his rough exterior, Ray was good people, and Mel adored him when he wasn't driving her completely mental. Perhaps this was why the thought of him dating Detective Harpy didn't work for her on any level. Ray deserved someone who was kind, who liked cannoli and spending her weekends at the track betting on the horses, a woman who saw the best in him, not some shrill screecher who got her jollies by persecuting Mel.

"Oh, no, Ray. Say it isn't so," she said.

"What?" He struck a pose of innocence that Mel didn't believe for a hot minute.

"You are here for her," she said.

To his credit, Ray didn't deny it. But before he could say anything at all, Dwight pushed Mel through the gate.

"Much as I hate to interrupt your gossip sesh, we need to go. DeLaura." With a nod at Ray, Dwight led Mel out to the sidewalk to where his Jeep was parked at the curb. He opened the door and hustled Mel in. She had barely gotten her seat belt clipped when he shot out into traffic.

"That was abrupt," she said.

"Your uncle wanted you out of there," he said. "I'm assuming he had his reasons."

Mel sighed. "Yes, but now I have to go have dinner with my mom."

"Joyce? She's a peach." Dwight gave her a look like she was an ungrateful brat. Not totally wrong but he didn't know the whole story.

"A few months ago, my mother was convinced I was pregnant," Mel said. "You have no idea how crazy she is going to make me when she finds out Angie *is* pregnant, which I'm sure she already knows because my mother knows everything. It's her superpower or she's a witch, hard to say."

"Maybe you should ask her how your artist friend died then?"

"You're annoying, you know that?"

He flashed her a grin, which turned his usually foreboding face into an almost handsome one.

"It's my gift."

Dwight dropped Mel off without coming into the bakery. He patted his abs and said he was on his way to the gym. By choice. Mel stepped out of the Jeep, marveling that they had become friends when they so clearly had nothing in common.

"Hey, Mel," Dwight called through his open window as she reached the front door. "Be careful, okay?"

Mel felt her lips curve up. That was as close as Dwight was ever going to get to admitting he cared. She nodded and yelled, "You, too."

He waved in acknowledgment and took off.

The smell of cupcakes, gloriously sweet decadent cupcakes, engulfed Mel as she stepped through the door to the accompaniment of the clang of the bells tied to the inside door handle. There was a moderate line of customers, and Marty was manfully behind the counter filling orders. Mel glanced around looking for Oz. There was no sign of him. Huh.

She hurried behind the counter, grabbing her apron off the hook as she went. "Where's Oz?"

"Darned if I know," Marty said. "He had another 'appointment.'" He made air quotes as he said the word. "And he was in a tie—again."

Mel felt her heart sink. It sounded as if Oz was definitely going on job interviews. The thought of losing him killed her. He was her right arm and sometimes her left arm, too. How was she going to run the bakery without him? But she had to face the fact that his suited-up disappearances likely meant that he was looking for a new position elsewhere.

Maybe they could offer him more money, his own franchise, creative control over their product. No, that was the line she couldn't cross. The creation of cupcakes, while she was open to experiments and new ideas and was happy to share, the overall product had to remain hers. Maybe that was what was driving Oz out. He wanted to be the chief creator. She understood, she did, but it still hurt.

"Hey, Tate and Angie told me about Rene," Marty said. His eyes were kind. "If you want to take off, I can handle this by myself."

"No, it's better to be busy," she said.

Marty nodded in understanding. "Let me know if you change your mind." He patted her back and continued to work.

Mel helped Marty clear out the customers. They were just closing up the bakery when Joe walked in. He was still in his dress shirt and tie from the office and on a leash was their Boston terrier, Peanut, adopted when his human had been the victim of a homicide.

"Peanut!" Mel knelt down and hugged her snorty, drooling baby girl to the front of her apron. "Did you come to see Mama at work, did you? Did you? Who's my pretty girl? Is it you?"

Peanut started to wiggle her waggle or waggle her wiggle, whichever case it was, as she danced around Mel in a circle of pure undiluted canine joy.

Joe leaned down to kiss Mel and then explained, "Uncle Stan told me we're having dinner at your mother's tonight, and I am under orders not to show up if I don't bring her granddog. Joyce wanted me bring her grandcat, too, but when Captain Jack saw the cat carrier, he did that weird slip-into-the-second-dimension thing that cats do when they hide in plain sight, and I couldn't find him."

Mel laughed. "He's done that to my mom, so I'm sure she'll understand. Did Uncle Stan tell you why we're having dinner?"

"He was very cryptic," Joe said. "But he said attendance was nonnegotiable. I suspect it has something to do with Rene."

"You mean Rene's death," Mel said. Her voice caught, and Joe immediately held out his arm. Mel stepped in for a comforting hug.

Joe pressed his head against the top of hers while Peanut collapsed on her feet. And for a second or two Mel felt okay. Then she thought of how horrible Peter must be feeling, and grief pierced the solace with its jagged edge, making her feel heartbroken and miserable once again.

Joe leaned back and glanced at her face. His chocolate

brown eyes went soft and he said, "I'm sorry about Rene. I know she was more than an artist to you. She was your friend." He kissed her hair, and Mel felt her throat get tight.

"You remember when you and I were first getting together, and you dumped me because you thought I might get whacked because of the mob case you were working?" she asked.

Joe cringed. "Biggest mistake of my life."

"Indeed. Rene was the one who told me to give you a second to come to your senses. She liked you. She believed in us."

"She was a wise and remarkable lady," Joe said. His voice was low and rough.

"That's why she made the topper for our wedding cake and now she won't be here to be a part of it," Mel said. "I just can't believe it. I mean, I just saw her last week."

"And from what you said it's clear she was suffering," Joe reminded her. "Do you think . . . and I'm really sorry to ask this . . . but do you think she was using?"

"Using what?" Mel asked.

Marty's bald head poked up from behind the glass bakery case. "You know, get-go, speed, ice, crystal, crank, meth."

Mel's eyes went wide. "How do you know all those names?"

"I watched *Breaking Bad*," he said. He glanced at Joe. "She was on amphetamines, wasn't she?"

"Toxicology won't tell us for a while, but given the erratic behavior Mel described and the crushing work schedule she'd been keeping, it's not out of the realm of possibility that she went looking for a boost to push through and ended up overdosing."

"Is that what they're saying it is?" she asked.

Joe shook his head. "The only thing confirmed so far is cardiac arrest. We're still waiting for the report, but I'm sure Uncle Stan has a million questions for you."

Mel sighed. She hoped her mom was serving her home-made mac and cheese tonight, because she was going to need her go-to comfort food.

"I'll lock up," Marty said. "You two head out."

"Oh, you don't have to," Mel said.

Marty waved her off. "Oz already cleaned the kitchen. All I need to do is shut off the lights. I've got this. You go."

"Thanks, Marty." Mel took off her apron and gave him a quick hug. "I don't know what I'd do without you."

His bald head turned a shade of hot pink and his voice was gruff when he said, "You'll never have to."

Joe led Mel and Peanut out the door to his waiting car. Mel's mother lived in a nearby neighborhood, the same one Mel and Joe lived in, and it took less than ten minutes to get there. Joe parked on the street in front of the house, and Mel opened her door, letting Peanut dash out. There was no sign of Uncle Stan's car and she wondered if he'd been de-layed at the gallery.

Joyce hurried outside to meet her granddog, whom she spoiled horribly. Bending over, she held her arms wide and Peanut raced toward her. In a greeting that was remarkably similar to Mel's and Peanut's, Joyce let the puppy kiss her face and she stood up and laughed. Her blue-green hazel eyes, the same color as Mel's, were sparkling.

"She's such a love," she cried. She slid a dog biscuit out of her pocket and gave it to Peanut, who fell on it with ca-nine rapture.

"It's a waste of breath to tell her not to spoil her, isn't it?" Mel whispered to Joe.

"Completely."

"Okay, then." Mel stepped forward with her arms wide. "Hi, Mom. Thanks for having us over for dinner."

"Of course," Joyce said. She hugged Mel and then stepped back, cupped her face, and studied her features. "You look tired. Are you getting enough sleep?"

"Yes, Mom."

Joyce gave her a doubtful look and then turned to Joe with a brilliant smile and her arms held wide for a hug. "Dear Joe." She squeezed him tight and asked, "Is she getting enough sleep? Because she looks tired to me. I know you take excellent care of her but we both know how stubborn she can be. Don't let her push you around."

Joe grinned at Mel over her mother's shoulder. Mel gave him a put-upon look. Her mother had been calling Joe "dear Joe" since they'd first started dating, and there were days that Mel was certain her mother preferred him to her own daughter.

He stepped back and met Joyce's gaze. "She is getting enough sleep, I promise. But today has been a rough day so she might look tired when she's really just sad."

"I'm standing right here," Mel said. "It's not like I can't hear you talking about me." Joe and Joyce ignored her. She glanced down at Peanut, who had consumed her biscuit and was standing on her back legs, pressing her nose into Joyce's hand in case there were more.

"Why is she sad?" Joyce asked.

"Her friend passed away."

"A friend? Who?" Joyce whirled towards Mel. "Was it someone I know?"

"I don't think so," Mel said. "Her name is Rene Fischer-Klein, she is . . . was a glass artist in Old Town."

"The one with the exhibit that is opening over the canal tomorrow?"

"Yes, that's her."

"Oh, no, I read about her in the paper. Her work is stunning."

"She was very gifted. She even made the cake topper for our wedding as a gift," Mel said. The words caught in her throat and she swallowed hard. "I have it in a box at the house."

"Oh, honey, I'm so sorry," Joyce said. She opened her arms and Mel stepped in for a hug. While both Uncle Stan and Joe gave great hugs, there was nothing like a hug from her mom. Those bracing arms had seen her though childhood illnesses, the awkward bullied years of middle school and high school, and the death of her dad. Her mom's fragrance, Chanel No. 5, was as familiar to her as the citrus trees blooming in March, and it always centered her.

She squeezed Joyce in return and then stepped back. She sniffed, and Joyce handed her a tissue from her pocket. Ever prepared.

"Thanks. I'm okay, Mom, or I will be."

Joyce studied her face and then nodded, seeming satisfied.

"Come inside, make yourselves comfortable," Joyce said. "I just need to glaze the chicken. Stan says he'll be here in a few minutes, but I don't want it to dry out."

The low-slung ranch that had been Mel's childhood home looked exactly as it had while she was growing up. Large windows looked over a grassy lawn that in the daytime offered an unparalleled view of Camelback Mountain. Citrus trees, older than her, lined the perimeter of the yard, which was enclosed by a brick wall.

She and Joe took Peanut outside so she could sniff the backyard to her heart's content. Joe looked thoughtfully at the darkening night sky while their dog dashed among the trees as if she couldn't decide which one needed a sniff down the most. Mel felt the corner of her mouth curve up. Thank goodness for her animals, they always lifted her up.

"Feeling any better, cupcake?"

She turned to find Joe watching her. She shrugged. "She helps. Mom helps. You help." She slipped her hand in his and said, "I just keep thinking about last week. How different Rene was. The paranoia and suspicion that I thought were from work stress and exhaustion, and now they think she overdosed on amphetamines? I just can't imagine. That's not the Rene I knew."

"Drugs change people," Joe said. "Addiction causes them to do horrible, out-of-character things. It's an epidemic. We just had a meeting at the office and went over the latest stats from the Federal Bureau of Prisons. Forty-five percent of all incarcerations are because of drug offenses. That's almost seventy-five thousand inmates. And in Arizona, all we do is incarcerate for minor nonviolent possession charges, when we know it doesn't work." He ran his free hand through his hair, which was his go-to mannerism when he was exasperated.

"Sounds like you're struggling as a county prosecutor," Mel said.

"I just think there are better ways to treat the drug epidemic than prison, especially in nonviolent cases where addiction is the problem," he said. "Uncle Stan and I have talked about it and he agrees."

"Agrees about what?" Uncle Stan asked from the open doorway to the kitchen.

"The uselessness of incarcerating nonviolent offenders in drug cases," Joe said.

Uncle Stan cringed. "Yeah, it's a mess. Ask any cop worth his salt, and they'll tell you that drugs are the cause directly or indirectly of ninety percent of the crime we deal with every day. Nothing like trying to uphold the law when the law is stupid, overly punitive, and lines the pockets of those invested in privatizing prisons."

This surprised a chuckle out of Joe. "The slippery slope of being a public servant."

Uncle Stan narrowed his eyes at Joe. "What we need is some hotshot young lawmakers in office, focusing on rehabilitation instead of incarceration."

Before he finished his sentence, Joe started to shake his head. "I am not running for office."

Mel felt her jaw drop open. "Office? What office?"

Joe heaved a sigh and looked at Stan. "Now you've done it."

Uncle Stan grinned and turned to Mel. "Me and the squad have been trying to get your fiancé to consider a career in politics. We need someone in the job who has walked the walk, not these out-of-touch, bottom-line local businessmen who don't know their a—"

"Dinner's ready," Joyce announced from behind them.

Uncle Stan coughed into his fist. "Well, you know what I mean."

Joyce glanced at the three of them, and Mel realized that if her mother knew what Uncle Stan was suggesting, she would be on it like a shark on a guppy. There'd be lawn signs to "vote for dear Joe" before the man knew what was what.

Mel squeezed Joe's hand. "We'll discuss it later."

"Or not," he said, returning the squeeze. "Because I'm not doing it."

"Not doing what?" Joyce asked.

"Taking up golf," Uncle Stan said. "The kid positively refuses to meet me on the green."

Joe gave him a look and Uncle Stan shrugged. Clearly, he was not at his best in the diversion department today. Without comment, Joyce led the way into the house, and Joe followed. Mel would have been right behind him, but Uncle Stan held her back.

"How you doing, kid?" he asked.

"Eh," Mel said. "This is going to take some time. Why did you want us here for dinner?"

Stan glanced at the house and then at her. "After dinner, we'll talk. You look like you're about to drop."

Mel glanced at the house and saw Joyce watching them. "Sounds good." She forced a smile and headed inside.

They washed up and sat at the dining room table, which Joyce had set with her favorite blue Fiesta ware. Uncle Stan sat in the seat that used to be Mel's father's, while her mother sat at the opposite end, with Mel and Joe across from each other. It had taken Mel some getting used to, but it felt more normal now to have Uncle Stan sitting at the head of the table. There was no doubt Stan had been a stabilizing force in Joyce's life, and she'd gotten him to take his health more seriously, which had been long overdue. Mel couldn't even remember the last time she'd seen him demolish a roll of antacid tablets.

Dishes were passed, including homemade mac and cheese, and plates filled. Joyce beamed at them and Mel knew that her happiest moments were when her family was sitting at the table together. It was too bad Mel's brother

Charlie lived in Flagstaff with his wife and two sons. It would have filled Joyce's happiness bucket to overflowing to have them here, too.

Because Joe's family was so large and boisterous, Mel sometimes felt as if her family was too quiet in comparison. Joe reassured her that he found the difference to be a welcome relief. The DeLauras couldn't seem to get through a month without someone having drama, and Joe was usually the first on call. It was a nice change for him that Mel's family didn't really have that, well, except for Mel's penchant for stumbling across dead bodies.

She wondered why she couldn't be cursed with the gift of finding money. It would be so much less stressful. Technically, she hadn't been the first to find Rene, so that was a nice change. But still she knew her, had just seen her, was technically working for her, and still couldn't believe that someone as driven as Rene would have risked her life or her health on the eve of her biggest exhibition. That was the thing that had been bothering her all day. Rene overdosing, either intentionally or not, made absolutely no sense.

"Did my chicken do something to offend you?" Joyce asked.

Mel followed her gaze down to her plate. Her beautifully sliced chicken breast with the orange glaze looked like it had been massacred, chewed up and spat out, and left to rot. Shredded to itty-bitty pieces and fit only to be stuffed into a tortilla. Even though she knew she was obviously responsible, Mel had no idea how it had gotten that way.

"Sorry, no, it's delicious. I just got lost in thought," she said.

"Probably not a good idea with a knife in your hand," Uncle Stan said.

Joyce gave him a look and then reached across the table and put her hand over Mel's. "Were you thinking about your friend?"

Mel sighed. "Yes, I just don't understand how this could have happened. Rene was a force of nature. I can't imagine that she died of a drug overdose."

"It's still speculation at this point," Joe reminded her. "Until we have the medical examiner's report, we don't know anything for certain." He turned to Uncle Stan. "Did her husband, Peter, say anything that would explain what happened?"

Uncle Stan shook his head, and Mel knew he wouldn't talk about an ongoing investigation in front of her and her mother. She tried not to be frustrated, but Rene was her friend and she wanted to understand. Uncle Stan surprised her then.

"Her husband was incoherent," he said. "We couldn't get anything out of him. He was so overwrought, refusing to allow the medical examiner to take her body, that he had to be sedated and sent home with the gallery owner, Sunny Davidson."

Mel made a face. Uncle Stan's gaze narrowed. "You know something about her?"

"She's mean," Mel said. "At least, she was the other day when I stopped by to meet with Rene. She flat out forbade me from 'bothering' her even though I was there for work."

"Is she normally that protective of her artists?" Joyce asked.

"Not that I'd noticed before," Mel said. "I assumed she was agitated about the installation, as her gallery would benefit from the exposure, but maybe she knew more of what was happening with Rene."

"We questioned her, and she insisted she didn't know anything," Stan said. "In fact, she made it sound as if she hardly knew Rene and Peter outside of a working relationship."

"That's weird," Mel said. "They've been exclusively represented by her gallery for years. I know that the three of them used to have wild trips across Europe, looking at art. Rene told me about their drunken shenanigans in Paris, Milan, and Prague, just to name a few."

Uncle Stan looked thoughtful while he chewed his dinner. "I figured," he muttered. "I should have pressed her harder."

"You'll have another chance," Joe said. "I don't see this case going away anytime soon. It's too high profile given that the artist is local and the installation is for the city."

The doorbell rang, and Joyce started. She frowned at the clock. This was an incredibly late supper by her standards but still it was supper, family time, and whoever was at her door at this time of night, interrupting their meal, was not going to be warmly welcomed.

"I'll get it," Uncle Stan said. He pushed back his chair, wiped his lips with his napkin, and headed for the door.

"Thank you," Joyce called after him. Then she turned and said, "Now, dear Joe, tell me how Angie is feeling."

Mel felt her eyes widen. Had her mother heard about Angie's pregnancy? How? From whom? And how was it possible that she hadn't said a word until now? It had to have been from Mrs. DeLaura. Given that Angie was the youngest and the only DeLaura daughter, Mel knew her future mother-in-law was probably worried to death about her.

"She's doing great," Joe said. He shoveled some mac and

cheese into his mouth as if that would stop Joyce's line of questioning. Mel shook her head. Did the man not know her mother at all?

"Does she know how far along she is? Do you think they'll find out if it's a boy or a girl or do they want to be surprised? How about an obstetrician? Has she picked one yet?"

The questions came like cannon fire. To Joe's credit, he didn't drop his fork and cover his head. Rather, he finished chewing, swallowed, and said, "I'm not sure."

"About which?" Joyce asked. She cast Mel a side eye. "I'm only asking you because my daughter forgot to mention it to me even though she knows Angie is like a second daughter to me, and I would have been overjoyed to hear the news."

"Easy there, Mom. Dial back the guilt machine. I've been waiting for Angie and Tate to give us the go-ahead to share the news," Mel said. "Some parents like to wait until the first trimester is over before they announce their pregnancy."

"Of course they wait to share with the public at large, but I am family," Joyce said. Her voice wobbled when she added, "At least I thought I was."

Joe looked stricken. Tears were not his bag. Mel, on the other hand, had been on the front line of Joyce's mama drama too many times to play.

"Of course you're family," Mel said. "Don't be silly. As a matter of fact, Angie told me that she wanted to tell you herself, so now you're going to have to pretend that you don't know, because otherwise she'll be terribly disappointed not to be able to see your initial reaction to her news for herself."

"She was?" Joyce dabbed her eyes with her napkin and clasped her hands over her chest. "Oh, that sweet, lovely girl."

Mel saw Joe's lips twitch and she quickly looked away from him so she wouldn't ruin the moment by laughing. She turned back to Joyce. "How'd you find out anyway?"

"I was at the florist, picking some flowers for the table"—Joyce paused and gestured to the vase of colorful gerbera daisies, before she continued—"when Ray walked in. He was buying a lovely bouquet of tea roses, and we got to talking. He was so proud. He told me Angie is planning to name the baby after him."

Joe choked on a green bean, and Mel had to cover her mouth with her hand to hide her smile.

"Dear Joe, are you all right?" Joyce asked. "Here now, raise your arms up in the air, it'll help."

Joe was hacking and Mel supposed she should have been concerned, but Joyce had left her seat and was now assisting Joe in getting his arms up in the air like he was five, and it was just too much. A laugh broke free. Joe scowled at her as he tried to clear his throat and fight off her mother at the same time.

"What the hell is going on in here?" Uncle Stan asked.

"Stan, language," Joyce huffed. She dropped Joe's arms.

"Sorry, but we have company," he said. He jerked his eyes to the side, indicating the person behind him. Mel could tell from his expression he wasn't happy about whoever had arrived. She tried to peer around him but couldn't see in the dim hallway light.

"Well, invite them in," Joyce said. She patted Joe on the back, two hard wallops that launched him into the table but effectively ended his coughing fit.

He straightened up and gave Mel a surprised look. Despite her build, Joyce packed a punch. As Mel's brother Charlie liked to say, she was small but mighty.

Stan turned around and asked, "You hungry?"

"No, thank you," a woman answered. Mel was intrigued. "I just want to speak with your niece and then I'll be on my way."

Mel frowned. *She* was Stan's niece. Who wanted to speak with her?

Uncle Stan entered the room as if the woman had a gun to his back. When he stepped aside, Mel took in the professional woman standing behind him. She was of average height and build, wore her blond hair in loose waves that framed her face and ended at her shoulders. Her suit was a navy blue jacket over a white shirt with a dark tie. On the left breast was a police shield and on the shoulder was the patch for the Scottsdale Police.

Mel had never met the woman looking at her so sternly, but she'd seen her interviewed on the nightly news. It was police chief Lori Rosen. Mel felt her stomach sink into her feet. This could not be good.

Eight

Joe and Mel both rose from their seats. She gave him a panicked look, which he ignored.

"Chief Rosen," Joe said. "What brings you by?"

"DeLaura." The chief's face remained neutral and she turned to Joyce. "Sorry to interrupt your dinner. I just want a quick word with your daughter."

"Oh, all right," Joyce said. She wasn't a complete pushover to authority as she turned to Stan and said, "Explain."

"It's about the incident at the art gallery," he said. "Chief Rosen has some concerns."

"About me?" Mel asked. Her heart started hammering in her chest. The chief of police was here asking about her. This was not good, *not good*.

"If we could speak privately in another room?" Chief Rosen asked.

"Yeah, sorry, Chief. That's not going to happen," Joe said. He glanced at Stan, who was obviously in a rock and a hard place between his boss and his niece. "I'm coming with you."

One of the chief's perfectly arched eyebrows rose. Joe met her stare head-on.

"Very well then." Chief Rosen turned and left the room, clearly expecting them to follow.

"Wait," Joyce hissed. "I don't understand what's happening. Why is she here? Why does she want to talk to Melanie?"

"It's all right," Uncle Stan said. "It's just a talk and Joe is with her."

"A talk—but why?" Joyce persisted. "Are you in trouble, Mel?"

Mel glanced at Joe. How to answer? She didn't think so, but she wasn't sure and didn't want to give her mother false information. Sensing her dilemma, Joe turned around and said to Joyce, "Don't worry. I've got this."

Much to Mel's chagrin, Joyce's shoulders dropped, and she beamed at him in relief and said, "Of course you do, dear Joe."

Mel turned on her heel and went to follow the chief, with Joe behind her, sounding suspiciously like he was trying not to laugh. He leaned forward and said, "I love your mom."

"As you should," Mel said. "She's your number one fan for life."

"And I'm hers. After all, she brought you into the world and you're my everything," he said.

Mel caught her breath. She glanced at him over her shoulder. "If you're trying to sweet-talk your way out of me being peeved with you because my mother thinks you do no wrong, it's totally working."

He chuckled but it was cut short as they joined Chief Rosen, who was standing in the living room, looking decidedly unamused.

Mel crossed her arms over her chest, feeling awkward and vulnerable. There was a pulse of power that came off the chief that she wasn't used to. Joe seemed impervious to it, so she tried to follow his lead.

"Have a seat, Chief," he said. His voice was firm as if he was meeting her as an equal. Suddenly, her mother's worship of Joe made perfect sense to Mel. He really was her hero.

The chief gave him a curt nod and sat on the edge of one of the leather armchairs. Mel and Joe took the sofa. They sat in the middle, close together. Mel thought Joe was making a statement that he was on her side. When he took her hand in his, she knew it for sure.

"How can we help you?" he asked.

The chief's glance slid from Joe to Mel. She tipped her head to the side and studied Mel. "You're an interesting woman, Melanie Cooper."

Was that a euphemism for something bad? Mel wasn't sure, but she did know that the only person who called her Melanie was her mother.

"Mel," she said. "And in what way am I interesting?"

"Owner of a national cupcake bakery franchise and at such a young age," the chief said. She tapped her chin with the tip of her index finger as if giving Mel careful consideration.

"I have a very savvy business partner," Mel said. She felt defensive and, not surprisingly, suddenly wanted a very decadent, very gooey cupcake like a triple vanilla or a deep blue velvet with cream cheese frosting.

"Tate Harper, I know," Chief Rosen said. "He comes from quite the wealthy and powerful family. Lots of money there. And he's married to your other partner, your friend Angela DeLaura." She turned to Joe. "Your sister, correct? How cozy this all is."

Mel felt a shiver ripple down her back. She didn't like the way the chief was looking at them, as if they were up to something and she was onto them. Had Mel inadvertently made an enemy of the chief of police? How? She'd never had so much as a parking ticket in her entire life.

"I don't see—" Joe began, but Mel squeezed his fingers, quieting him. It was suddenly very important to her not to appear weak in front of this woman, who as chief of police was likely a badass. She didn't want to hide behind Joe. She wanted to be her own advocate.

"You wanted to speak with me and here I am. So, please tell me, have I done something?" Mel asked. "Because this feels a bit like an interrogation, and I can't think of any reason why I'd be on the receiving end of one."

"Does it?" the chief asked. Both eyebrows went up and Mel felt her temper get short. She didn't like games.

"Chief Rosen, I would appreciate it if you could just be straight with me," Mel said. "I'm a hardworking small business owner who has never broken a law in her life, so what is it exactly that you need to talk to me about?"

Joe squeezed her fingers in approval, and Mel took heart and sat up straighter. She was no one's doormat.

"Fair enough," Chief Rosen said. "I have some concerns about you, Ms. Cooper, number one of which is, why are you always present when a dead body is discovered?"

"I'm not," Mel protested. "Not really. There have just been a couple of weird circumstances."

"Really?" Chief Rosen asked. "Let's see if I remember some of the highlights I read about you today. Christie Stevens? Wasn't she Tate Harper's fiancée before he married Angela DeLaura? So interesting that you found her body and, hey, aren't Tate and Angela married now?"

Mel felt her heart start to beat hard in her chest. She didn't know what to say. It had been horrible to find Christie, and certainly none of them had wished the woman dead.

"I fail to see—" Joe began but the chief ignored him.

"Let me see, wasn't there an 'incident' with Baxter Malloy?" she asked. Her eyes were as hard as glass. "He was on a date with your mother, Joyce, when he went toes up, as I recall."

"That was an unfortunate coincidence—" Mel began but the chief steamrolled right over her.

"And how about Vic Mazzotta, your mentor?" Chief Rosen asked. "Another unfortunate coincidence, I suppose?"

A flash of pain punched Mel right in the chest. She still missed Vic.

"Don't—" Mel protested but, again, the chief barreled on, regardless of the parade of pain she was causing Mel.

"And Blaise Ione, the photographer? He was one of several who died, all of whom were hired for . . . wait for it . . . Angela and Tate's wedding," Chief Rosen said. She stared at Mel as if she'd been the one to commit the murders, which was ridiculous. "And that was just one of the latest. There were more murders, and you were there for every one! How do you explain your involvement with all of these deaths?"

Mel's hands were sweating. Her throat was tight. It looked awful, she knew that, but she truly had nothing to do with any of these murders.

"Bad luck?" Mel suggested.

"No one is that unlucky," Chief Rosen said.

"No, really, she is," Joe said. "I've seen it."

Mel turned to look at him and he shrugged. "Sorry, but it's a fact, cupcake. You have the worst luck of anyone I've ever known when it comes to stumbling across dead bodies, and that includes all of the homicide detectives put together."

She looked at the chief. "I can't help it if my business brings me into strange and weird situations."

"You bake cupcakes," Chief Rosen said. Her teeth were clenched. It was hard to understand the words, but Mel got the gist.

"Yeah." She nodded. "Cupcakes and death are apparently not as uncommon as you'd think. Who knew?"

The chief shook her head. "Yeah, I don't buy it."

"Buy what?" Joe asked. "She can't help it if she's been in the wrong place at the wrong time a few times."

"A few times? Were you not listening? She's been murder adjacent at least ten times. How does that happen to a normal citizen?"

"When you put it like that, it sounds bad," Mel said.

"It *is* bad," Chief Rosen said. "You baked cupcakes for Rene Fischer-Klein every week for years and now she's dead. I find that highly suspicious, especially given your past. I've decided to call an independent council of police officers to do a review of any and all cases that involve you, however indirectly."

"What?" Joe snapped. "That's ludicrous."

"But why?" Mel asked.

"Because I have sworn to protect and serve the citizens of this city, and I have to consider the very real possibility that perhaps some or all of these deaths have been caused by you," Chief Rosen said.

"But that's insane," Joe protested. "What exactly are you accusing her of?"

"Nothing . . . yet," Chief Rosen said. "But we'll see what the council discovers."

"You're serious." Mel gaped. "You're going to have officers investigating my past? This is ridiculous. I've never done anything."

"Are you denying that you had a relationship with Vincent Tucci?" Chief Rosen asked.

"Yes!" she said. "He and I both studied baking in Paris at different times, that's all. Plus, he tried to kill me."

"How convenient," Chief Rosen said.

"Not really," Mel said. "It wasn't."

"What exactly are you looking for?" Joe asked. His color was high; he looked furious. In all the years Mel had known him, she'd never seen him look so angry.

"Not looking, just gathering facts. Food enterprises are notorious for fronting drugs and laundering money," Chief Rosen said. "If this sort of thing were happening within the bakery, it would explain why Mel seems to be constantly getting mixed up in murder."

"Money laundering?" Mel thought she might have a stroke. "I don't even balance my checkbook, and now I'm a money launderer?"

"You seem awfully defensive. Let's talk about your partner, the investment whiz kid, Tate Harper," Chief Rosen said. "He supposedly left his father's firm with nothing. *Why* would he do that? And now, he's made your enterprise a multimillion-dollar success and in just a few years. *How* did he do that?"

"Tate is one of the best people I know. Hardworking, honest, and kind. He also happens to be a financial genius and convinced me to let people buy franchises of the bakery," Mel said. "Much to my surprise, although it shouldn't have been, it was a brilliant business move."

"Yes, and one of those franchisers was a Vegas showgirl, Holly Hartzmark, with quite the sketchy past if I remember the report right," the chief said. "An explosion killed one of the men trying to find a location for the bakery, correct?"

Mel pressed her lips into a thin line to keep from saying something profane in her mother's house that might also land her in jail overnight. As if he sensed her inability to articulate her ire politely, Joe filled the tense silence.

"Chief, if you have a problem with my fiancée, feel free to investigate her, her business, and her friends and family to your satisfaction," he said. "She has nothing to hide and neither do we."

"Are you talking as a county attorney?" Chief Rosen asked. She looked patronizingly amused.

"No, I'm talking as a man who knows that he has the best woman in the world, and I'll defend her with everything I have, even if it means suing the Scottsdale PD for slander."

That wiped the sly smile off of the chief's face. "Tread carefully, DeLaura."

"I'd advise the same to you," he said.

Chief Rosen stood. Mel and Joe did, too. The chief looked dissatisfied and a bit annoyed, which was fine with Mel. She could have told the chief not to go up against Joe.

He'd been mediating his brothers' disputes his entire life. He was a pro and he never lost.

"This conversation isn't over. The independent council will be in touch," the chief said. She glanced at Mel. "I imagine you'll want to clear your calendar for some depositions."

The manners Joyce had drilled into her since birth had Mel moving to the front door. She held it open and said, "Good night, Chief Rosen."

The chief paused to give her one more measured glance before she stepped out into the night. Mel shut the door behind her and collapsed against it. Joe was right there, pulling her into his arms. To Mel's surprise, she discovered she was shaking.

"It's okay," he said. "I'm not going to let anyone come after you. Not now. Not ever."

Mel leaned back to study his face. "I love your confidence but that is the chief of police, and she thinks I'm a murderer, an accomplice to murder, or quite possibly a serial killer!"

"She's wrong," he said. "And even though she's the chief, she's still just a human, and humans make mistakes."

"A human? Really? Because her resemblance to a fire-breathing dragon can't be discounted," Mel said.

"Ha!" Uncle Stan joined them in the foyer with Joyce right behind him. "That's what we call her at the station, the dragon."

"How did it go, honey?" Joyce asked. "Is everything all right?"

"You mean you weren't listening at the door?" Mel asked.

"No, of course, we were," Joyce said. "But we missed some parts. The dragon is a low talker, very annoying."

Mel smiled. If the dragon wondered where Mel got her buttinsky tendencies from, it was Joyce. She glanced at Uncle Stan to share the joke, but he was frowning.

"Is that why you wanted me to come over for dinner tonight?" Mel asked. "Were you going to warn me about the chief?"

"She was at the art gallery today," he said. "Once your name came up and a few of the officers mentioned prior cases you'd been linked to, she became like a dog with a bone and was determined to interview you. The independent council is a bit of a surprise, however."

"Does she really think I had something to do with all of those murders?" Mel asked. "I mean, that's mental, right?"

"Right. To be honest, I'm not sure why you're on her radar, given that your uncle is on the force and your fiancé works in the courts, but I don't like you being in her sights, Mel," he said. "You're going to have to be very careful, and stay as far away from the case surrounding Rene as you can."

"But Rene was my friend," Mel said. "I don't think I can do that."

"It could cost you if you don't," Uncle Stan said. "And honestly, kid, I don't know if Joe and I can protect you from the chief."

Mel saw the concern in his eyes mirrored in her mother's. She nodded. She didn't want them to be worried. "Okay, I'll steer clear of the situation as much as I can. I have no idea what Peter's planning to do about the opening tomorrow, and I have all of those cupcakes, but I'll just donate them to a women's shelter if I don't hear from him."

"Thank you, dear," Joyce said. She reached up and brushed Mel's bangs out of her eyes. "I know it's hard for you, but I think it's for the best. Now, who wants some of my homemade apple pie with vanilla ice cream for dessert?"

"Make mine a double," Uncle Stan said. He turned and headed back to the dining room.

"No, I won't make yours a double." Joyce followed him. "At most you can have a smidgen more than a regular portion."

"But I'm a big man," Stan said.

"You'll just have to find another way to satisfy your appetite," Joyce said.

Awkward silence greeted this pronouncement, and Mel glanced down at her shoes. This was one of those things a child never wanted to know about their parents and their partners, the dreaded S-E-X.

"It's all right, I didn't hear a thing," she called after them. "I'm not scarred, no need for therapy here, nope, I'm totally fine."

She could feel Joe trying to hold in a chuckle while Stan and Joyce escaped the weirdness by ducking into the kitchen as fast as their feet could carry them.

Joe pulled her in close and tight, and Mel hugged him back. As his laugh subsided, he leaned back and studied her. "That was a nice thing you did."

"What's that?"

"Fib to Joyce and Stan about staying away from the investigation of Rene's death," he said.

"Joe DeLaura, are you calling me a fibber?"

"If the fib fits," he said.

She sighed. "It wasn't a total fabrication. I am a little

worried that the chief seems so obsessed with my uncanny ability to be in the wrong place at the wrong time, and it's disconcerting to hear how many murders I've been tied to. I mean, even I'm starting to think maybe I'm cursed or everyone around me is."

"No," Joe said. His tone was firm and reassuring. "I think it's just the company you keep: me, a prosecutor; Uncle Stan, a detective; and the rest of the cupcake crew. We've all brought you into situations you wouldn't have had anything to do with otherwise, and the independent council will prove it, you'll see. If she wants to investigate you, I say bring it on."

"Maybe."

"No maybe about it."

Joe met and held her gaze. "Hey, I'm serious. It's not you. You're not cursed."

"And yet, still another friend of mine is dead," Mel said. She put her hand on the side of his face. The grief she'd been pushing down all day bubbled up. "After what happened between me and Rene last week, how can I not feel responsible? I should have done something, said something, insisted she see somebody."

"I think you're taking a bigger bite out of that responsibility than is your share," Joe said. "Peter said she wasn't herself. He knew she was struggling. If anyone should have stepped in, it was him."

"You're right. And why didn't he?" she asked.

Joe shook his head. He didn't know the Kleins as well as Mel and couldn't hazard a guess. "That's Uncle Stan's job to find out."

"I think Peter is more likely to talk to me than Uncle Stan," she said.

Joe sighed. "Well, that promise to steer clear lasted a whole five minutes."

"Fibber," Mel said with a shrug. Then she turned and headed to the kitchen, where Joyce's apple pie awaited her, because apple pie, just like cupcakes, always made everything better.

Nine

"Then what happened?" Angie asked.

Mel, Angie, and Oz were working in the kitchen while Marty manned the front counter. Mel was telling them about her alarming meeting with Chief Rosen.

"She left, and Joe tried to tell me that all of these deaths had nothing to do with me, but I still feel weird about it. I mean, it is weird, right? Normal people don't have dead bodies spilling out at them from every nook and cranny."

"That's ridiculous," Angie said. "You can't help it if you're in the wrong place at the wrong time, right, Oz?"

"Well, she is in the wrong place an awful lot," he said. He loaded his pastry bag with frosting.

"Oz!" Mel cried. She glanced at him. She was still getting used to being able to see his eyes. Had he always had long thick eyelashes like that? Why did men always get the best eyelashes? They were wasted on them. It wasn't fair.

Oz ignored her and piped a thick swirl of mocha buttercream onto a coffee-flavored cupcake. He paused and sifted some cocoa powder on top and then placed one chocolate-covered espresso bean at the peak of the frosting. They looked fabulous, smelled even better, and Mel knew without tasting them that they would melt in her mouth and the cake-to-frosting ration would be perfection. Oz was a magician and she was never going to find another assistant as great as him. The realization was crushing, and protocol aside, she couldn't stand not knowing any longer.

"You're quitting, aren't you?" she asked. The words flew out of her mouth unfiltered.

Oz dropped the sifter. Cocoa powder went everywhere in an explosion of brown dust that made him cough. He brushed the cocoa off his face and blinked. His eyes were wide when he asked, "What? How did you . . ."

"The haircut, the suits, it really wasn't brain surgery," Angie said.

"Oh." Oz looked crestfallen. "I wanted to tell you. I was going to tell you. I mean, I planned to tell you before they started calling my references. You're it, by the way. I just—"

His voice trailed off and he looked more like the boy from the tech high school who had arrived for a job a few years ago than the grown man with the culinary degree that he was now.

"It's all right," Mel said. She raised her hands, indicating that he should calm down. "We all suspected what was happening, but no one wanted to say anything until you were ready to tell us. I wouldn't have said anything now, it's just that things have been rough around here lately and I just needed to know. So, are you leaving? Have you had an offer? Will you accept a new position somewhere nearby? It's okay if you do."

"Except for Olivia," Angie interrupted. "I'll go full Italian if you leave us for her." She looked at Oz with teary eyes and then blinked. She sniffed, and in her best mobster voice, she said, "'Watch who you trust. Even your teeth bite your tongue every now and then.'"

"*The Godfather,*" Oz said, identifying the movie. His voice sounded gruff. "And for the record, that was a terrible Vito Corleone."

"What are you talking about?" Angie protested. "I do a great Brando."

"Oh, was that was supposed to be Brando?" Oz rolled his eyes. "I thought it was Pesci from *My Cousin Vinny.*"

Angie picked up his pastry bag and pretended she was going to blast him with it. He held up his hands as if to ward her off. They both laughed.

Mel noticed that he looked relieved by the teasing. As if by joking about his leaving, they were telling him it was okay. It wasn't. She was crushed. But just like her mentor Vic Mazzotta had let her go when she was ready, she needed to do the same for Oz. He had dreams of his own to pursue, and she would never stand in his way even though her heart hurt when she thought about him leaving their bakery family.

"So, where are you thinking you'll likely go?" she asked.

Angie handed him the pastry bag, and Oz resumed working. He frosted three cupcakes before he answered. "There's a resort that's looking for a pastry chef."

"Which one?" Mel asked.

"The Sun Dial," he said. "I'll have my own brand-new state-of-the-art kitchen and four assistants."

Mel was quiet, absorbing this news. There was absolutely nothing they could offer him that would be better than this experience. If he wanted to make a name for himself in the world of pastry, this was his ticket.

"The Sun Dial. They're new," Angie said. "I saw a write-up about them in the paper. Pretty high-end resort."

"Yeah," Oz said. He stared down at his cupcakes.

Mel waited but he said nothing more. She felt as if her nerves were at the breaking point. She glanced at Angie, who looked as anxious as she felt.

"So, they made an offer? Are you going to take it?" she asked.

Oz put down the pastry bag. He glanced up at her, looking ill at ease, which on his six-foot-four stalwart frame gave him a vulnerability that made Mel want to hug him.

"I wanted to tell you when the time was right," he said. "But with everything that's happened, oh, who am I kidding? Around here, there never seems to be the right moment."

Mel felt her throat close up, but she pushed the words out. "You can tell me now."

Oz nodded. In a voice that was thick with emotion, he said, "All right, then this is my official two weeks' notice. They're going to call you sometime in the next few days, which they told me was just a formality, but I'd appreciate it if you'd give me a good reference."

A single tear slipped out of the corner of his eye, and he swiped it away with the back of his hand. The sight broke Angie, who let out a wail that sounded like someone had pilfered her last cupcake. The swinging doors to the kitchen slammed open, and Marty appeared, with one eyebrow high as he scanned the room.

"What is that noise?" he demanded. He glanced at the three of them. "What's going on? Why is everyone crying? Did someone die? Did *I* die?" He patted his chest. "I feel okay."

Oz laughed. Then he sobbed. "I'm going to miss you, old man."

"Who are you calling old?" Marty protested. "Wait, what do you mean you're going to miss me?"

The three of them were silent. No one knew how Marty would take the news. He and Oz had become the best of friends over the past few years, and it was going to be strange to have one without the other. Mel glanced at Oz, and he returned her look with an imploring one. She could see he wanted her to deliver the bad news. Oh, joy.

"Oz has given me his two weeks' notice," Mel said. "He's going to be moving on to a bigger job, a career move."

Marty's mouth formed an O. He looked at Oz and then nodded. His voice was gruff when he said, "Well, duh, of course you've got to strike out on your own. That's as it should be, but you'll still live above the bakery, right?"

Oz glanced at Mel, and she nodded. Of course he could live in her old apartment as long as he wanted. He grinned, and she knew that he'd been afraid that by quitting his job, he'd lose his home, too. Never that. Even if he left, he'd always be family.

"Well, all right then, that's not so bad. We'll still see each other every day," Marty said. He cleared his throat and looked stern. "In the meantime, I've got a line of customers out front and I could use some help. Get off your keisters and give an 'old man' a hand."

"On it," Oz said. He handed Mel his frosting bag and Angie his sifter and followed Marty out to the front.

Mel and Angie were quiet for a moment, focusing on the table full of coffee-flavored cupcakes in front of them. Finally, Angie asked, "You okay?"

"No, but I will be," Mel said. "Eventually."

Mel and Angie set to work and finished the cupcakes, putting them into the walk-in cooler. As they cleaned the kitchen, Angie said, "You know we need to throw him the biggest send-off party this place has ever seen, right?"

Mel nodded. "It'll be our first send-off party. He deserves a really good one. We can invite his family and his girlfriend, Lupe."

"And close the bakery early and fire up the jukebox," Angie said. "It'll be a righteous bon voyage."

"Sounds good," Mel said. She forced a smile.

"You hate this," Angie said.

"With every fiber of my being," she sighed. "Not the party, just losing Oz. Aside from the fact that he's like family, he's irreplaceable. He's a long-distance marathoner when it comes to work. He's never sick, he's happy to work at the crack of dawn, take the van out to special events, and invent new flavors. I mean, I don't think I fully appreciated him, and now he's leaving."

"He is going to leave a giant Oz-sized hole in the operation."

"Where am I going to find someone to take his place?

"No idea," Angie said. She sounded forlorn. "He's one of a kind."

Mel thought about the boy who showed up from the technical high school wearing a Ramones T-shirt, several piercings, and his bangs down over his eyes. "He is at that."

As if he knew they were talking about him, Oz returned to the kitchen, bursting through the swinging doors from the bakery like he was running from the law.

"Mel, we have a situation," he said.

"What do you mean? Are we being robbed?" she asked. "Is Marty okay? What's going on?"

"Marty's fine. You're not. You need to go. Now."

"Oz, calm down," Angie said. "Where's the fire? Wait, is there a fire?"

"No. Trust me," Oz said. "You want to slip out the back. Go hide out in my apartment for a while."

"What? Why?" Mel asked. "What's happening?"

"Reporters," he said. His eyes were round. "Loads of them and they all want to interview you."

"Me?" she cried. "Why?"

"The first one through the door said he heard that you're a person of interest in the murder of Rene Fischer-Klein, and asked if you would like to make a statement about that," he said. He grabbed her hand and dragged her to the back door. He was about to open it, when a fist rapped on the door, startling them both.

"Susan Estevez, with Channel Seven. I'm looking for Melanie Cooper," a woman said.

"Ah! Too late. They're here," Oz said as he twisted the lock on the doorknob, securing it. He pushed Mel behind him as if he could shield her if the reporter kicked the door in.

"Back! Back, I say!" Marty cried from the swinging door that led into the bakery. Angie jumped off her stool and darted across the kitchen. She peeked through the round window in the door and spun back around. "Marty's fending them off, but I don't think he can do it alone. I'm going out there!"

"No!" Mel cried. "You're pregnant. You could get hurt."

Crash!

The noise came from the bakery, followed by muffled shouts and the sound of a scuffle. Angie went to look but Oz moved her aside, grabbing a spatula and twirling it through his fingers like he was wielding a lethal weapon. He pushed the door open and peered out. Mel felt Angie press up against her side as if the two of them could fight off whatever was out there by becoming one.

Oz's shoulders relaxed. He spun around with a grin and said, "It's all right. The brothers are here."

"What?" Angie raced forward. She pushed past Oz with Mel right on her heels. When they entered the bakery, it was to find Sal, Tony, Al, and Paulie escorting the last of the reporters, none too gently, out the door.

Al locked the door after the last one and flipped the sign to CLOSED. The brothers exchanged a round of high fives and clapped one another on the back.

"Bruhs," Marty said and joined in on the high fives. "Excellent timing."

Angie stood with her arms crossed over her chest, and her head cocked to the side. "Yes, really amazingly excellent timing. How did you know?" She turned on Tony. "Did you bug the place? Are there cameras?"

"Well, duh," Tony said. He gestured to the camera that Joe and Tate had insisted be functional and not just for show after a crazy man with a gun tried to shoot Mel in the bakery a few months ago. "But that's not how we knew the reporters had descended upon you."

"Like a scourge, seriously, I've only seen creepers like that in Minecraft," Al said. He shuddered.

"Then how did you . . . ?" Mel began, but Tony interrupted.

"I got a tip from a friend," he said.

Tony was the DeLaura family CIA operative—not really—who kept his personal life on complete lockdown. It drove their mom crazy, but Tony's entire life was a closely guarded secret. If he dated, no one knew. If he had friends outside the family, they were kept compartmentalized and secret. Even his job, technical director, meant nothing. No one knew what technical he was directing or for whom. They didn't have a clue how he spent his time or whom he spent it with. It drove Joe bananas.

"What friend? You have friends?" Al asked. He was the closest to Tony, and even he didn't know anything.

"Yes, he has friends," a voice said from the kitchen door. They all swung around to see a drop-dead gorgeous redhead standing there.

"Susan," Tony said. "You were supposed to wait outside."

She shrugged a slender shoulder and tossed her glorious hair. She studied her manicure, a pale peach color, and in a voice as low and mellow as golden honey said, "I got bored. Plus, you need a better lock." She held up a credit card, showing how she'd gotten in.

"Damn it, I should have turned the dead bolt," Oz said.

"Who is this?" Paulie gaped. His eyes were bulging like a cartoon character. Mel was surprised they didn't bounce in and out of his sockets like they were on springs.

"A friend," Tony said.

"A friend?" Susan asked. "Tsk-tsk, I thought we were more than that."

She moved as if she were made of liquid, gliding into the front room like a supernatural being. Mel glanced at the men. They looked gobsmacked. All except for Tony, who smiled at her with an indulgent look.

"Dial it back, Suz," he said. "My brothers aren't equipped to handle you."

This set off a chorus of protests. The loudest being Sal, who protested quite loudly that he was more than capable of "handling" the sexy siren before them.

Susan let out a sigh. She reached into her purse and pulled out a pair of large round-framed glasses and slipped them on. Then she twisted her hair into a tight topknot on her head and buttoned her blouse to her throat.

"Aw, man, that's not any better," Sal complained. "The sexy librarian look is a killer."

"Wait for it." Tony held up a hand. "How can I help you, Susan?"

"You promised me an exclusive." The high-pitched whine that came out of her mouth made Mel want to clap her hands over her ears.

Oz did just that, while Marty looked confused. "Is she talking? I can't hear anything."

"I think the frequency is too high for you," Oz said. He looked pained.

Collectively, the DeLaura men glanced away, their impression of the hot girl completely decimated by her real speaking voice.

"How do you two know each other?" Al asked. His face was still scrunched in a wince, but he obviously wasn't through with Tony yet.

"Work," Tony said. As if that answered anything. "Now, if things are good here, why don't you all head out and I'll stay and make sure everything stays that way. M'kay? Great. Lovely afternoon out there. Don't be strangers. There you go."

And just like that, in a matter of moments, Tony had the brothers outside the bakery looking in, which was why he pulled down the window shade with a little finger wave.

"Okay, then," he said. He turned around to face them.

"What is going on, Tony?" Angie asked.

"Susan is here on my invitation," he said. "Isn't that right?"

"Correct," she said. They all jumped. Gone was the Minnie Mouse voice and the sexy siren. Instead, she sounded like a perfectly normal professional woman. She shrugged at their surprise. "I do a lot of undercover work." She put her hand to her throat. "The voice is just another tool."

"I'm feeling dizzy," Marty said. "I need to sit down."

"Same." Oz and Marty slumped into the chairs at one of the small café tables. They propped their chins on their hands as if they were watching a show, a very confusing show in a foreign language with no subtitles.

Tony laughed. "She has that effect on people."

Susan swatted his arm and turned to Mel. "Ignoring him, as we should, let me explain," she said. "I really am a reporter, but I'm not here to claw a story out of your pain like those other jackals. I'm here to warn you."

Mel lifted her eyebrows. "Okay. Should we sit down for this?"

"Yes," Tony said. He pushed out chairs for Mel, Angie, and Susan, seating himself last.

"What do you know?" Angie asked.

"I know that the police think Rene was murdered," Susan said. "There is no record of her being a drug user, and the heart attack that killed her was completely unexpected, especially since she had a physical just six months ago and was given a perfectly clean bill of health. I also know that they think Mel had something to do with it. I know that the chief of police in particular is interested in why you crop up at so many murders and is planning an inquiry by an independent—"

"Council. I actually know about that," Mel said. "The chief stopped by my mother's house last night to have a chat. Chief Rosen's not happy with me."

"Wait," Angie said. "Go back to the part where they think Mel had something to do with the murder. Why would they think that? Mel has nothing to gain from Rene's death."

"It seems someone talked to the press and mentioned an altercation between you and Rene the week before she died over your misplaced affection for her husband," Susan said. She gave Mel a pointed look.

"Don't even," Mel said. She raised her hand in a stop gesture. "Do you know who I'm engaged to? Like I would ever in this life care about anyone besides Joe DeLaura."

Tony looked at Susan and said, "Told you so."

"And I agreed with you," she said. "No woman in her right mind would throw over a perfect specimen like Joe DeLaura for that anemic weakling Peter Klein."

"That being said," Angie interrupted. "Peter is our friend."

"Really?" Susan asked. "Even if he killed his wife?"

Ten

"Ah!" Mel and Angie gasped together.

Susan looked at Tony in exasperation.

"They're very sheltered," he said.

"No, we're not," Angie said. "We've been around way more murders than you."

"You sure about that?" he asked.

Angie stared at him as if she didn't know him.

"Exactly," he said.

Angie looked at Mel as if she wasn't sure which way was up or down. Mel was right there with her. What was going on here?

"The spouse is always suspect number one," Susan said. She shook her head at Mel and Angie. "Surely, you know that."

"Of course we do," Mel said. "But we like Peter. We've

known him for years just like we know . . . knew Rene. You have to understand, we saw the love, the caring, the friendship. The man brought her cupcakes every Friday *for years*. They were relationship goals to us."

"It's true," Marty chimed in. "They seemed very happy together. I can't imagine that he killed her."

"Unless, he's been portraying the doting husband all these years just to make himself not seem like the suspect when he murdered her," Susan said.

"But why would he?" Oz asked. "Why not just pack up his stuff and go?"

"Because his fame was attached to her fame," Tony said. "He's a failed painter and he was riding her coattails. Without her success he's nothing."

"Kind of harsh, dude," Oz said. His knee jogged up and down. "I mean, a guy can be less successful than his girlfriend, erm, wife and still be a contributing member of society."

"How old are you, kid?" Tony asked.

"Twenty." Oz stuck his chin out. "And I'm not a kid."

"Sure, check back with me in ten years and we'll see if you feel the same."

Mel glanced at Angie, who was looking at Oz with the same speculation Mel felt. Was this it then? Was Oz's need to prove himself because his girlfriend, Lupe, was pre-med at college and he felt like he wasn't doing anything as big as that?

"Back to the subject," Marty said. "Why would Peter kill Rene? Insurance money? Was he cheating? Was she going to divorce him?"

"Who knows? Which is why reporters and detectives investigate," Susan said. "There's been nothing discovered so far, but you can bet your last cupcake the police are looking at all of that."

"I don't understand," Mel said. "I was told she died from a heart attack, and while I understand that it's suspicious and they're investigating the cause, I can't help wondering, if she was murdered, how could the murderer have caused a heart attack?"

"They're waiting for the medical examiner to weigh in," Susan said. "Poison is the number one suspicion, but added to that it could have been stress, abuse, exhaustion, a combination of all of those things. If it is murder, the killer could have been working towards this goal for months, again, making the spouse the number one suspect because he would have had the most access to her. We'll have to wait and see. In the meantime, it might interest you to hear that Peter is going ahead with the grand opening of her art installation over the canal tonight."

"Really?" Mel asked. She glanced at the others in surprise. "Have we heard from him?"

"I'll check the voice mail," Oz said. He bounced out of his seat, went behind the counter, and picked up the landline. He tapped in the code and waited, listening.

"I mean I guess it only makes sense since it was already installed and the opening night party planned," Angie said.

"Klein said at a press conference this morning that he wants it to be a memorial to Rene and her life's work," Susan said. "So it will stay up for a few months as originally scheduled. They've had to hire guards to watch the glass pieces twenty-four-seven, as they're afraid someone will try to steal them."

"Because art is always more valuable once the artist is dead," Angie said. She looked grim.

"Who would gain financially if she was dead?" Marty asked. "I mean, does Peter inherit everything? Because that would also be a powerful motive if he wanted out of his marriage."

"We don't know," Susan said. "But it'll come to light soon. There are a lot of knots to untie in this case."

Mel tried to imagine Peter abusing his wife or poisoning her. She couldn't see it, but perhaps it was because she didn't want to see it. She didn't want to believe there had been anything wrong in the marriage she had held in such high regard.

"I'm going to be crushed if he did it," Angie said. "Absolutely crushed."

"I know," Mel agreed. "I just don't feel it." She glanced at Susan and asked, "You said someone told the press about my *very slight* misunderstanding with Rene."

Susan nodded.

"Who was it?"

"An anonymous tip," she said. "The woman called it into all of the news stations, clearly wanting to make certain it was in today's news cycle."

"A woman?" Mel asked. Susan nodded, and Mel turned to Angie. "I know who it was."

"Bernadette," Angie said. "It makes sense. She's trying to deflect blame from herself."

"Wait, hold up," Tony said. "Are you saying you think this Bernadette killed Rene?"

Mel nodded slowly. She could absolutely see Bernadette killing Rene more so than Peter. The woman was scary. "There was bad blood there."

"Interesting," Susan said. She took out her cell phone and started to type. "I don't suppose you have any proof."

"I don't but I know who might," Mel said. "Rene's assistant, Emersyn. She was the one who told me that Rene hadn't been herself, that she'd changed over the past year."

"Emersyn? The cute young thing that was incoherent with tears on the news last night?" Susan asked.

"Was she?" Mel asked. "Poor kid. She was planning to quit after the installation. From what I witnessed, Rene was pretty hard on her."

"Hard enough for Emersyn to want to kill her?" Tony asked.

"Emersyn? No." Mel shook her head. "She's an intern. I think she was more hurt and confused than angry. What possible motive could she have?"

"Maybe she snapped. Being in a pressure cooker day in and day out could do that to a person," Angie said. She glanced at Oz. "You know, like a corporate kitchen where everyone from the hostesses to the waitresses to the executive chef is breathing down your neck nonstop."

Oz still held the phone to his ear but pulled it away to shake his head at her. "No."

Tony glanced between them. "I feel like there's a subtext here that I'm not getting."

"Really?" Marty asked. "Because Angie's about as subtle as a hammer."

"It's not related to the situation at hand," Mel said. "It's an in-house thing."

Tony turned to Susan. "So what do you think? What strategy should we employ to keep the bad press at bay?"

"I think Mel needs to go on the offensive," she said. She turned to Mel. "If the chief of police has her eye on you because of your proximity to other cases, then you need to make a stand. You're dating a prominent county attorney, and public perception is important. Remember, this could affect his career, too."

Mel felt her stomach drop. Joe had said he wasn't interested in running for office, but if he ever changed his mind, Mel being targeted by the chief of police as a suspect in a murder case would not help him in any way, shape, or form. Damn.

"It's a go," Oz said from behind the counter. "Peter left a message for us to bring the cupcakes to the art opening as we'd originally planned."

Double damn. She hated the thought of facing down public scrutiny. Mel looked at her crew. "Everyone okay with that?"

As one, they all nodded.

"It's actually perfect," Susan said. "Being seen in public with your head held high will push back against the rumors. Then I can run a piece on you, establishing you as a friend of Rene's and an innocent bystander."

Mel was about to leap on the offer, but Angie held up her hand. "Not to be a doubter, but why? To put it plainly, what's in it for you?"

Susan's perfectly arched auburn eyebrows lifted and she looked at Angie with respect. She turned to Tony and said, "You were right, she's delightfully suspicious."

"It comes from having seven older brothers," Angie said. "I still don't enter rooms without checking behind doorways."

"Because we raised you right," Tony said.

"Enough with the sibling banter," Marty cut in. "How can we trust you'll write a positive piece about Mel and not twist it so she looks guilty?"

"Firstly, because I owe Tony a favor," Susan said. Tony

nodded in affirmation. "And secondly, because I don't believe she's guilty. My money, as I mentioned, is on the husband."

They all stared at her. Susan wasn't fazed at all. Instead, she relaxed back into her chair, lifting her chin up as if she had all the time in the world for them to mull over her offer.

Tony broke the silence by addressing Mel. "This is one way to get ahead of the narrative the press is likely to build around you as a person of interest."

"Minus the throng of reporters who were here earlier, do you really think I'm a suspect in Rene's death?" Mel asked. "Just because Bernadette, and I'm betting it was Bernadette, called all the news outlets and said Rene and I had a spat about her husband, does that really make me newsworthy?"

"Yes," Tony said. His voice was flat, and Mel got the feeling that he and Susan knew something they weren't sharing.

"What aren't you telling me?" she asked.

Tony considered her. She had the feeling he wasn't going to enlighten her any more than her uncle Stan would. She hated to do it, but leverage was leverage.

"You know, I don't think we've ever banned anyone from Fairy Tale Cupcakes before," she said. She sat up straight and turned to look at Angie, Marty, and Oz. "Would I be correct in that?"

"You wouldn't!" Tony said. He looked at Angie. "Help a brother out."

"Can't." She shrugged. "This is Mel's call."

"Hardball, I like it," Susan said. Her eyes twinkled.

"Whose side are you on?"

"Tony, Tony, Tony, you know me," she said. "I'm always on the winner's side, and right now that's looking like Mel's."

Tony glowered and then shook his head. "Fine. But this information doesn't leave this room."

They all nodded, leaning forward to hear what he had to say.

"I have it from a very reliable source that there was some concern about the cupcakes you brought to the gallery yesterday and that the medical examiner took them with him to the crime lab for further analysis."

Mel looked at Angie to find her staring back. At the same time, they asked, "What happened to the cupcakes we brought?"

"I don't know," Mel said.

"Me, either," Angie cried.

"Oh, no, this is bad, so bad," Mel said. She jumped up from her chair and began to pace. She pressed her fingers to her temples as if she could squeeze the memory of what they'd done with the cupcakes out of her brain.

Angie hopped up from her seat and started to pace as well. "This is all my fault. If I hadn't been throwing up—"

"No, it's my fault," Mel said. "I was the one who decided to race over there, because I just had to butt in and see if I could help."

"Hey, now," Marty said. "You're being awfully hard on yourself for trying to be a good friend."

"Was I?" Mel asked. "Was I being a good friend? Or was I just being nosy and insinuating myself in yet another crime scene? Maybe the chief is right, maybe I am the problem."

"You're not the problem," Tony said. "Whoever murdered Rene is the problem."

"*If* she was murdered," Angie said. Tony gave her a sympathetic look. "Until the medical examiner says otherwise, I refuse to accept it." She glanced at Susan. "And that includes believing that Peter did it."

"Suit yourself," Susan said. "We still need a strategy to get Mel off the hot seat."

"What do you suggest?" Mel asked.

"To start with," Susan said. "Go to the opening and agree to the interview, an exclusive."

Mel cringed. "Not going to be about cupcakes, is it?"

"No," Susan said.

Mel sighed. "I hate this."

"You'll hate it more if it costs Joe his career," Tony said.

"Okay, sure, what else?" Mel asked.

"You need to work the opening tonight," Susan said. "Meet and greet like you've never done before. The best thing you can do to squash the rumors is march in there, looking like a grief-stricken friend who is seeking solace with other mourners."

"Oh, boy," Mel said. "This is going to be awful, isn't it? It's too hard. I don't know if I can do this."

"I'll be with you," Angie said. She gave Mel a half hug. "And so will Tate and Joe."

"We'll be there, too, working the cupcake table," Marty said. He gestured between himself and Oz, who nodded in agreement.

"There you have it," Tony said. "An entourage."

"But don't forget to keep your guard up," Susan said. "If Rene was murdered, I'd be willing to bet her killer is there, too."

"Are we sure this is a good idea?" Joe asked. He was wearing a suit and tie and kept his hand at Mel's back as they made their way down the sidewalk towards the entrance to the art exhibit, which was beyond a small park adjacent to the canal that ran through the south side of Scottsdale. Mel had chosen a soft dark blue dress that draped becomingly, floating around her knees and showing off her low-heeled sandals. She hoped she had successfully crafted the look of "innocent woman" and not "guilty-as-sin woman."

A jazz band was playing while waiters moved through the crowd with wine and beer. Mel was too nervous to drink or eat, which was a big indicator of her anxiety because food was usually her go-to choice to feel better.

She glanced behind her and saw Tate and Angie. He was in a suit as well, and Angie was wearing a dark purple chemise. She looked tired but resolute. Tonight was going to be difficult for all of them. Still, Mel was glad they were here. The sight of her friends made her feel better, knowing she had a crew to lean on if things went sour. There was no sign of any reporters, and she wondered if Peter had barred them from entering. It would be a boon if he had.

A line of pop-up canopies had been set up for the food stations. Serving dessert, Oz and Marty, in dress shirts and ties under their aprons, were at the end of the line after the steak kabobs, stuffed mushrooms, cheese in olive oil, and fried peppers.

People were already in line in front of their station, so Mel decided to wait for a break before going over to talk to them. The guys had planned to chat up as many people as they could and find out what was being said about Rene's death. Knowing that Marty wasn't the smoothest operator, Mel was relieved to have Oz with him to contain him.

What were they going to do without Oz? She had to push the thought aside, or the crushing sadness she was already feeling at the loss of Rene was going to finish her.

She glanced down at the glossy postcard that had been handed to her when they entered. On the front was a spectacular shot of Rene in her studio, looking happy, bubbly, and full of life. On the back was a collage of several pieces that made up her masterpiece *Seasons*. Included with the photographs was her artist's statement: *Life is beautiful but so very fragile. I try to capture both elements in every piece and in doing so, I hope to remind us all to love each other with gentle kindness.*

Upon reading the words, Mel shed more than a few tears, as did Angie. The words seemed horribly prophetic now that they were all here to say good-bye to Rene more than to celebrate her, and Mel was once again consumed by the feeling that she should have done more.

Per Susan's advice, Mel looked for faces in the crowd that she knew, and she and Joe, along with Tate and Angie, shook hands and commiserated with their friends and neighbors from Old Town over the loss of one of their own. Unlike at other art openings, there was no laughter or chatter. The jazz band played subdued songs that had a note of melancholy running through them. But to Mel's relief the story that she was a person of interest had clearly not been leaked to this crowd. No one seemed suspicious of her. In fact, the locals who knew her well knew that Rene had been her friend and were wonderfully sympathetic.

Rene's exhibit had been in progress for months. The installation itself had taken up the final weeks with workers stringing heavy cables across the canal to hang her sculpture high enough to be out of reach but low enough to be seen and appreciated. It had been finished just in time with the last piece being installed yesterday, right before the celebratory champagne. If there was anything that Mel was grateful for, it was that Rene had been able to see her greatest work finished before she died.

The entrance to the canal exhibit was closed off by two enormous blue satin curtains that were suspended from a tall iron archway. Mel glanced at her watch. They had twenty minutes to go until the big reveal. She was eager to see it but also reluctant, because seeing the piece would bring home the fact that this was Rene's final work. There would never be another, and that was devastating not only because her work was brilliant but also because it hammered home the reality that Rene was gone. Forever.

"Are you all right?" Joe asked. He squeezed her fingers in reassurance.

"I've been better," she said. "I can't help feeling like Rene should be here, enjoying all of this acclaim, and it makes me angry that she's not. Then I think of how she behaved the last night I saw her, and I wonder if she would even want me here."

He let go of her hand and put a protective arm around her shoulders. "Don't think that. Never that. Rene was your friend, and regardless of what was happening to her at the end, you have years of history together. You deserve to be here as much as anyone."

He met and held her gaze until Mel nodded. He was right. She had to focus on the memories of Rene that filled years. Sharing after-hours drinks in the gallery courtyard when the art walk had closed down, beginner cupcake batches gone horribly awry that Rene had insisted she would eat anyway, and local merchant meetings where they had sat in the back of the room and been hit with a fit of the giggles. Mixed in all of that, Mel could see Peter and Rene looking at each other as if they shared a love that was so unique and rare that common mortals couldn't possibly understand it.

It was that memory that made her search the crowd for Peter. No matter what Susan had said about Peter being nothing without Rene and a spouse being the most likely suspect, deep down, Mel just couldn't believe that he could have had anything to do with Rene's death. Angie pressed up against her side, and Mel knew she was feeling the same onslaught of emotions.

"Have you seen Peter?" Angie asked. "I know this must be so hard for him."

"No," Mel said. "I can't imagine he wouldn't be here, but maybe he's going to have someone else do the unveiling. It might be too hard for him."

Mel scanned the crowd beyond the fellow merchants that she knew. It appeared to be mostly socialites and moguls, glittering in the wink and sparkle of their diamonds. The smell of their extravagance scenting the air in thick clouds of Kilian Hennessy perfumes and Tom Ford colognes.

Personally, Mel would have preferred the scent of fresh-baked bread or a whiff of vanilla buttercream. Simple pleasures.

"Oh, hey, there's Mick," Angie said. She smiled. "Okay, he's the last person from Old Town that I expected to see in a suit, but given that he did Rene's bird tattoo, I suppose it makes sense."

Mick Donnelly, Old Town's most sought-after tattoo artist, stood in a somber black suit. His shaved head sported a rising phoenix tattoo on the back, which made him easy to spot in the crowd.

Mel noticed that most of the finer folks in attendance were giving him a wide boundary line, and she couldn't blame them. Even without the ink, he was a fearsome sight to behold at six foot four and with enough body piercings dripping off his lobes, eyebrows, and nostrils that she doubted he'd ever get through a metal detector on the first pass.

Angie grabbed Mel's hand and led her over to where Mick stood alone, listening to the music while he sipped a pint of beer. Joe and Tate followed as they wound their way through the crowd.

"Mick," Angie greeted him. She opened her arms and hugged him. "It's so good to see you."

"Angie, Mel." His stern demeanor lifted, and he offered them a small smile, hugging them each in turn. "Tate, Joe." He shook their hands and motioned to the blue curtain. "I gotta say, I'm not really sure how to feel about this."

"I know what you mean," Angie said. "It's the best way to remember Rene, appreciating the project that consumed the last year of her life, and yet . . ." She gestured to the stiff-necked crowd, none of whom seemed to be grieving the artist. "It seems mercenary."

"Exactly," Mick said. His lip curled as a well-heeled couple strolled past. "These weren't her people."

"Maybe not," Tate said. "But they're the only ones who can afford her now."

"I miss how it was," Mick said. "Back when we were all just starting out. I had my parlor, you had the bakery, and Rene was just hitting her stride as an artist. It was all living on a shoestring and a prayer, but we were in it together." He paused. "Mostly, I can't believe she's gone."

"Me, too," Mel said. "When was the last time you saw her?"

"A few weeks ago," Mick said. "I was cruising through Old Town on my Harley, and there she was, standing on the sidewalk and having it out with some—" He paused and glanced at the entrance to the pavilion. He frowned and said, "I'll be damned. It was that woman over there. Rene was having an argument with her."

As one, they all turned, following the direction of his gaze. A tall, lithe young woman, wearing a red satin gown with a slit up to mid-thigh and her honey-colored hair piled on top of her head, sauntered into the gathering as if she expected people to back up and make room. The force of her presence was such that people did.

"Red, really?" Mick said. He sounded offended. "Who wears red to a memorial?"

"Someone who is not very broken up about the departed departing," Joe said.

On a hunch, Mel pulled her phone out of her purse and did a quick search. She limited it to images, and sure enough, the woman was exactly who she'd expected. Willa Kincaid, rival glass artist from Phoenix, the one with whom Rene had been obsessed.

Eleven

The red dress caught more than their attention. Out of nowhere, Emersyn appeared. She was pale and red-eyed, wearing a black dress that looked two sizes too big for her, and she charged right up to Willa and hissed, "Get out."

Willa looked Emersyn over and, apparently deciding that she wasn't even worth speaking to, made to walk around her. Emersyn wasn't having it, however. She stepped into Willa's path, refusing to be ignored. The entire crowd grew quiet in order to watch the scene unfold.

"You're not welcome here," she said. Her voice trembled with emotion, but her spine was stiff, and Mel had a feeling she would take the other woman down if need be. "Please leave."

Willa put her hand to her throat in a gesture of hurt. "But I was invited."

"Since I'm the one who sent the invitations, I find that very difficult to believe," Emersyn said. "You were no friend to Rene, and I'll ask you just one more time to leave."

They stared at each other in a standoff that had Mel holding her breath.

"Emersyn, it's all right," Peter said. He stepped out from behind the curtain and caught the intern by the arm. Emersyn yanked her elbow out of his grip. He looked embarrassed but forged on. "It's all right. Ms. Kincaid is here by personal invitation from me."

Emersyn gasped and looked at him as if he'd sprouted horns. "But . . . why?"

"She was Rene's peer, she deserves to be here to pay her respects," he said. His voice was quiet but firm.

Emersyn looked at him as if she couldn't comprehend this level of betrayal. She shook her head and then turned on her heel and stormed off into the thick of the crowd.

The group watched surreptitiously as Peter took Willa's hand in his and leaned close. He was whispering, and she nodded as if in understanding and then they walked away together, behind the blue satin curtain and out of sight.

"Um . . ." Angie started to speak but then stopped. She looked at Mel and said, "What was that?"

Mel shrugged. Peter being nice to Rene's rival, a woman that Mel had heard Rene raged about, made absolutely no sense. None. Unless . . .

"Do you think that Peter thinks Willa had something to do with Rene's death?" Mel asked. "Maybe she's here so that he can keep an eye on her or lure her in so the police can nab her?"

Joe looked surprised. "I'm not sure how you jumped onto that high-speed locomotive, but it's a heck of a theory."

"It's about the only thing that makes sense," Tate said. He looked at Angie. "I can't imagine inviting a person you despised to, heaven forbid, a memorial service for you."

"That's because you know I'd haunt you," she said.

No one doubted for a moment that this was true.

"Mick?" A woman in a simple black sheath approached. She wore her highlighted dark hair in a French twist, cat-eye glasses, and ruby red lipstick. She looked professional and poised as if nothing could rattle her calm demeanor.

"Delilah," Mick greeted her. He leaned down to kiss her upturned cheek. "I haven't seen you since opening night at the opera."

"Chamber of commerce season in the valley," she said. "Busy, busy, busy." She gestured behind her towards the canal. "I curated this show."

Mel met Mick's gaze and gave him her most winning smile. He grunted, clearly taking the hint that introductions were in order.

"Delilah Henry, I'd like to introduce my friends, Melanie Cooper, Joe DeLaura, and Angie and Tate Harper."

They all shook hands with Delilah, who studied each one in turn. Her eyes narrowed on Mel and Angie. "You're the local cupcake bakers, aren't you? Fairy Tale Cupcakes? I remember reading about you in *Southwest Style* magazine."

"That's us," Mel said. "We were also good friends with Rene."

"Of course you were," Delilah said. "Old Town is quite the small community."

There was a pause and then Angie asked, "Did you enjoy curating her show?"

Delilah looked as if she was about to say yes with a

canned smile, but she glanced at Mick and said, "No, I didn't. I would even go so far as to say it was the worst experience of my professional life."

No one knew what to say. Mick coughed into his hand. Tate opened his mouth to say something but then shut it. Mel squeezed Joe's hand, hoping his mediation skills would kick in and he'd know exactly what to say. A glance at his face and she knew he was flummoxed.

"Was Rene very difficult?" Mel asked. She figured someone had to go there while they had the chance.

Delilah heaved a sigh. "I'm sorry, I shouldn't have said anything. It was horribly unprofessional of me, I'm just . . . I'm so overwrought."

A crack in the professional façade appeared, and Mick put his arm around her and pulled her into his side. "It's okay, we all loved Rene, but we know that her last few months were tough."

"She was the most brilliant artist I've ever worked with," Delilah said. Her words were choppy as sobs choked her. She swallowed hard. The look in her dark eyes became steely as she glared at the curtain. "If it wasn't for him . . ."

Mel frowned. "Him who?"

"Her husband, Peter," Delilah said with a moue of distaste. "Awful man."

"Peter?" Angie clarified. "Peter Klein?"

"Does she have another husband?" Delilah asked. Mick handed her his pocket square and she used it to dab her eyes.

"No."

"Then that's the one," Delilah said. "He is a horrible, horrible man."

Mel clutched Joe's arm. She felt as if Delilah were yanking the carpet right out from under her feet.

"I don't understand," she said. "Peter was Rene's biggest fan."

"Pfff," Delilah scoffed. "Look into the water beneath the installation and you'll find several pieces of Rene's that were smashed."

Mel thought of the glass leaf that Rene had thrown at her head. "By . . . ?"

"Peter!" Delilah spat. "He is the reason she's dead, I'm sure of it."

"What makes you say that?" Joe asked. His tone was even, very conversational, but Mel could hear the underlying county prosecutor gauging Delilah's words, sifting out the truth from the lies.

"Because I have been working with her for months," Delilah said. "And I saw how he treated her. He was demanding and cruel, and if he didn't think her work was up to her usual standards, he berated her, even going so far as to toss some of her work into the canal. He was emotionally inaccessible and several times—"

She broke off and Mel almost screamed in frustration. What was she going to say? Mick put his hand on her back and said, "It's all right. You're among Rene's friends here."

"He's a liar," Delilah said. Then she shuddered as if she was trying to shake off the memories. "And it wasn't just me he lied to, he was cheating on Rene. It was so obvious, he barely bothered to keep it a secret, and she was devastated by his betrayal, mostly because he wouldn't tell her who the other woman was."

"How do you know this?" Joe asked. "Did she confide in you?"

Delilah glanced away. She looked ashamed. "No, I overheard them arguing one night at the gallery. It was a particularly bad fight, and I didn't leave because I feared it might get violent."

"You think he was abusing her?" Mick growled. He looked like he wanted to go find Peter and do him an injury.

"No," she said. "I was afraid Rene was going to go after him. It was ugly. She'd found a woman's bra, not hers, mixed in with his laundry, and she demanded to know whose it was. He refused to tell her. When Rene threatened to divorce him, he laughed in her face and told her to go ahead since he'd get half of everything she'd ever earned.

"She lost it then," Delilah said. "And I couldn't blame her. He worked her like a plow horse, living off her success, and then he was unfaithful, and did everything he could to undermine her. All because he was so bitter that he was a nothing, a nobody, a loser. Ugh, I loathe him."

They were all silent, taking in her words with various levels of shock. Joe seemed the least surprised. Because of his occupation, there wasn't much human awful that he hadn't had a front row seat for.

"I had no idea," Mel said.

"Me, either," Angie said. She glanced at Tate. "All this time I thought they were the perfect couple."

"Not perfect," Delilah said. "Not even close." She looked at Mick. "Sorry, I didn't mean to unload on you all. It's just, this is harder than I thought it would be. Rene was so talented, she had such vision, and now she's gone."

She broke off on a sob and turned her face into Mick's shoulder. He put an arm around her, making sympathetic shushing noises. Mel met his gaze and gestured that they would leave them alone. Mick nodded.

Mel took Joe's hand and led him away, leaving Angie and

Tate to fall in behind them. This night was quickly unraveling, and she had no idea if she could handle much more of it.

The musicians finished their piece, and a murmur rippled through the crowd. Mel glanced across the courtyard to see Peter walk through the blue satin curtains. Willa Kincaid wasn't with him. A small podium with a microphone had been placed to the side and he positioned himself behind it. Mel noted that Byron, Bernadette, and Sunny were standing just behind him, the entire Desert Winds Gallery saying good-bye to one of their own.

She studied their faces. Aside from Byron, who appeared to be struggling with his emotions, they were stonefaced and silent. Even Peter looked restless, as if he was eager to get his speech over and done. He cleared his throat, once, twice, then he reached for a bottle of water and took a long swallow. Had Mel not just talked to Delilah, she would have believed it was grief that was making him struggle. Now she didn't know.

Had Delilah told them the truth? Mel couldn't think of any reason for her to lie. Assuming what she'd said was true, then it was likely that Peter wasn't grieving at all, or if he was, it was more for the money he would be losing now that Rene was gone. Mel felt sick to her stomach.

She glanced at Angie. She looked absolutely green. "Are you okay?"

"No, I think I'm going to be sick, but I don't want to make a scene," Angie said.

Tate looked at her face and said, "I don't care if you do, I'm taking you home. I'll carry you out of here if I have to."

"Please don't," Angie said.

"Joe and I will cover you," Mel said. She positioned Joe

beside her, blocking Tate and Angie from view. "Go ahead and slip through the crowd. I'll call you later."

Covered in sweat and pasty pale, Angie nodded. They were working against the crowd, but they managed to wend their way out of the crush.

"Think she'll be all right?" Joe asked. A frown marred his forehead.

"Tate will make certain of it," she said.

They turned their attention back to Peter at the podium. He had a fistful of note cards, his hands were shaky, and when he spoke, his voice wavered.

"Good evening, everyone," he said. He paused to clear his throat again. "We're here tonight to pay tribute to my . . ." He stopped. He lowered his head. A murmur of sympathy ran through the crowd. It was clear that Peter was struggling to come up with the words.

Mel waited, wondering what he could say that would wash away the things Delilah had said. She felt as if she'd had blinders on and suddenly the real Peter Klein had been revealed to her. Had there always been a cruel twist to his lips? Had his smile never reached his eyes? Was she just imagining it because of what Delilah had said?

"No, not mine," he said. "She belonged to the world. And so we're here to pay tribute to the brilliant artist, Rene Fischer-Klein, my wife, my best friend, my partner in all things, and the light of my life."

Mel hissed in a breath. If what Delilah had told them was true, then everything that Peter was saying now was a lie. Maybe some part of him loved Rene, but he'd cheated on and betrayed her, and Mel knew she would never look at him the same way again. Joe gently squeezed her fingers with his. "Steady," he said.

Peter continued to talk, listing all of Rene's accomplishments, somehow managing to work himself into every bit of it, saying behind every talented woman there was a man doing the dishes. Some people laughed but Mel felt her temper heat much like the furnace Rene used to fire her glass sculptures.

As if sensing that her temper was slipping, Joe leaned close and said, "As a prosecutor, I understand how you're feeling, but you can't convict on hearsay. Delilah's information is concerning but we need to know more about her and her relationship with Rene and Peter before we run with everything she told us."

"I know, but it makes so much sense," Mel said. She leaned closer and whispered, "Rene's erratic behavior. Why she was accusing him of cheating with everyone. He probably was. You saw him with Willa Kincaid, her rival. What was that about? Is she another fling? Is that why Rene hated her so much?"

"Shhh." A woman nearby shushed Mel.

Whatever Joe was about to say was interrupted by Peter's final announcement. "I give you the finest work, the masterpiece, of Rene Fischer-Klein."

He swept his arm in the direction of the towering curtains, and they began to open. A ripple of excitement spread through the crowd. People craned their necks and rose up on their toes trying to get glimpses of the installation as it was revealed. Gasps sounded at the front of the crowd as those in the front began to walk into the exhibit space.

Even from the back, Mel could tell that Rene had outdone herself. Mentored by some of the world's greatest glass artists like Dale Chihuly, known worldwide for his unique large-scale sculptures, and Lino Tagliapietra, who had taught Rene how to make her own colors, she had created a breathtaking feast for the eyes.

Mel took Joe's hand as they followed the throng past the curtains into the roped-off area that ran along the canal. Overhead, lit up to dazzling effect, was a glass sculpture that ran the length and width of the canal park over which it was suspended. Huge ornate pieces of glass in swirls and spirals and waves of intense color seemed to float high over the water, which reflected the art above, doubling its impact.

It took Mel a moment to realize she was holding her breath, and she gasped, sucking in air in awe and delight.

Seasons. The glass sculpture was aptly named as it shifted from stark white to soft hues, much like crocuses breaking through snow in spring, until it erupted into a glorious riot of summer color that faded into the fiery red and gold of autumn leaves, which bled back into the white of winter. The piece was crafted in a large wide loop, and as the crowd below watched, it slowly began to rotate above them, giving the piece no beginning or end.

Mel felt the tears trickle down her face before she realized she was crying. Each piece of glass was stunning in its own right, but put together, it was so achingly beautiful as it moved seamlessly from one season to the next that it overwhelmed. Her gaze moved to each section, taking in the curves and the textures of delicate glass from large flat round pieces to whimsical spirals. She knew it was the sort of sculpture that would require hours of study to fully appreciate the very specific details in each piece of glass and their meanings. It was quite simply a masterpiece, and it hurt so much to look at it that she had to duck her head and let out a mournful sob.

Rene should be here. And the pain she felt at her friend missing this moment, her finest hour, simply crushed her.

Joe pulled her close. He cleared his throat and she glanced up and noticed the sheen in his eyes as well. He reached up and gently brushed a tear from her cheek. The understanding in the gesture almost undid her completely. Her chest ached, and she put her knuckles against her sternum as if she could ease the pain.

"This," she whispered, glancing up at Rene's work, "is everything."

"Yes," Joe agreed. "It is."

They stood under the glass sculpture, which had been strung on heavy industrial cables and a framework that allowed it to turn, for a long while. When a breeze moved the air, the sculpture rotated just a little bit faster. Each precisely placed piece rode gently on the wind, giving the sculpture a feeling of life. It was incredible, and the crowd gasped as one. Mel had no doubt that Rene had engineered the sculpture to do exactly that, and she was blown away by the absolute genius of her friend.

"I have a feeling Rene ordered that breeze especially for tonight."

Mel turned around, and standing behind her was Peter. A million questions flew through her mind. She wanted to demand that he tell her what Delilah had said wasn't true, and then she wanted him to say that he'd had nothing to do with Rene's death, that he hadn't been awful, he hadn't worked her to death, or cheated on her, or caused her so much stress that she overdosed on uppers or whatever. But, of course, she couldn't do any of that.

Sensing her conflict, Joe tightened his arm around Mel

and pulled her into his side. He reached out to Peter and shook his hand. "No doubt you're right."

Peter nodded. He looked shaken and pushed his glasses up on his nose. "Thank you both for coming. It would have meant a lot to Rene to have you here."

"Of course," Mel said. It took everything she had to keep her voice neutral. Because she knew it was expected of her, she asked, "How are you holding up?"

"As good as can be expected," he said. "I just wish . . ." Mel waited.

"I would trade every bit of this." He gestured to the crowd. "To have her back with me."

"Would you?" Mel asked. "Would you really?"

Twelve

The questions were out before she could hold them back. Peter frowned at her from behind his wire frames as if he couldn't believe she even had to ask.

"Why, yes, of course," he said. "You know how much I love . . . loved her."

"Did you?" Mel persisted.

Joe squeezed her hip, pulling her in hard and tight. Mel knew he was trying to get her to rein it in, but she was so furious at having Peter standing in front of her, soaking up the limelight of his wife's brilliance, that she could barely contain her raging emotions.

"Mel, are you all right?" Peter asked. She didn't answer but concentrated on her breathing, striving for calm. "Listen, I just wanted to thank you for providing the cupcakes tonight. Rene loved them so much, it wouldn't have been right not to have them." He glanced up at the sculpture, and his voice was soft. "I don't know what I'm going to do on Fridays when I'm supposed to be picking up her cupcakes."

His voice cracked, and he turned away. As if he couldn't bear to stand with them anymore and think about the future without her, Peter walked away with his head bowed. Mel reached out to stop him, but then lowered her hand. She didn't know what to say. She didn't know what to believe. And the hurt inside of her chest cavity felt as if it was never going to mend.

"It's best to let him go for now," Joe said. "You don't want to give anyone anything to gossip about right now, not with the police chief keeping an eye on you."

"Is the chief here?" Mel asked.

Joe scanned the crowd. "I don't see her, but I'd be shocked if she wasn't."

Mel closed her eyes and leaned against him. "I don't think I can take much more of this. Do you really think she'll do what she said and hire an independent council to review every homicide case I've been associated with?"

Joe opened his mouth and then closed it. It looked like he wanted to say something, but he wasn't sure how it would be received.

"Yes or no, Joe, don't candy-coat it for me," she said.

"Yes." His tone was grim.

"Okay, maybe a few sprinkles or possibly a cherry on top would have helped," she said.

"Don't worry," he said. "You have no connection to what happened to Rene, and those other cases have all been solved satisfactorily. She can have her council look at them upside down and inside out and it won't change the facts.

And the fact is you are innocent of any wrongdoing and we all know it and soon Chief Rosen will, too."

Mel hugged him. This was one of the many reasons she loved Joe DeLaura. When the world was spinning out of control, he had the rare and unique ability to make it stop.

"Ms. Cooper." A voice interrupted their moment. She lifted her head from Joe's shoulder and turned around.

A man in an ill-fitting suit, with frosting on his fingers and a glass of wine in hand, was staring at her. Maybe he was a customer that she couldn't place.

"Yes?" Mel asked.

"Is it true that you were having an affair with Peter Klein and that you and Rene Fischer-Klein fought bitterly about it just last week?"

Mel blinked.

"What did you say?" Joe's voice was a low growl, daring the man to repeat his question.

The man's eyes went wide, and he looked at Mel. "Well, Ms. Cooper, do you have a statement you'd like to make for the paper? I could give you an exclusive, you know, tell the story from your side."

Shock had Mel rooted to the spot. Joe took a menacing step forward but was cut off by a waterfall of autumn hair.

"No, let me," Susan said as she slid in front of him. "This story is taken, Kevin." When the man looked as if he'd protest, she snapped her teeth at him. His eyes went wide, and he scurried away.

She turned back around and smiled as Tony joined them, handing her a glass of wine.

Joe frowned, glancing between the two of them. Mel knew he was trying to figure it out. He wasn't alone there.

"They're just friends," she said. Susan and Tony shared a look that seemed way more than friendly. "I think."

"Susan Estevez, Joe DeLaura," she said. While they shook hands, she turned to Tony. "I didn't know you were going to be here."

"Neither did I, but Susan felt it was necessary."

"And I was right," she said. "I knew there'd be some reporters worming their way in here, trying to steal my scoop."

"I'm a scoop?" Mel asked.

"A very tasty one, too," Susan said. She glanced around the exhibit, watching the people. "Has anything happened that we should know about?"

"If you mean were there any scenes, only a small one when Willa Kincaid arrived," Mel said. "But we talked to the curator of the show, and that was enlightening."

"Do tell," Susan said.

"Not here," Joe cautioned. Tony caught his eye and nodded.

"He's right," he said. "We should go somewhere else. Are you two ready to leave?"

Mel glanced up at the exhibit one last time. She'd be back, she knew, to sit in quiet contemplation at another time, when it was less crowded. She turned to Joe and nodded.

"All right then, let's go back to our place," he said. "We can talk there."

They turned and started to work their way through the crowd. Mel took Joe's hand so that they wouldn't be separated. She glanced at the faces of Scottsdale's finest soaking in Rene's work. Some expressions were thoughtfully contemplative of the meaning of the piece, others were aggrieved for the loss of such a promising genius, and some were conspicuously covetous. It occurred to Mel that she didn't know what would happen to *Seasons* when it was done. She hoped there were bigger plans for it, because the thought that it might be dismantled and sold off in pieces was unacceptable.

They were near the entrance, when a movement out of the corner of her eye caught Mel's attention. It was Bernadette, standing in the center of a small group of artsy-looking people, their hair colorful, their outfits bold, their shoes pointy. Bernadette was holding a pink martini and laughing. Abruptly, the sight of Bernadette's big smile flipped a switch of anger inside Mel that she couldn't snap off.

She dropped Joe's hand and veered through the crowd, heading straight for the wire sculptress. She wanted to know if Bernadette was the one who'd called the media and reported the story about her tiff with Rene and, if so, why.

Mel approached, not slowing her roll, not checking to see if Joe, Tony, or Susan was following her. This situation was between her and Bernadette, and she wasn't leaving until she got some answers.

"Bernadette, you're just who I was looking for," Mel said. She stopped in front of the other woman. "Had a busy day, have we?"

Bernadette didn't flinch. Instead, she slowly took a sip of her drink, eyeing Mel over the rim. She was in a dark fit-and-flare dress that made the most of her figure and her legs. Her dark hair was loose, her eyes were lined to resemble a cat's, and her lips were ruby red. She put the *voom* in *va va va voom*. Mel wondered if she'd kissed Peter on the lips again or if that had just been for Rene's benefit—when she'd been at her most vulnerable.

"Are you the one who called the press?" she asked.

Bernadette glanced at her companions and tipped her head to the side. As one, they scuttled away into the crowd like cockroaches down a drain.

Mel felt Joe come up behind her. She suspected he wasn't happy, but she didn't care. She needed some answers and she needed them right now.

"This is not the—" he began but Bernadette interrupted him.

"What is it, Little Bread Girl?" Bernadette asked. She took an e-cigarette out of her pocket and clicked it a couple of times. Then she sucked on it, holding the vape in her mouth before letting out a stream of smog that curled around them like a pungent cloud of cotton candy. Her expression was one of extreme boredom, and Mel had to fight the urge to give her a hard shove into the canal.

Mel glared. "Answer the question. Did you call the reporters about my visit to the gallery last week?"

"Why would I do that?" Bernadette asked. She glanced past Mel at Tony and Susan. Her eyes narrowed as she took in Susan's beauty. It was clear Bernadette liked to be the only queen bee in the hive.

"Oh, I don't know," Mel said. "To take suspicion off yourself by manufacturing a motive for me."

Bernadette scoffed. "Oh, please, as if I'd pick you to be the one to have an affair with him. If I'm going to accuse someone of taking my sloppy seconds, I'm going to make it someone worthy."

Mel blinked. "Sloppy seconds? So, you're admitting to having a relationship with Peter?"

The curvy woman looked her over as if she thought Mel was too stupid to live.

"It's common knowledge in the art scene. Denying it would only make me look like I have something to hide, and *I* don't," she said. "Besides, it was a while ago. It's not relevant now."

So, Peter and Bernadette really had an affair. Mel knew she shouldn't have been so shocked. People cheated on their partners all the time, but even though her image of Peter as the doting husband was tarnished, there had been a teeny apart of her still clinging to the image of Rene and Peter as the perfect couple.

"Do you think he was the only one in that marriage who stepped out? Rene was secretly meeting Neil Johansson for months. She wasn't discreet. Everyone knew about it and we knew why."

"Neil Johansson, the art collector?" Susan asked. One auburn brow arched in interest.

"The one and only, multibajillionaire and hot as a buttered biscuit," Bernadette said. "He owns the Imagine Gallery on the other side of Old Town, and he and Rene had a thing."

"What sort of thing?" Mel asked. Bernadette gave her a hard stare.

"Do you mean he and Rene were . . . ?" Mel couldn't finish the question.

"No, I mean they were playing canasta. Duh, grow up." Bernadette rolled her eyes. She looked at Joe, letting her gaze sweep over him from head to toe in what could only be described as a leer. "If ever you get tired of dating this Girl Scout, call me." She blew him a kiss, and without saying another word, she turned on her spiky heel and strode away.

"Oh, gross, I think I need a shower," Joe said.

"And I think I'm offended," Tony said. "We're brothers, we even look alike. What makes you such a catch and me not so much?"

"Because she's trying to hurt Mel," Susan said. "She has nothing to gain by coming after my escort, but they're engaged and she'd likely revel in hurting Mel, who was friends with Rene, just like she clearly enjoyed hurting Rene."

"I don't like her," Mel said.

"Justified," Tony agreed.

"Perhaps, but it makes my gut feeling that she's telling the truth even more annoying. She seems to be fully embracing her role as the other woman. I imagine she'll be more than happy to tell any and all about her torrid affair. It gives her notoriety to be the woman who took Rene's husband. I hate that she's going to use a sordid hookup as a launchpad to greater fame."

"Perhaps it will backfire on her," Susan said. "Rene was loved in the art community and Bernadette not so much. Maybe what she'll find is that a good old-fashioned shunning awaits her. If she gets a taste of that, it might check her behavior."

"I hate to say it, but attention seekers rarely weigh the cost of the limelight," Joe said. "She'll move forward before she thinks it through. The lure of notoriety will be greater than she can resist."

"I agree," Tony said. "And I don't think she was the one who called the press about you, either. She seems the type who would own any pain she caused."

"Does that make her less of a suspect if we discover Rene was murdered?" Mel asked.

"No," Susan said. "She remains on the short list until we know more." She looped her arm through Mel's as they left the exhibit area. She glanced over her shoulder at the men. "Is it just me, or is anyone else in need of a cupcake?"

"Make mine a double," Tony said.

They crossed the park to the line of food vendors. The Fairy Tale Cupcakes table was wiped out. Oz and Marty were packing up the last of the empty cupcake tiers.

"Snap," Joe said. "I really wanted one of the crème de menthe cupcakes."

"There are a few back at the bakery," Oz said. "I made extra."

"I knew I liked you for a reason," Joe said. "What do you say? Strategy session at Fairy Tale Cupcakes?"

"Lead the way," Tony said.

Mel took a minute to thank Oz and Marty for their hard work. They told her that they hadn't seen or heard anything about Rene's death other than people feeling shocked and saddened. The food tent had been so busy, they hadn't had a chance to dig any deeper. While it was one more dead end, Mel wasn't terribly surprised. Rene's death had been suspicious, but murder? She just wasn't sure.

While Joe drove them back to the bakery, Mel did a quick search on Neil Johansson on her phone. The picture that came up was of a distinguished-looking man in his mid-fifties. Tan, fit, with a thick head of gray hair and spar-kling blue eyes, he had a lot of appeal. She said as much to Joe, who grunted.

"What?" she asked.

"Is he single?"

"Yes," she said. "No previous marriage is listed in his bio, either."

"That seems weird," Joe said.

"What do you mean?"

"A mega-rich guy in his fifties with no exes?" Joe asked. "Why would he hook up with Rene?"

"What's that supposed to mean?" Mel asked. "Are you being ageist? She has no value because she's older and not of childbearing years?"

"Um, no," he said. "You know me better than that. What I mean is why hook up with a woman who is still married? He couldn't find someone who was single? Why go for the complicated, potentially hazardous relationship?"

"Maybe he loved her and thought she was worth it," Mel said.

They paused at a red light, and Joe checked the rearview mirror to see that Tony was still behind them.

"If he did, then it seems like it was unrequited. If Rene was equally as crazy about him, why was she so paranoid about Peter cheating on her?" he asked. "If they were in love, why would she care who Peter was involved with?"

Mel thought about it. She remembered how scathing and suspicious Rene had been. Joe was right. A woman who was in love with someone else didn't act that way about a man she was planning to leave behind.

"Could she have wanted both of them?" she asked.

Joe shrugged. "I suppose. It could have been an I-don't-want-you-but-no-one-else-can-have-you-either situation."

"That seems selfish and kind of mean, neither trait of which I would have associated with Rene," Mel said. She glanced at Joe while he drove. "Have I told you lately how glad I am that I'm marrying you?"

"No, but it's always nice to hear." Joe reached for her hand and gave it a quick squeeze. "I feel the exact same way."

He turned the car into the parking lot behind the alley of the bakery, and Tony parked beside him. The four of them got out of their cars and crossed the lot to the bakery, where Mel used her key to let them in and then switched off the alarm.

Joe, at home in the bakery, went into the walk-in cooler and delivered everyone's requested cupcakes while Mel brewed a pot of coffee. By mutual agreement, they tabled the discussion of Rene and her death, focusing on the current state of the Arizona Cardinals and their chance at making the playoffs.

When the last of the cupcakes had been consumed, and the four were lingering over their coffee, Mel turned to Susan and said, "All right, I did as you asked. I meeted and greeted with everyone I could at the exhibit. Do you think it helped?"

"Yes," Susan said. "And when I run the exclusive interview with you about your friendship with Rene over the years, it will seal your image as a hardworking local businesswoman who lost a dear friend. It'll be that much tougher for Chief Rosen or the independent council to make you look like a serial killer or whatever it is she's trying to prove."

Mel studied Susan's face. She was a beautiful woman, but even more than that, her eyes were kind. Mel trusted her.

"Okay, thank you," she said. "When do you want to do the interview?"

"How about tomorrow?" Susan asked. "I can meet you here around ten?"

"Sounds good," Mel said.

"And you might want to wear business attire," Susan said.

"Oh, all right." Mel frowned. "We're not doing pictures, are we?"

"No, but while we talk, we are going to do some art gallery recon."

Mel looked at Susan and shook her head. "I don't think it's a good idea for me to go back to Desert Winds anytime soon."

"Clearly," Susan said. "Good thing we're going to Imagine Gallery instead."

Thirteen

Mel disliked business clothes. They were hot, itchy, restrictive, and she hated having to pick up, drop off, and pay for dry cleaning. But when Susan arrived, looking like she'd just walked off the cover *Vanity Fair* in a tailor-made sea foam green silk suit and beige heels, she was glad she'd upped her fashion game. A dress and then a skirt two days in a row was too much, but for Rene, she'd do it.

She wore a cream-colored blouse tucked into a pin-striped navy and ecru skirt with navy heels. She hadn't worn this particular outfit since her corporate days and she was pleased that it still fit, although it was a little snugger in the hips than she remembered. Susan nodded at her in approval when she entered the bakery.

"Are you ready?" Susan asked. "I have an appointment to meet with Mr. Johansson at eleven."

"What?" Mel asked. "I thought we were doing recon. You know, pretending to be art buyers or bored housewives or something."

Susan laughed. "We are. We're just doing it with an appointment so I can be certain that he's there. We don't have time to waste chasing him around town if he isn't in the gallery."

"Oh, good point," Mel said. "Sorry, I'm usually much sharper about these things."

"It's all right, you're grieving," Susan said.

She stated it so matter-of-factly that Mel caught her breath. It was true. She was grieving, and she probably would be for a long time. The worry about what had happened to Rene, and the question of who had tried to make it appear that Mel was involved, had kept her from fully sinking into her grief, but it was there just below the surface. The effort required to push it down was exhausting, but Mel knew if she didn't that she would cry for days, and that wouldn't do Rene any good.

Susan drove them to the gallery. It was a square building made primarily of sheets of rusted steel, concrete, and thick floor-to-ceiling panes of glass. Technically, Mel supposed it was modern architecture, but so many buildings had been constructed of the same material that it was beginning to feel very turn of the century and not as innovative as it once seemed. She kept her opinion to herself, however, as they entered the building.

It was a large open space, as most galleries were, but this one was full to bursting with freestanding partitions displaying the artwork. There were so many such walls that the place had the feel of a maze. She wondered how they would find anyone to greet them, but maybe that was on purpose. They were forced to walk by all of the art, and perhaps that's how Johansson managed to sell. He threw up his artists as barricades.

Finally, when they turned the corner around a wall that held hand-painted tiles done in abstract colors, one of which was banana yellow with a red pepper on it, they found a small lounge area. Sitting in one of the stylish black leather chairs was Neil Johansson. Mel recognized him from his picture. He was just as handsome in person as he'd been in his online profile.

When he heard them, he stood up with a smile. "Good morning, ladies. Ms. Estevez, I presume?"

Susan tossed her hair and gave him a smile at full wattage. To his credit, Johansson didn't lose his powers of speech at the sight, for which Mel gave him big points.

"A pleasure," Susan said and extended her hand. "And this is my friend Melanie Cooper."

Johansson turned to Mel and they shook hands. She knew she didn't have the same impact as Susan, but she gave him what she hoped was a sincere smile, and Johansson smiled back with a twinkle in his bright blue eyes. So far so good. He hadn't pointed at them in horror and declared them frauds at least.

"I understand you're in the market for some sculptures," Johansson said. "Could you tell me a little about your preferences, what you look for in a piece, artists that you admire, that sort of thing?"

Susan looked at Mel with a small smile and then turned back to Johansson and declared, "I am simply, madly, passionately in love with Rene Fischer-Klein."

Johansson's eyes widened. His face flashed emotions like a warning signpost: shock, dismay, sorrow, grief. Full stop. He glanced down at the tips of his shiny black shoes. He cleared his throat. He took a deep breath and then raised his head. The cycle of emotions had been neatly tucked back away behind a face that was fully contained, showing no hint of emotion.

"She is . . . was . . . a genius," he said. "I assume you've heard the horrible news of her recent death."

"Yes, which is why I am desperate to own something of hers," Susan said. "I'll pay any price."

"Regretfully, I am not in possession of any of her work," he said. "And, honestly, even if I was, I don't think I could bear to part with it."

"Nothing?" Susan asked. "I had heard . . . I assumed . . . were you not . . . ?" She broke off with what Mel believed was feigned embarrassment and then Susan pressed on. "It was my understanding that you and Rene enjoyed a special relationship."

Johansson studied them, his blue eyes suddenly cool, and Mel suspected this was the moment he would toss them out on their behinds. Surprisingly, he didn't. Instead, he nodded.

Susan didn't move and neither did Mel, but she knew they were both thinking the same thing. That he was about to admit to having a relationship with Rene. As much as Mel wanted to know the truth, she didn't want it confirmed that Rene had cheated on Peter like he had cheated on her. It would destroy the last little bit of magic she'd thought their relationship had.

"Rene and I did have a special relationship," Johansson said. He glanced around the gallery, which was quiet, and gestured for them to sit down.

Susan sat on a leather love seat, and Mel took the space

beside her. She felt as if she was just going along for the ride, like a handbag, which was probably for the best because it was taking everything she had not to cry.

"And yet you have none of her work?" Susan asked. He gave her a dark look that Mel suspected was to hide his hurt. "Forgive me, I know I'm being terribly rude. I'm just desperate. I thought I'd always have time to acquire the right Rene Fischer-Klein piece and now, well, now I'm just undone."

Johansson relaxed ever so slightly. Susan was speaking his language as a collector. Mel felt herself relax as well.

"Rene and I were friends," Johansson said. "Good friends. She had so few of those. I don't think anyone understood how terribly lonely she was."

Mel felt the sharp metaphorical point of a knife slide in between her ribs and pierce her heart. Rene had been lonely?

"What makes you say that?" she asked. Her voice came out sharper than she intended but Johansson was studying the top of the coffee table and didn't notice, or if he did, he didn't react.

"Artists are different creatures," he said. "And an artist of Rene's caliber is different than most. You saw her canal piece I assume?"

They nodded.

"The amount of creative energy and intelligence it takes to conceive and execute such a heroic work of art is, well, monumental," Johansson said. "She spent so much time in her own head, thinking and thinking and thinking about every single element, how to craft them, put them together, and then assemble them in a loop, giving the piece no beginning or end. It's positively genius."

He gazed at them and then past them as his mind filled

with thoughts of Rene and her talent. Finally, he brought his gaze back to theirs.

"We used to meet for coffee in the morning, before the sun was up, and we'd walk the canal and talk, just talk," he said. "Sometimes, it was about current events like the weather, other times it was her trying to figure out how to work a particular piece, and some moments we shared a bit about our lives. The last year of her life, I knew she wasn't happy, but no matter what door I held open for her, she wouldn't step through."

Mel and Susan were silent. Mel was undone. She didn't know how to respond and felt like an absolute failure of a friend. How had she not known how lonely Rene was?

"When you talk about doors," Susan said. "Exactly which ones were you holding open for her?"

Johansson shrugged. It appeared he had said all he was going to say. It wasn't enough. Mel needed to know all of it.

"Mr. Johansson," she said.

"Neil, please."

"All right, if you'll call me Mel and her Susan," she said. He nodded. "I have a confession to make and I should have told you the moment we arrived."

"You were friends with Rene," he said. "You're Melanie Cooper, the cupcake baker, whose cupcakes she adored."

"You knew."

"Not until I mentioned how lonely she was and saw the look of devastation that crossed your face. Only someone who cared very much for her would have looked so crushed," he said. "Then I remembered that she used to talk about a Mel who baked cupcakes in Old Town, and I assumed it was you."

"Smart man," Mel said.

"I notice things," he said. He turned to Susan. "And what is your truth?"

"Reporter," she said.

He nodded. "I should have guessed. Your questions were quite to the point."

"Clearly, I'm going to have to work on my skill set," she said.

They were all quiet for a moment, accepting that the charade was over but not really knowing where to go from here.

"Would you mind if I asked you some questions?" Mel asked. "As Rene's friend?"

Neil Johansson studied her for a moment. His blue eyes, which had seemed so kind before, were now sharp, assessing her, determining her worth. Mel assumed that's what made him such a good gallery owner. He could see what lay beneath.

Finally, he said, "Yes, but I give you fair warning that I may not answer, and I expect it to be kept off the record."

Susan nodded.

"Thank you," Mel said. "Did Rene ever indicate that she was afraid of anyone?"

"No," he said without hesitation. "If she had, I would have gone right to the police. But I've racked my brain, going over every bit of conversation we ever had, and there's nothing."

"What about Peter?" Mel asked.

"What about him?"

"Did your friendship bother him?"

"He didn't know about it," Neil said. "Rene preferred it that way. Peter, as her manager, discouraged her from having any friendships outside of their rather insulated world."

Mel frowned. This was a controlling side of Peter she had never known about. "Do you think he was trying to keep her isolated?"

Neil shrugged. "I don't know. Rene was an intensely loyal person. I offered to help her leave him, leave Desert Winds, to strike out on her own on the world stage, but she couldn't do it. She couldn't make herself leave."

"I've heard that their marriage wasn't as solid as I'd always believed."

Neil glanced away. "She said she forgave him."

"For the affair? Did you believe her?"

"I had no choice, as she rejected the alternative that I gave her," he said.

Mel knew without him saying so that a life with him was the offer he'd made. She was surprised by his candor, especially given that it didn't go his way.

"Why did she stay?" Mel asked. She just didn't understand why Rene would have chosen to stay in a less-than-ideal marriage when she could have had so much more.

Neil shrugged. "Theirs was a unique pairing. They got together very young and their lives were so entangled. They were very dependent upon each other in so many ways and yet, they also seemed to try to tear each other down, too. It was dramatic and passionate, and I think they were addicted to the drama. I could never offer Rene that. I'm not an overly demonstrative man."

"You were in love with her," Mel said.

"From the very first time I set eyes on her," he said. "She was working in the courtyard of Desert Winds. Her hair was pushed back from her face with a deep pink headband. She was wearing a tank top and jeans with Doc Martens.

She was covered in sweat, and her concentration was completely on the piece she was twisting into shape, a beautiful deep purple spiral. I was riveted. I couldn't take my eyes off her, but she had no idea that I was even there. It was like she was in this creative second dimension where it was just her and her work, nothing else existed."

His gaze was cloudy with the memory, and Mel nodded. She'd seen Rene at work and in the same state. It was as if she had her own portal to the universe, a gateway to creativity that was hers alone, and once she opened that door, she lived on a separate plane of existence.

"Did she know how you felt about her?" Susan asked.

"Yes, I told her," Neil said. "I couldn't not, but her heart belonged to Peter and I loved her enough to respect that."

"Even though it broke your heart," Mel said.

"It did," he agreed. "But she remained my friend, that's how loyal she was, and I took comfort in being her confidant, the person who wanted nothing from her but to spend time with her."

The words were so poignantly spoken that Mel felt her throat get tight. There was such grace in Neil's feelings for Rene. It hurt to hear about it. She could feel the tears well, and she desperately did not want to lose it in front of Neil and Susan. She rose to her feet and said, "Excuse me, I just need to—"

The words got stuck on the knot in her throat. Neil seemed to understand. He gestured to a door neatly tucked into the corner. "The washroom is right there."

Unable to speak, Mel nodded and hurried to the restroom. She opened the narrow brushed steel door and slipped inside. It was larger than she'd expected with a cream-colored chaise lounge and side table in the front room and the sink and toilet beyond another set of doors. She let the door swing shut and sank onto the chaise.

She bent forward, letting the grief bubble up through her as if it could release the pressure of the pain. Today had been a revelation. A person she'd considered a friend turned out to have a life she knew nothing about. She thought about Rene as the cheerful, eccentric artist who encouraged everyone around her to pursue their passion to the fullest, and yet, her life was being revealed to be an isolated existence controlled by the person Mel had thought cared about her the most.

It was hard to wrap her head around it. She wanted to reject it completely, but between Bernadette's admitting to an affair with Peter, Delilah's insistence that Peter wasn't who he seemed, and Neil's confirmation of both of the previous statements, Mel started to feel as if the person most responsible for Rene's death was the man that she and Angie had been so sure was the perfect husband. The thought made her dizzy and not a little sick to her stomach.

Being a believer in pastry as a cure-all for whatever ails a person, she was wishing with every cell in her body that she could have a cupcake at the moment. A big one, extra large, with sprinkles. Instead, she let a few tears fall and concentrated on her breathing until the knot in her throat eased. When she was calmer, she used the sink to wash her hands and pat cold water on her face. Using a paper towel to dry her hands, she tossed it into the trash and reached for the door handle but paused.

Hanging on a coat hanger on a hook on the back of the bathroom door was a red satin gown. She let go of the doorknob and touched the fabric as if to prove to herself that it was real and she was actually seeing what she thought she was seeing. The recognition came fast and furious. Willa Kincaid had been wearing this very dress last night. Mel dropped the gown and yanked open the bathroom door, storming back to the lounge area where Neil and Susan waited.

She stood in front of Neil and glared down at him. "You're good, very good, and you almost had me."

"Excuse me?" His eyebrows rose in surprise.

"Oh, that whole song and dance about your love for Rene, I find that very difficult to believe when it seems you are involved with her biggest rival, Willa Kincaid," Mel snapped.

Fourteen

Understanding lit Neil's eyes, and he rose from his seat, forcing Mel back a few steps. Susan was looking at her as if she'd lost her mind, but Mel didn't back down. She knew that dress and she knew what it meant for that dress to be hanging in the gallery's washroom. Willa and Neil had a relationship, and if he'd been pretending to be Rene's friend, then it had to have been based on an ulterior motive, like destroying Rene's career to make room for the new rising star Willa Kincaid.

"Follow me, please," Neil said. Much to Mel's surprise, his tone was very polite. He led the way through the gallery, leaving Mel and Susan to follow. Mel glanced over her shoulder at Susan, who shrugged.

They worked their way to the front of the gallery. A

partition containing several empty steel bases was placed in front of the tall windows. A sign on one of the bases read: *Willa Kincaid, coming soon.*

"Oh." Mel felt her face grow warm. "So you're representing her."

"When I couldn't get Rene to join my gallery, I offered the space to Willa and she accepted," he said. "And, before you ask, yes, I told Rene."

"And how did that go?" Susan asked.

"About as well as you'd expect," he said. "She told me she hated me, threw her coffee at me, and stormed away." He paused, looking forlorn. "Those were the last words she ever spoke to me."

There wasn't much to say after that. Neil said that he'd tried to talk to Rene after, but she refused to see or speak to him. Using Emersyn as a messenger, she made it clear that she considered him a traitor and would never forgive him.

If Mel had felt guilty for not being the friend she thought she ought to have been to Rene, then she could only imagine how awful Neil felt.

On their way to the door, she had to ask him one more question. It was rude and intrusive, but she thought it would answer a host of other questions, such as why he would ever sign Willa to begin with, knowing how Rene felt about her.

"Did you offer representation to Willa because you knew it would infuriate Rene?" she asked.

"I'm not sure what you mean," he said. He avoided her gaze, however, so Mel figured he knew exactly what she meant, but sure, if he wanted, she could spell it out more plainly.

"Were you hoping to get Rene to notice you by making her jealous?" she asked.

A faint pink stained his cheeks, and Mel knew her question had just been answered.

"For a man who is not overly dramatic, you certainly attempted an emotional coup there," Susan said.

"Attempted and failed," he said. "The only thing it got me was shut out of Rene's life for the final weeks of it, and I didn't know . . . I thought I'd have more time."

There was such raw pain in his voice that Mel couldn't resist reaching out and squeezing his arm. Unfortunately, she had no words of comfort to give because she, too, thought she'd have more time.

\/,\,\

"What do you make of that?" Susan asked once they were back in her car.

"Gut wrenching," Mel said.

"Yes, but do you believe him?"

Mel thought about it. Did she think Neil was telling the truth? She couldn't imagine why he'd lie. His representation of Willa was right there out in the public. His relationship with Rene couldn't be proven but the emotion in his voice—she didn't think he was that good an actor.

"Yes, I believe him."

"Me, too."

"So, what's next?" Mel asked.

"I think we need to hear what Peter has to say about his relationship with Bernadette," Susan said. "And given that you're a longtime friend, I think you are just the person to ask him."

"Oh, goody," Mel said. "Can we stop at the bakery first? With Angie feeling so sick, I need to check on things."

"A cupcake wouldn't be out of the equation, either," Susan said.

Mel decided she liked this woman. They parked in a spot in front of the bakery and strolled in the front door. Susan was in the lead and took two steps and then whirled around, trying to push Mel back outside.

"What's wrong?" Mel asked.

"Nothing," Susan insisted. "I just think we should come back later. It looks busy in there."

Mel frowned at her. "It's okay, I'm pretty sure I can jump the line."

"No, that would be terrible customer service, trust me—"

"Mel!"

Mel knew that voice. It was loud, it boomed, and at the moment it sounded distinctly grumpy. She glanced past Susan. Sure enough, there he was.

"Uncle Stan?" she said. "What are you doing here?"

"Looking for you." He stepped forward so he was looming over Susan.

"You found me," she said. "This is my friend Susan Estevez."

Stan glowered. "We've met."

Susan looked at Mel. "I might have written one or two pieces about the Scottsdale Police Department."

"Oh."

"Not very flattering pieces at that," another voice said. Mel looked past Uncle Stan. Chief Rosen stood there, looking like the picture description of unhappy. "If we could have a moment of your time, Ms. Cooper?"

Mel had a feeling that her definition of "a moment" and the chief's varied widely.

"Sure," she said. She glanced at Susan. "Let's run that other errand a bit later, shall we?"

Susan glanced from the chief to Mel and back. "Gotcha. You have my number."

"I'll call you."

Susan nodded and then walked past Uncle Stan to get in line at the bakery counter. "I'm still getting a cupcake."

Mel smiled. She glanced at Uncle Stan, who was not smiling, and Mel felt the corners of her mouth droop down. He jerked his head to the side, indicating that he wanted Mel to take them to the kitchen in back. She passed the counter of yummy goodness, smiling at Angie and Marty as she went. Neither of them looked reassured.

The kitchen was empty, and Mel pushed the door open, holding it for Uncle Stan and Chief Rosen. The chief was, again, in her navy blue suit with the appropriate patches, badges, shield, and stars. So, this was a formal meeting.

"Can I offer either of you a cupcake or a cup of coffee?" Mel asked.

"I'll have a coffee," Uncle Stan said.

"Nothing, thanks." The chief looked at her watch.

Mel went to the coffeepot in the corner that looked to have been just brewed. The bakery kept a fresh pot in constant rotation, not only for the customers but for themselves as well. She poured a cup for Uncle Stan, fixing it just the way he liked, and handed it to him.

She gestured for them to take seats at the steel worktable, which was thankfully empty and had been scrubbed down after her last baking bender.

"What can I do for you?" she asked.

"We came to tell you some news actually," Uncle Stan said. "Some of it I think you'll be relieved to hear."

Mel waited. She didn't want to say anything that might jinx his saying that she was free and clear of suspicion since it was clearly ridiculous to hold her accountable just because of a misunderstanding between her and Rene the week before she died.

"The medical examiner tested the cupcakes that were picked up as evidence on the day that Rene died," Uncle Stan said. Mel felt her heart beat a little faster and her throat went dry. She could feel the chief watching her, but she refused to give the woman the satisfaction of seeing her squirm.

"What did he find?" Mel asked. "Was my cake-to-frosting ratio not up to scratch? Or did I use too much confectioners' sugar?"

Uncle Stan gave her a quelling glance, but she saw the twitch of his lips indicating that he was trying not to laugh. The chief was not nearly as amused but huffed out a breath of impatience.

"Are you done?" she asked.

"For the moment," Mel said.

"The cupcakes were clean," Uncle Stan said. "There weren't any traces of substances that should not have been there."

Mel considered him. "What is it that they're looking for?"

"I'm not going to tell you that," he said.

"Clearly, it's something," Mel said. She stared first at Uncle Stan and then at the chief. "Was Rene poisoned? I'm her friend. I deserve to know."

"And you will," the chief said. Mel blinked in surprise. "When the findings are official, and the report can be made public."

Mel stared at Uncle Stan and he shrugged. He was not going to be any help here. Mel glanced back at the chief. There was something going on here. This woman clearly did not like her, with her independent council nonsense, and Mel was sure her time was too valuable to be spent visiting bakeries, especially when she was not even indulging in a cupcake or four.

"While I appreciate the in-person update," Mel said, "what's really going on? Why did you want to talk to me? Because there is no way it was to tell me that our cupcakes were clean." She glanced at Uncle Stan. "That could have been conveyed in a text."

Uncle Stan and Chief Rosen exchanged a look. Then he said, "She's got more access to the players than we do."

Chief Rosen made an annoyed gesture with her hand. It was a dismissive wave as she cut through the air as if she wanted to slap someone. Mel got the distinct feeling it was her.

"What is said in here goes no further than this room," Chief Rosen said. Mel nodded. She'd have agreed to anything to find out what had happened to her friend. She knew it was the only way she'd ever feel absolved of not noticing how much turmoil Rene was in.

"The evidence indicates that Mrs. Fischer-Klein was poisoned," Uncle Stan said. "Until the medical examiner tells us what with, we are operating on speculation."

"So, you know, or you think you know, but you can't declare it yet, is that right?" Mel asked. She glanced at the chief. Her mouth was in a tight straight line. It looked as if it physically pained her to nod.

"And you're sharing with me because?"

"We need you to wear a wire and use your friendship with Peter to see what you can get out of him," the chief said. It lacked finesse, but it was to the point.

Mel turned surprised eyes to Uncle Stan. "And you're okay with this?"

"No, but we're out of options," he said. "We need to know what was happening between him and Rene, if she was about to leave him or divorce him or vice versa, something that would have tipped the scales in the relationship, causing him to harm her."

"And you think he's just going to share his intent to kill his wife with me?"

"No, but he might drop a hint, a clue, or a lead in conversation with you," Chief Rosen said. "Believe me, I do not like this plan at all, but we are passing the forty-eight-hour mark, and my gut tells me that Rene Fischer-Klein was murdered. Now are you willing to help us or not? I will consider dropping having you investigated by an independent council if you do."

"Huh." Mel was surprised. The chief didn't strike her as someone who backed down, ever. "Just so you know, I would have helped whether you dumped the investigation or not, but since you've offered, I accept." Uncle Stan gave her a look of approval. "Now what do you need me to do?"

"Have a conversation with Peter Klein," Uncle Stan said.

"Interestingly enough, I was already planning on that," Mel said.

"And wear a wire while doing it," Uncle Stan added.

"Okay," Mel said. "Sure. I mean, a wire is no big deal, right? And if he's a homicidal maniac who killed his wife and discovers me wearing a wire, I'm sure it will be no problem. Right? Right."

"Are you done freaking out?" Uncle Stan asked.

Mel walked away from him and yanked open the walk-in cooler. Done freaking out? She hadn't even begun, but as in all things, a cupcake would help. She reached for a cookie dough cupcake, no, two cookie dough cupcakes and came out of the cooler, double fisting.

"I'm not freaking out," she said. "I'm merely mentally preparing myself for the sting."

"It's not a sting," the chief said. "You're having a conversation, and that's it."

"Uh-huh." Mel bit into the cupcake. The sugar, the butter, the crunch of the chocolate chips, all of it helped soothe her mild case of panic at the thought of pretending to be chummy with a longtime friend who may or may not have killed his wife. She took another bite and sighed.

Uncle Stan gave her an irritated look and strode over to the cooler. He yanked open the door and grabbed two more cupcakes. He joined her at the table and thrust one of the cupcakes at Chief Rosen. When she stared at him in revulsion, he waved the cupcake under her nose.

"Take it," he said. "Trust me, you're going to need it."

\\'⁄,\\'\\'

"Clip this to your bra," Tony said. He handed Mel a small flat plastic device not much bigger than a large paperclip.

Mel reached under her shirt and secured it to the fabric of her bra, making sure it didn't poke or mar the line of her black scoop-necked shirt.

Tony looked at her, examining the placement, when Joe nudged him aside. "Eyes back in their sockets. I'll check it."

Tony smirked at his brother, but Joe ignored him. He stood in front of Mel and said, "I don't like this, cupcake."

"I know, but Uncle Stan asked, *he asked* me to do this," she said.

"Which makes me like it even less," he said. "If Stan is willing to pull you into this, then they're clearly struggling to tie anyone to Rene's death. Whoever caused her heart attack, if that's what happened, might get desperate if they feel the police are closing in."

"Why would they?" Mel asked. "The police have only said that her death is under investigation. They haven't arrested anyone, not even Peter, who as her spouse is the most likely suspect."

"I still don't like it," Joe said. His frown looked like it was going to be permanently etched in his forehead.

"That's why I'm here, Bro," Tony said. He removed the headphones he'd been wearing, letting them sit around his neck. "We'll be using my state-of-the-art equipment and keeping her safe, don't you worry."

"Too late," Joe said.

"DeLaura, what is taking so long?" Uncle Stan barked as he pushed his way through the swinging door into the bakery.

Tony and Joe both glanced at him in question. And then Tony turned to Joe and said, "I'll field this one if I may."

Joe waved his hand in assent.

"We're actually ready," Tony said. "The device is voice

activated, so it's already begun recording. It's saved onto a tiny hard drive, but also to a cloud, so even if Mel gets caught and the perp finds it and smashes it, we'll have backup of the audio."

"I'm not going to get caught," Mel said. "I'm meeting Peter at the installation, as we arranged. He suggested that I would enjoy seeing the piece in daylight, and he offered to meet me so we could share our grief over the loss of Rene."

Joe looked at her in sympathy. "Are you sure you're up for this? It's going to be tough."

"I know," she said. "But if it's the last thing I can do for my friend, then I'm going to do my best."

Joe leaned forward and kissed her forehead. "That's my girl. Remember that we'll be listening nearby. If you get freaked out in any way over anything, you leave. You don't owe him an explanation, just go."

"And if you're in trouble and you can't get out of there, use your safe word," Uncle Stan said. "The one we agreed upon."

Mel nodded. "Got it."

They headed out the back door in single file. Joe held Mel back for a second and asked, "Wait, what's your safe word?"

"Cornflakes," she said.

"Seriously?" he asked.

"Yes, it's a good one," she insisted.

"How do you figure?" he asked. "You're supposed to be able to work it into a conversation naturally. How are you going to do that with *cornflakes*?"

"Well, I'm hoping I don't have to," she said. "But if I do, I'll manage it."

"Give me an example," he insisted.

Mel opened and then closed her mouth. She mulled it over and then looked at him and said, "Hey, look over there! Is that a cornflake on the ground?"

Joe rubbed his hand over his face. "Yeah, that was seamless, not weird at all."

"It'll be fine," she said. She waved her hand at him. "You worry too much."

"I can't imagine why," he said, his tone as dry as a, well, cornflake.

Fifteen

Mel took her own car to the canal. It was early morning and cooler, the desert having enjoyed a nice seasonal rainstorm the night before. She wondered how Rene's piece had fared. The wind had been intense at the beginning, lessening in strength as the rain came, but the severity of the storm might have done some damage. She wondered if that's why Peter had wanted to meet at the exhibit when she reached out to him the day before under the watchful gaze of Uncle Stan and Chief Rosen.

She'd called Susan to tell her about the change of plan, and thought Susan, as a reporter, would be disappointed not to be going with her as they'd discussed. Instead, her voice sounded cautious. She ended their call by saying, "Be careful, Mel."

This did not help Mel's case of nerves at all. Peter had been her friend for so many years. It had been awful to realize that the man who presented himself as the doting husband every Friday was actually a controlling, cheating, manipulative jerk. She wasn't sure how she was going to pretend that she didn't know these things.

She parked her car, noticing that Joe had parked a few spots down from her with Tony in the passenger seat. Per his instructions, she spoke out loud, "What a beautiful day."

Tony gave her a thumbs-up through the windshield, meaning that her listening device was working. Great. Now it was showtime.

Mel sucked in a breath and strolled through the park. It was empty of food vendors and rich people dressed to the nines. There were a few people headed toward the exhibit but not the crowd that had been here a few nights ago. The thought rocked her. Had it only been a few days since Rene's death? She felt as if she'd aged exponentially since she and Angie heard the news.

She left the park and walked under the wrought iron arch that indicated the art space. The sun was still low in the sky, but that didn't stop it from sending shafts of light through Rene's piece, making the colors dance on the water below. Mel caught her breath as she took in the massive work as it slowly rotated overhead. She had a feeling that no matter how many times she looked at it, she would see something new and amazing. It made the loss of Rene all the more poignant. What else might she have done with her amazing talent? They would never know.

"Mel!" She glanced up to see Peter standing down the canal from her. He raised his arm to wave her towards him, and Mel waved back and started walking. As Rene's work glided overhead, moving with her, Mel felt as if it was Rene promising to have her back.

"It looks to have survived the heavy rains last night," Peter said as she joined him.

"It looks even more beautiful that it did the other night, and that's saying something," Mel said.

Peter nodded. "Rene wanted it to be primarily a daytime exhibit, but the lights at night give it a special something."

"Is the gallery pleased with how it was received?" Mel asked. "I imagine people are flocking there to see more of Rene's work."

"Not just see it, they want to buy it," Peter said. He put his hand on the back of his neck. "I was up all night last night, grabbing everything I could out of the gallery because Sunny planned to sell all of it and at these insanely inflated prices. I couldn't . . . I just . . . Rene's only been gone a matter of days. I felt as if the vultures were circling and the hyenas were stalking. I changed the locks on the studio, and I have Emersyn helping me pack up everything."

Mel studied his features. Behind his wire-rimmed glasses, his eyes were sunken, and his face looked gaunt. Did regret do that to a person? Did it carve out the excess flesh and leave just the bones behind?

"Sunny can't have been happy about that," Mel said. "She strikes me as a person who is used to getting her way."

"Understatement," Peter said. "She runs that gallery as if it's a factory and the artists are just supposed to punch out the desired number of pieces for her to sell. Rene hated it."

"Then why didn't she leave?" Mel asked.

"Loyalty."

"Sunny discovered her?"

"She gave Rene her first show," he said. "Rene never felt like she could leave after that."

That fit with what Neil had told Mel about Rene refusing to come to him.

"What about Byron and Bernadette, are they happy at the gallery?"

"Byron is like a big puppy," Peter said. "He's happy wherever he can get a pat on the head and a belly scratch."

Mel gave him a look, and Peter had the grace to look embarrassed. "Sorry, that wasn't fair. It's just that Byron, well, he's more showman than artist, if you get my meaning."

"I think what you're saying is that Byron is a whole package, hot guy who does clay sculpture, more than he is an artist," Mel said.

"Exactly."

Mel started to walk and Peter fell in beside her. There were other people there to study *Seasons*, and Mel maneuvered around them, walking back towards the park.

"What about Bernadette?" she asked. "How does she feel about the gallery?"

Peter shrugged. "I'm sure I don't know."

Mel was disappointed. Mostly because he chose to lie, but also because now she was going to have to be a hard-ass to get the information out of him.

She decided not to pull her punches. She turned to Peter, and said, "You had an affair with her, didn't you?"

"This is not the place for this conversation," he said. He glanced at the people nearby who were admiring the sculpture, as if he was afraid they might recognize him.

Mel didn't care if they did. She'd been dragged into this

mess because of the job she'd promised to do for Rene and also because of her friendship with the couple, but she wasn't going to pretend she was okay with anything that had happened since that disastrous Friday night.

"It may not be the place, but it's time," Mel said. She stopped walking and turned to face him, hoping that whatever he said could be picked up on that dinky mic Tony had given her. "Bernadette told me the truth the night of the exhibit opening. She said you two had an affair and that most of the art scene knew, so I'm guessing Rene knew, too?"

Peter looked like a wild animal caught in a trap. He leaned close, his voice frantic as he said, "Bernadette lied."

Mel shook her head slowly from side to side. She didn't believe him. Bernadette had nothing to gain by admitting to the affair, and she was right that if the local art scene knew, it would become public knowledge one way or another soon enough.

"No, she didn't," Mel said.

This time, Peter didn't argue. He simply looked crushed under the weight of the truth that he could not push off or pretend wasn't there.

"Is that why Rene was so suspicious of me, of Emersyn, of anyone you came into contact with? Was the truth of your affair eating her up inside?" Mel asked.

"No," Peter said. "It was a mistake. Rene and I worked through it."

Mel gave him a look and he sighed.

"We were trying to work through it. I can't believe Bernadette told you," he said. "We agreed—well, never mind. As my *friend*, I will expect your utmost discretion on this."

"Of course," Mel choked, thinking about the recording device in her bra. She said it too quickly, with an edge of panic, and Peter looked at her in doubt. She kept her expression neutral and, finally, he nodded.

"I am ashamed to admit that there was a brief flirtation between me and Bernadette," he said. "I don't know what I was thinking. It was during a time when Rene was traveling a lot and I was lonely. Bernadette seduced me, and I succumbed to her charms."

Mel breathed slowly in through her nose and out her mouth, trying to keep calm while Peter blamed the other woman for his own failings. She might not like Bernadette, but if a man responded positively to a woman's invitation, the woman wasn't solely to blame. Peter was just as culpable as, in fact more than, Bernadette. He was the one who had vows to uphold, not her.

"Your flirtation sounds more like an affair," Mel said.

Peter gave her a hurt look, but Mel refused to back down.

"Either way, it was over before it even began, but the damage was done. Bernadette made sure of that. Rene never trusted me and, in fact, became quite paranoid that I was fooling around with every woman I came into contact with—as you know. Our marriage was never the same, and I could never get her to look at me with the same love in her eyes."

Mel was silent, waiting for him to say more.

"Marriage, love, a true partnership is like these glass pieces," he said. He paused and gestured to Rene's work overhead. "They are so beautiful, and they appear to be so strong, able to withstand anything, but they're not. Trust, the core of any relationship, is as fragile as glass, and once it's shattered, it can never be mended, not really. I lost Rene the day I admitted to the affair. She refused to let me come near her or the studio ever again. She didn't know what she wanted to do about our marriage and said that any decision she made would come after this show, but I knew in my heart that our marriage was over, and I was the one who killed it."

"Do you think she was going to divorce you?" Mel asked.

"Yes, no, maybe," he said. He sighed. "I suppose I'll never know."

Beneath the glory of his late wife's greatest artistic achievement, Peter stood before her a broken man, left with nothing and no one. Mel wanted to feel sorry for him, but she couldn't. She'd known Rene and Peter before Rene's career took off, and there had been so much love between them. How had it gone so spectacularly wrong?

"I heard some things about you," Mel said. She didn't want to go there but she couldn't ignore what Delilah had told her. "That you were cruel to Rene, that you treated her like a plow horse, that you smashed some of her work."

To Mel it felt as if every word she uttered was like a hammer blow. Which was good, because she wanted to reduce all of the lies and posturing, all of it, to rubble. She wanted to see the truth revealed.

To her surprise, Peter nodded. "I was cruel. We fought all the time, and I was angry. It was terribly immature of me, but the more she shut me out the more I wanted to hurt her, so I pretended to care only about her production schedule, not her. It was all a lie."

"How much did you want to hurt her?" Mel asked.

Peter's eyes went round behind his glasses. "Not like that. Never like that. I loved her. You have to believe me, Mel. She was my everything."

Mel did believe him. Sadly, she'd thought his confession

of the affair and the fallout afterwards would make everything that had happened make sense, but it didn't.

She believed that Bernadette hadn't called the press about her, which left her wondering who had. She also concluded that Rene's erratic behavior was more than just an angry woman acting out because she'd been betrayed. There had been levels of paranoia that were not normal. Also, she genuinely believed that Peter regretted the affair. When she glanced at his face, it was clear he was devastated.

"Do the police know about the affair?" she asked.

"No," he said. He shook his head and glanced away. "I didn't want it to become public. But if Bernadette told you, then it's clear she's going to drag Rene's legacy through the mud. This is exactly what I didn't want. I could ki—"

"Don't finish that thought," Mel interrupted. She knew Uncle Stan would have a hissy fit, but she wasn't going to let Peter entrap himself in something because of her. "Nothing good comes of that sort of thing."

"You're right," he said. "I'm just so frustrated. I knew Rene wasn't well, but I thought it was because of me and what I'd done. I was afraid to confront her because I didn't want to make it worse. I let her push me away, hoping that after the show, she'd give me a second chance, and now we're never going to have one."

Tears coursed down his face. He looked completely destroyed. Mel couldn't imagine having to live with the load of guilt he was going to have to shoulder for the rest of his life. She squeezed his arm in sympathy, and after a moment he patted her hand in response.

"What do you think caused Rene's heart attack?" she asked.

"The night she died, I thought it was stress," he said.

"Our marriage was unraveling at the same time as the biggest show of her career. If I had it to do all over again . . ."

"And now?" Mel asked. "What do you think now?"

"I think she was murdered," he said. "I think someone wanted her dead."

Mel sucked in a breath. "Who?"

"I don't know, but I'm looking, and when I find out—" His hands clenched into white-knuckled fists. He looked as if he planned to rip apart whoever had harmed his wife.

"Is that why you invited Willa Kincaid to the opening night?" Mel asked. "You were trying to figure out if she could have had something to do with Rene's death."

"Not just her," he admitted. "All of them, the hangers-on, the artists, wannabe artists, collectors, gallery owners, everyone who wanted a piece of Rene, who took her time and her energy, who wanted to own a little bit of her for themselves, never mind how it left her with nothing. I'm looking at all of them, and I will find the person responsible."

Mel looked at the fierce light in his eyes, and she knew he was telling the truth and he meant it. She wondered if this was how he was assuaging his own guilt at not being the husband Rene had needed at the end. She didn't say as much, however.

"Do you have any idea who it might—" Mel began but his head snapped to hers, causing the word to jam up in her throat. The look in his eyes was frightening, and Mel felt her pulse skip a beat or two. Could it be that this was just an elaborate ruse? Could it be that Peter was the one who had facilitated Rene's death, and now he was playing the grieving outraged husband to mask his guilt? An uneasy feeling skittered through her.

"No, I don't," he said. He turned away, staring across the canal at the buildings on the other side. Luxury apartments and shops, where the wealthy liked to live and play. "But I will."

Mel took the opportunity to start walking. Peter fell in beside her. They didn't speak until they returned to the park.

"Can I offer you some advice as a friend?" Mel asked.

"Only if you understand that I probably won't take it," he said.

Mel smiled. Her heart rate slowed. There was the old friend she knew.

"I think you need to go to the police with everything," she said.

Peter met her gaze, and she knew he understood that she was telling him that he needed to talk to the police so he could get ahead of the situation. Peter nodded once. He looked at Mel and opened his mouth to speak, but he seemed to have no words. When he spoke, she suspected the words weren't so much for her as they were for Rene.

"I'm sorry this happened," he said.

Mel nodded. She believed he meant it. "Me, too."

Before, they would have parted as friends, sharing a hug. But not now, not here, probably not ever. Their friendship had been irrevocably changed. The rumors and insinuations had altered the ease that had always existed between them, making it prickly and awkward.

The information that he had cheated on Rene had tainted it as well. Mel knew that people made mistakes, she did, and she knew it wasn't her place to judge, but Peter had not only broken Rene's trust, he'd broken Mel's, too. He wasn't the man she'd thought he was, and she didn't think she could ever look at him in the same way again.

"That," he said. "That look."

Mel tipped her head in question.

"That look of disappointment in your eyes," he explained. "That's how Rene looked at me after I told her about Bernadette. It killed me. And when she was dying in my arms, even then, that look of disappointment was still there. I have to live the rest of my life knowing I'm never going to get the chance to make it up to her."

He looked utterly defeated, and then he turned and walked away from her, heading back to the exhibit. She supposed it was because it was the place where he could be closest to Rene and her greatest creation. How incredibly sad.

Mel tipped her head up and soaked in Rene's work, one last time. She knew it would be hanging here for a few more months, but she suspected she wouldn't be able to bear coming back to see the last bits of her friend, hanging in the sky, because it just hurt too damn much.

After one last long look, she turned and walked through the park. She hoped Tony had managed to save the conversation between her and Peter, because she didn't think she could remember it verbatim. When she approached her car, Joe stepped out of his own. He pulled her close and kissed her head, before tucking her into the passenger seat, obviously planning to drive her home.

"Ready to go?" he asked, his voice gentle as if he knew exactly how hard it had been for her to face Peter.

"Yeah," she said. "Let's get out of here."

"Good job, Mel," Tony said as he climbed out of Joe's

car and leaned against her open window. "We heard the convo. What did you think of what Peter said? Do you believe him?"

"I . . . I don't know," she said. "I wish I did, but I just don't know."

Sixteen

Mel spent the rest of the week doing some much-needed baking therapy. Uncle Stan and the chief thanked her for her participation in recording her conversation with Peter and then warned her away from approaching him or anyone close to Rene again, because of course they did. It grated.

When Friday rolled around, a week after Rene's death, Mel kept busy making a batch of specialty passion fruit cupcakes for a baby shower the next day. She wondered if Angie would want passion fruit cupcakes for her baby shower. The sound of retching from the staff bathroom interrupted her thought, and she assumed the answer was no, at least for now.

The cupcakes in front of her were a light fluffy coconut cake infused with a passion fruit mousse and topped with a vanilla buttercream, drizzled with a passion fruit puree. They were a bite of tropical breeze yumminess, and Mel resisted the urge to taste test another one. She'd already had two and they were good—no—great.

She finished drizzling the puree on the last one and then set the best-looking two dozen on a tray and stored them in the walk-in cooler. They would be boxed for delivery later that day. The remaining six cupcakes she put on a plate and stored it on the shelf in the walk-in cooler where she and Oz put their extras or their experiments, so the staff could have a treat or give feedback as needed. She did not need feedback on these, however, because she knew they were the bomb.

When she stepped back into the kitchen, it was to find Angie at the steel worktable, looking pasty and wan. Mel poured her a glass of water from the cooler in the corner of the bakery and put it in front of her.

"All right, Ange?"

"'I'm back. Puke and rally!'"

Mel wrinkled her nose. "Ugh, you did not just quote *Varsity Blues*."

"Oh, yes, I did," Angie said. She sipped her water, looking pleased with herself.

"That makes me want to puke," Mel said.

"Well, don't," Angie said. "You might start off a chain reaction." She put her hand over her stomach. "The doctor said the baby should calm down in a few more weeks. I am counting on it." She glanced down and addressed her belly. "Did you hear that, sprout? You need to settle in. We've got about thirty weeks to go here."

"Thirty weeks?" Mel asked. "That's a little over seven months."

"End of April or early May," Angie said. She looked at Mel with a small frown in between her eyebrows. "You're going to have a rather large matron of honor, unless of course you want to replace me, which I completely understand."

"Never," Mel said. "You and Tate are my best friends, and since Joe has scooped Tate for his best man to keep the brothers from coming to blows over the honor, that leaves you for me, and I can't think of anyone I'd rather have as my wing woman." Mel paused. "Unless you don't want to do it because of the stress. I mean, it's going to be a super-low-key wedding but you might be too tired, and your attention really should be on the baby."

"Mel—"

"I won't be mad, don't worry about me," Mel said. "I'm sure I can find a replacement." She ignored the panic at the thought of not having Angie by her side and put on her big girl brave face. "Really, whatever you want is fine."

"I love you," Angie said. Mel felt her heart squeeze. This was where Angie told her that being in a wedding was too much so close to giving birth and she was going to politely decline. Mel braced for it, even trying to turn up the corners of her mouth into a frozen smile that she hoped didn't crack. "But you are an idiot."

Mel blinked.

"You are my best friend," Angie cried. "Of course I'm going to stand up for you. I don't care if you get married two days before I'm due. I don't care if I go into labor in the middle of it—"

"Um, let's not borrow trouble," Mel said.

"Hush, I'm not done," Angie said in her most cranky pregnant voice. "What I want to say is that I am thrilled that you are finally going to be my sister. I feel as if I've been waiting for this since I first figured out you had a crush on Joe."

"Not like it was hard, because I was pretty obvious," Mel said.

"Why do you say that?" Angie teased. "Just because you lost your powers of speech, turned a lovely shade of aubergine, and looked like you were going to faint every time he came into the room?"

Mel laughed. "Sometimes I still feel like that."

Angie smiled. "I know what you mean." She shook her head. "Can you believe it? We're living our best lives with the men of our dreams. Sometimes I have to pinch myself just to make sure it's legit."

"If we'd known in middle school what we know now . . ." Mel began but Angie interrupted.

"I would have been a jerk to the tenth power," she said. "So, it's good that I had to do some pining and have some hardship first. It makes me appreciate what I have."

"That's true," Mel said. "Sometimes you don't appreciate what you have until it's gone."

Her thoughts flitted back to her conversation with Peter earlier in the week. Is that what had happened to him? Had he not realized how much Rene and his marriage meant to him until she was gone?

Mel had checked in with Uncle Stan every day. There had been no news about the cause of Rene's death, but they were still treating it as suspicious, given that Rene had no previous medical conditions, was young, and minus the past few months, had always been in great shape.

"You're thinking about Rene," Angie said.

"I can't seem to stop," Mel confessed. "I just feel like I'm missing something."

"Something like what?" Angie asked.

Mel shook her head and spread her arms in an I-have-no-idea gesture. "I just don't think Rene died of natural causes. She wasn't herself and everyone admits it, but no one seems to know what exactly was wrong with her. It wasn't the show, it wasn't because she was working too much, although that probably didn't help."

"So you think someone murdered her?" Angie asked. "For real."

Mel took a deep breath. "Yes."

"Who? Peter?" Angie looked horrified. "I mean, I know he cheated on her, but murder? Wouldn't his life be better if she were still alive as the primary breadwinner?"

"It would," Mel said. "And also, I think he still loved her and was genuinely sorry about his fling with Bernadette. I really think he wanted to make it up to her."

"Sorry shmorry," Angie said. "Maybe Rene would have forgiven him, but I never would."

"Agreed," Mel said. "But they had a lifetime together. Who knows what other baggage they carried."

Angie paused to sip her water. "If we give Peter a pass and look for who else had a motive, who do we come up with?"

"That's the thing," Mel said. "Everyone is better off with Rene alive, everyone except Willa Kincaid."

"Her rival? The one in the red dress?"

"Neil Johansson is representing her now," Mel said. "He took her on to try and get Rene to notice him."

"Which totally backfired, as it always does," Angie said.

"But now Willa is in the South Scottsdale art scene," Mel said. "And with Rene gone, she has no competition."

"Do you think the police have interviewed Willa?"

"Uncle Stan won't tell me anything," Mel said. "But I think I may have a work-around."

"Do tell." Angie rested her chin on her hand as she listened.

"The person closest to Rene over the past few months was her intern Emersyn. If anyone can tell me what sort of contact Rene and Willa had, it would be her."

"Sounds like a long shot," Angie said. "Unless, of course, Rene was being stalked by Willa, and then you're on it."

"Well, it seems quite a coincidence to me that Neil offered Willa representation when there are other glass artists in the valley," Mel said. "Why her? Why now?"

"Do you trust what Neil told you?" Angie asked.

Mel thought about it for a moment. "Honestly, right now, and until I know exactly what happened to Rene, I don't trust anyone."

"Probably wise," Angie said.

They spent the rest of the afternoon plotting how Mel could approach Emersyn without causing any suspicion. Mel figured the best way was to stop by the gallery with a box of cupcakes, as had been the Friday ritual forever. She hoped she could pull enough heartstrings to get Emersyn to talk to her about what she'd seen and heard during her time as an assistant.

✶ ✶ ✶

Mel left the bakery late in the afternoon. Angie and Marty were tending the front of the shop, while Oz was out delivering special orders, including the baby shower coconut and passion fruit mousse cupcakes.

As had become her habit, Mel entered the gallery from

the back. She didn't want to run into Sunny and risk having her head ripped off. Frankly, she'd seen enough of that woman to last a lifetime. She stepped into the courtyard to find Byron, alone, unloading his kiln. He wasn't wearing a shirt, and his skin was coated with sweat. His muscles rippled as he lifted enormous clay pieces and placed them on the ground around him. Oblong vases done in streaks of mesa red filled the area, and Mel marveled at his talent to wrest lumps of clay into such noteworthy pieces.

"Afternoon, Byron," she said as she slipped through the gate.

"Hi, Mel." He glanced up and smiled. It was a subdued version of his usual rogue's grin, and Mel could feel his melancholy all the way across the cobbled courtyard.

"Missing her?" she asked.

"Every second," he said. "I keep turning around to tell her something, but she isn't there." He glanced at Rene's furnace, stone cold and likely to remain that way. Then he sighed. "What brings you by?"

"It's Friday," she said. "We always send cupcakes to the gallery on Friday."

"You miss her, too," he said.

Having a hard time finding the words, Mel nodded. She cleared her throat and held up the box, popping the lid open. "I brought you a lemon one."

His smile this time blinded her, like looking directly into the sun. "Thanks," he said. "You just managed to make my day a little bit brighter."

With a show of white teeth and soft lips, he took an enormous bite. Fearing that her brain might shut off if she stared at him for too long, Mel turned and headed for the stairs. "I'm just going to see if anyone else wants one."

"Keep spreading your sunshine, Mel," he said.

She waved in acknowledgment but didn't turn around, afraid she might get caught in his hot-guy vortex again. She darted up the stairs, taking them two at a time. She'd packed a variety of cupcakes, not knowing who wanted what, and was hoping one of them appealed to Emersyn, whom she hoped was still here.

In a perfect world, Emersyn would be here but no one else. She wanted to ask the intern unencumbered by others about the changes she'd seen in Rene over the past few months. Sure, Mel was certain the police had asked Emersyn the same questions and probably there was nothing new to be gained, but at least she would feel like she was doing something. Besides, she liked Emersyn and wanted to make sure she was okay since she hadn't seen her since her altercation with Peter over the attendance of Willa at the opening.

She remembered that Peter had said he'd changed the locks to keep Sunny out. Mel turned the doorknob and found it locked. She gently rapped on the wooden door, and called out, "Did someone order cupcakes from Fairy Tale Cupcakes?"

The door was yanked open and Emersyn was there in jeans and a ripped T-shirt, her long hair in a braid, with dirt smudges on her cheek and chin. She blinked at Mel from behind her glasses as if she was so relieved to see someone, anyone, that she couldn't quite believe Mel was there.

Mel held up the box. "Cupcake?"

And that's when Emersyn lost it, her face crumbling as she let loose a sob that sounded as if it had been trying to get out for a very long time.

Seventeen

"Oh, oh," Mel said. She stepped into the studio and dropped the box onto a nearby table. The door swung shut behind her, and she opened her arms to give Emersyn a hug. The young girl stepped close, and Mel held her tight and let her cry it out.

"I'm sorry," Emersyn babbled. "It's just so hard without her here, even though the last few months were tough, and Peter is never around and Sunny is always trying to come in, and Peter said I shouldn't let her in because she just wants to steal things to sell them, and I think I'm having a nervous breakdown."

Damn it, Peter, Mel thought. Why was he putting this kid on the front line in front of that vulture? Heck, even at her age, Mel was afraid of Sunny, never mind being just out of college and wanting a career in the field of art. What was he thinking?

"There, there," Mel said. "It's okay. I'm here and I brought cupcakes."

Emersyn sniffed and wiped the tears off her cheeks with the backs of her hands. "What flavor?"

"Chocolate, raspberry, orange cream, mojito, and almond," she said. "Byron already took the lemon." She gestured to the box on the table. "Help yourself."

Emersyn took the chocolate and the almond. "Two okay?"

"Are you kidding? You can have all five if you want."

A tiny smile lifted the corner of Emersyn's mouth. Mel put an arm around her and led her to the love seat in the back of the studio. She gestured for her to sit and then took the armchair nearby. She waited quietly while Emersyn polished off the first cupcake.

"So, I take it it's been rough," she said.

"And how," Emersyn agreed. She paused to swallow. She heaved a contented sigh. "Why do cupcakes make everything better?"

"I don't know, but they do."

Emersyn ate her second cupcake more slowly, savoring it instead of using it for comfort. While she calmed down, Mel thought of how to approach the subject of Rene without causing Emersyn to cry again. She didn't want to cause the young woman more grief, but she needed information, and as far as she could tell, Emersyn was the only one who might have it.

"I imagine you've been interviewed by everyone from the police to the local news," she said.

Emersyn nodded. "I did talk to the police, but I refused to talk to the reporters. It felt like it would be a betrayal, you know?"

Mel nodded. She knew exactly what she meant. She'd done her exclusive interview with Susan earlier in the week, and it had been hard to talk about Rene without feeling as if she was betraying her. Thankfully, Susan had kept the piece short and to the point, focusing on the friendships of all of the Old Town businesses. She'd made Mel look good, for which she was grateful.

"Stan Cooper is my uncle; did you talk to him?"

Emersyn's eyes went wide. "Detective Cooper? He's your uncle?"

Mel nodded.

"He was so sweet," she said. "He was very patient, and he didn't yell at me, not like the other one."

"Detective Martinez? Short, feisty lady, lots of attitude."

"That's the one," Emersyn said. "She had a lot of questions about you."

"I'm sure she did," Mel said. "We have a history."

Emersyn nodded. "That makes sense. Your uncle kept her in check, mostly."

Mel smiled. "What else did they ask you?"

"Mostly about who Rene was in contact with over the last few months of her life," Emersyn said. "I didn't have much to report, as she worked sunup to sundown trying to finish *Seasons*."

"It is a glorious piece," Mel said. "I saw you at the memorial."

Emersyn met her gaze with a startled one. Then she relaxed and said, "You provided the cupcakes."

"Yes, it seemed appropriate given how much Rene loved

them, and we had them baked and ready for the opening anyway."

"She would have liked that," Emersyn said. Her lip trembled but she sniffed and blinked and fought back fresh tears.

"Emersyn, I don't want to cause you any more sadness, but do you think you could tell me what you told the police, or at least what you remember about the last few months of Rene's life?"

"Why?" Emersyn's expression became guarded.

"Honestly, because I think someone hurt her. In fact, I know it. I just don't know who or how," she said.

"And you think I can help?"

"Maybe," Mel said. "I mean, it's worth a shot, right?"

Emersyn sighed. "I can't believe someone would have harmed her. I told the police that. I mean, Rene had a very small life in the time that I knew her. She was here at the gallery with Ms. Davidson, Bernadette, and Byron. Peter was here in the beginning but then she banned him." She paused. "It was pretty obvious why."

"Emersyn, did Peter ever hit on you or make you uncomfortable?" Mel asked.

"No," Emersyn said. Her eyes were wide. "I would not have put up with that."

Mel believed her.

"I usually got here at seven in the morning and Rene was already at work. She went for walks early in the morning and then came straight here. I took care of her correspondence and social media, and I assisted with the larger pieces. It was fun in the beginning. Then something changed, and Peter no longer came around except on Fridays when he delivered cupcakes, and Rene was angry all the time. She seemed to be so irritable, and I could tell she didn't feel good."

"Was she on any medications that you know of?" Mel asked.

"No," Emersyn said. "Not that she told me about, and I think she would have because she had me run errands for her, pay her bills, all sorts of stuff. The police asked the same thing. They wanted to know if she was on drugs, I suspect. But she wasn't. As far as I know, she didn't even take vitamins."

"So her one addiction was coffee," Mel said.

"She seemed to run on coffee and nothing else, well, except your cupcakes. In the time I worked for her, she lost weight, had dizzy spells, and she was always cold even when it was crazy hot outside."

"Did you tell the police that, too?"

"Yes, they were definitely curious about the changes in her," Emersyn said. "Detective Martinez really seemed to think Rene had a drug problem, but I'm sure she didn't."

"What did Rene talk about when you were with her?" Mel asked.

"How much she hated Bernadette and Willa Kincaid," Emersyn said without hesitation.

"Not Peter?"

"No, surprisingly, she didn't talk about him as much, but we all knew. Bernadette made sure everyone knew."

"About the affair?"

"Yes," Emersyn said. She looked incredibly uncomfortable.

Mel pondered the information. None of it was new. She wondered if it was possible for a caffeine overdose to cause a heart attack.

"Where did Rene get her coffee?"

"Other than her morning coffee, which she got herself, I got it for her," Emersyn said. "She had very exacting spec-ifications. I had to use a quarter of a cup of coconut milk, she was big on agave nectar instead of sugar, and the coffee had to come from a fair trade vendor. Sunny always had a pot brewing in the break room, because she and Rene were the heavy coffee drinkers."

"Where is the break room?" Mel asked.

"Downstairs," Emersyn said.

"All this talk about coffee is making me think I need a cup. Do you want one?" Mel asked.

"No, thank you," Emersyn said. "I have a Gatorade that Sunny brought me earlier. I think she was using it to try and get in here, but I stood my ground and made her hand it to me through a crack in the door."

"Well played," Mel said with a smile.

Emersyn returned it. "In my defense, it's hot in here."

Mel laughed. "If it's all right with you, I'm going to go downstairs and check out the break room."

"Sure," Emersyn said. She glanced at the clock on the wall. "Sunny usually takes off for dinner about now, so you should be fine, but I wouldn't linger."

"Noted," Mel said. "I'll stop back before I leave."

Emersyn sighed. "I'll be here."

Mel left the studio, noticing that Emersyn locked the door behind her. It seemed she hadn't exaggerated how tense things were around here. Great.

The staircase that led downstairs was in the middle of the hallway. Mel didn't want to announce her presence un-less she had to, so she skulked down the stairs, pausing at the bottom until she could get a sense of who was where in the building.

Byron was still outside. Bernadette's studio door was closed, but the sound of music was coming from inside, so Mel assumed she was working. The gallery was dark, and Mel stepped inside and glanced at Sunny's office. The lights were off. She figured Emersyn had been right and Sunny had gone out to eat. Good.

Mel wasn't a detective. She knew that. And there really wasn't anything she could do here that would help the police, but she was curious about the coffee situation. The very first day she had met Emersyn, the girl had been on a coffee run for Rene. With the coffee being kept down here, it made for easy access for anyone who wanted to tamper with it.

She walked through the silent gallery to the break room. It was a tiny space with a café table and two chairs, cupboards running along one wall, a small refrigerator, a microwave, and a sink. She stopped in the doorway. Huh. The counter where there had obviously been a coffeemaker, as evidenced by the packet of filters, was empty. Mel checked the cupboard above it just in case it had been put away. The cupboard was empty.

She knew, without texting Uncle Stan to confirm it, that the police had already been here and had likely grabbed everything in the break room to be tested. If what Uncle Stan said was true and they thought Rene had been poisoned, this was the most likely place to have gotten it done. The thought made Mel shiver.

She left the gallery and returned upstairs. Music was still coming from Bernadette's studio. She was halfway down the hallway when Byron appeared at the far end. Mel waved, and he waved back. His studio was before Rene's and he disappeared inside while Mel paused in front of Rene's door and knocked.

"Emersyn, it's me," Mel called. She didn't want Emersyn to worry that Sunny had come back, trying to lift more of Rene's work. There was no answer. Mel knocked again. "Emersyn."

That was weird. Emersyn had said she'd be here. Mel pressed her ear to the door. She heard a grunt and then a crash as if someone had knocked over a chair. She tried the doorknob. It was still locked. She banged on the door, pounding it with her fist.

"Emersyn! Open up! It's me," she cried. Panic was making her heart beat hard and fast. What could have happened in the ten minutes she'd been gone?

"Mel, what's happening?" Byron came striding out of his studio at the same time Bernadette appeared in her doorway.

"What is the racket?" she cried. "Some of us are trying to create."

Mel ignored her and turned to Byron. "Emersyn is in there. I just left her, but now she's not answering, and the door is locked and I heard a crash."

Byron tried the door. Locked. Without hesitation, he put his shoulder to it. It didn't budge.

"Back up," he said. Mel jumped back. Bernadette came down the hallway towards them.

"What is the drama now?" she asked.

They both ignored her as Byron got a running start and hefted all of his weight against the door. It shuddered on its hinges but didn't budge. He tried again and again.

Impatient, Bernadette snapped, "What are you doing?"

"Emersyn is in there and something's wrong with her!" Mel said. She glanced at the phone in Bernadette's hand. "Call 9-1-1."

Crack!

The wood on the doorjamb splintered and the door banged open. Mel looked past Byron, who was gasping for breath. Emersyn was on the floor, her body convulsing.

"She's having a seizure!" Bernadette cried while she frantically pressed numbers on her phone.

Mel hurried past her, and said, "Tell them to hurry."

While Bernadette made the call, Mel dropped to her knees beside Emersyn, with Byron by her side.

"Emersyn," Mel cried her name. Her glasses were gone, her eyes were wide, and she looked terrified.

"Help," Emersyn croaked through chattering teeth. "What's . . . happening . . . to . . . me?"

Byron and Mel exchanged a glance. He looked back at Emersyn and said, "You're having a seizure. Have you ever had one before? Do you have a condition?"

Emersyn's entire body convulsed, but she managed to gasp, "No."

"Don't worry, kid. We're here. We'll help you," Byron said. He turned to Mel and added, "This could be a drug-induced seizure." He nudged Mel aside and took over. He checked Emersyn's airways and her pulse, rolled her to her side, and barked at Bernadette, "Tell them to get here as fast as possible."

Within moments, Mel heard sirens. "I'll go meet them."

She squeezed Emersyn's hand, met her eyes, and said, "You're going to be okay."

On her way to the door, Mel stopped to pick up Emersyn's glasses from where they'd fallen. When she crouched, she kicked an empty Gatorade bottle. That had to be the one that Emersyn said Sunny had given her. Mel frowned and grabbed it, her instincts telling her to keep it in her purse with Emersyn's glasses.

She raced down the stairs and through the gallery. She unlocked the front door and shoved it wide right as an ambulance pulled up. Thank goodness the station was just down the street. A medic ran up to her, and Mel gestured to the stairs. "She's up there."

He didn't wait to chitchat but grabbed his medical bag and bolted up the stairs. Mel held the door open for more medical personnel and followed them, her heart in her throat as she wondered what could have happened to Emersyn in the few minutes she was gone.

She huddled in the hallway with Byron and Bernadette. No one spoke as they paced, waiting for word. Finally, Emersyn was put on a gurney and carried out of the building. Mel wasn't about to let her go to the hospital alone. She told the medic that she was her older sister, and they let her climb into the ambulance with her.

At the door, Byron said, "I'll follow."

"Thanks." Mel nodded. She moved to the bench beside Emersyn, gripping the young woman's hand in hers while they careened through Old Town to get to the nearest hospital.

Using her free hand, she texted Uncle Stan to let him know what was happening and asked him to call Joe.

The ambulance arrived at the hospital on Osborn Road within minutes, and Mel jumped out and then followed as Emersyn was unloaded and brought into the emergency room. She called Peter, because he was the only one she knew who would know how to contact Emersyn's parents.

"Mel, hi—" Peter answered but Mel cut him off.

"Peter, Emersyn is sick. We're at the hospital on Osborn, you need to call her parents right away," she said.

"What?" he cried. "How?"

"I'll explain later, but you have to get them to come here right away," Mel said. "It's bad, Peter, really bad."

"All right, I'm on it." He hung up and Mel felt herself calm down. Emersyn was at the hospital. They'd found her quickly. She glanced through the window of the swinging door. There were several doctors in there. It was going to be okay. It had to be.

She paced, back and forth, waiting for word. She had no idea how much time passed but it felt like hours.

"Mel!" She glanced up and saw Byron and Bernadette running towards her. "Is she all right?"

"I don't know, but she has several doctors in there," she said.

She was surprised to see the relief on Bernadette's face. Her expression must have shown her surprise because Bernadette shrugged. "What? She's a good kid. I'd hate to see anything bad happen to her."

Mel nodded in agreement.

"Do you know what happened?" Byron asked.

"No, I was with her, sharing cupcakes, then I stepped out for a few minutes and when I came back the door was locked, and she wasn't answering. Then I heard a crash, and I just knew she was in trouble."

"Weird," Byron said. "Any idea what caused her to get so ill so fast?"

"The same thing that caused Rene's death," Mel said. "I think she was poisoned."

"Ah," Bernadette gasped. "Was it Peter?"

"Was what Peter?" a voice asked.

They all turned to see Peter, striding toward them with Sunny at his side. Peter looked frantic, his clothes wrinkled, his hair mussed, and his glasses sliding down his nose. Sunny, on the other hand, looked calm, cool, and collected, as if she didn't have a care in the world, and why would she?

Sunny gave Emersyn the Gatorade. Emersyn, who worked beside Rene, who saw the dramatic change in her over time. The sort of changes that could signify a mental illness or perhaps something more sinister, like poisoning. Emersyn said that Rene powered through the last few months on coffee—coincidentally, the coffee was made by Sunny. It gave her a point of access to Rene that couldn't be discounted. The thought flashed into Mel's mind that if Sunny had murdered one woman and gotten away with it, she had no reason to believe she wouldn't get away with it again.

Peter and Sunny stopped beside them. Peter looked at Mel and said, "What's going on?"

"Emersyn was poisoned," Mel said. She wanted to see their reactions.

"Poisoned?" Peter's eyes went wide behind his glasses.

"Yes," Mel said. "With the same poison that I believe killed Rene."

Eighteen

Peter blinked, and she could feel the hard stares of Byron and Bernadette on the sides of her face.

"Mel, how do you know—" Peter asked but she cut him off.

"Because it was sheer happenstance that I was at the gallery today, and if I hadn't been, Emersyn likely would have died," she said.

Mel stared at Sunny, who was busily folding the cuff of her sleeve. Her dress today was a navy blue shirtwaist with tiny white polka dots with matching navy pumps. She looked the perfect part of a 1950s housewife, all innocence and light.

"But she's going to be all right?" Sunny asked. She glanced past Mel through the window in the door to the room beyond.

"We don't know yet." Mel stared at Sunny until the woman returned her gaze. "Why'd you do it?"

"Ah!" Sunny gasped and put her hand on her chest, the picture of shock. "How dare you!"

"Really?" Mel asked. "I'd say it's more like how dare *you*?"

"I'm not going to stand here and be verbally abused," Sunny declared. "You have some nerve accusing me of anything when we all know that you had a horrible fight with Rene the week before she died over your relationship with her husband. If anyone had a reason to poison Rene, it was you."

Mel crossed her arms over her chest. "So, now I know who called the press to tell them that I'd had a fight with Rene."

Sunny looked indignant. "I was merely relaying what was common knowledge."

Mel glanced past Sunny and saw Uncle Stan making his way towards their group. As always, his presence calmed her down.

Sunny sent Mel a scathing glance. "You can try and twist the facts all you want, but everyone knows there was something going on between you and Peter—"

"Hey!" Peter interjected, but Sunny ignored him.

"And you were feeding Rene poison through those cupcakes, planning to kill her. I refuse to stand here another second with a known murderer. Peter, take me back to the gallery."

Mel let her take a few steps down the hallway, making sure Uncle Stan was able to cut off any avenue of escape, before she reached into her purse and took out the Gatorade bottle.

"Why the rush to go back to the gallery?" she asked. "Looking for this?"

Sunny whirled around and saw the bottle in Mel's hands. A flash of alarm crossed her face, and she took a quick step forward as she reached out and tried to snatch it. Mel tucked it behind her back.

"Give me that!" Sunny demanded between gritted teeth.

"The bottle of Gatorade you gave to Emersyn today?" Mel asked. She blinked her eyes innocently. "Yes, she told me you gave it to her. Now why would you want it back so badly? It's quite the coincidence that she's been poisoned just like Rene, don't you think?"

"Give me it!" Sunny's voice was a low growl.

"Could it be because it has traces of the same poison you used to kill Rene?" Mel asked. She heard a strangled cry come from Peter's throat, but she ignored him. Sunny took a swipe at Mel, but she dodged. Byron tucked her behind him, and she peered out from behind his massive bicep.

"Move, Byron," Sunny demanded. "She's clearly insane. Don't you see? Move!"

"No," he said. He stood as solidly as a brick wall.

"Why did you go after Emersyn?" Mel asked.

Sunny ignored her and grabbed Byron's arm, trying to physically move him from in front of Mel. It was like trying to push a car. He didn't budge.

"Could it be that you were afraid the autopsy would show that Rene was poisoned, and when questions were asked, you feared that Emersyn would mention how you brewed Rene's coffee every day? That certainly gave you the opportunity, but, wait, what would be your motive?"

"Shut up!" Sunny snapped. "Give me that bottle."

"Why? What's in it?" Mel argued. "Did you use the

ever-popular antifreeze as poison? They say that it's the favorite among women who've snapped."

"That's a good guess, Mel, but not quite," Uncle Stan said as he joined them. "According to the medical examiner, we're looking for tetrahydrozoline."

"What the hell is that?" Peter asked.

Mel frowned. "I think it's eye drops."

"Bingo," Uncle Stan said.

"I thought those just made your stomach sick," Bernadette said.

"No, they're very dangerous," Uncle Stan said. His voice softened. "And in some cases, quite deadly."

Sunny spun around. At the sight of him, her eyes went wide. She tossed her hair and said, "You aren't going to listen to this nonsense, are you?"

"That depends." Uncle Stan looked past her at Mel and said, "You got the evidence?"

"Yep, she poisoned Rene's intern," Mel said. "And I have the empty bottle she drank from."

"Nice work."

"This is ridiculous!" Sunny raged. "Bernadette, Byron, Peter, you can't possibly believe them."

"Why?" Peter asked. He looked pale and shaky. "You of all people, Sunny, how could you do this?"

Sunny's face went pale and then red, bright red, as if she might explode from the fury coursing inside of her.

"Because she was going to leave me!" she cried. She glared at them. "Do you know how she spent her mornings? Taking long walks with Neil Johansson along the canal where her exhibit was going to hang. The two of them, sharing coffee and laughs, while they plotted against me."

"Sunny, she was never going to leave you," Peter said.

He looked horrified. "Rene was the most loyal person I've ever known." A flash of pain crossed his face as he acknowledged one of his wife's finer qualities. "You gave her her first shot. She would never have left you."

"Only because I kept her weak," Sunny said. "I put just enough eye drops in her coffee to keep her sick and needy and too ill to leave me."

"My god, all this time I thought she was sick because she was so brokenhearted about me wrecking our marriage," Peter said. "But she wasn't. She was being poisoned by you."

"You should thank me," Sunny declared. "If I hadn't kept her in such a weakened state, she would have left us both."

"You're a monster!" Peter cried, and then he lunged.

"Oy!" Uncle Stan cried as Sunny went down in a twirl of skirts. She tried to fight Peter off, but he grabbed her hands before she could claw at him, hauling her up so that her face was inches from his.

"I should kill you with my bare hands," he declared.

"Stop! Stop it! I didn't mean to kill her. She drank too much coffee the day before the exhibit opened and it was too much for her," Sunny pleaded. "Don't kill me. It was an accident. You have to believe me."

Peter shoved her at Uncle Stan, who deftly handcuffed her.

"Byron, Bernadette, don't let them do this!" Sunny cried. Tears were pouring down her face, ruining her makeup and the chunky silver statement piece of a necklace she wore. The veneer of rich gallery owner was smeared off to reveal the killer beneath. "Everything I did, I did for you, for all of you. Rene would have been nothing without me. You would be nothing without me. Nothing!"

She was screaming now, and Uncle Stan hauled her away, away from the door where a young woman still fought for her life.

Mel followed them, grabbing a plastic bag from the nurses' station. She stuffed the plastic bottle into it and handed it to Chief Rosen, who was just entering the hospital.

"What is this?" she asked.

"The evidence you need that ties Sunny to the murder of Rene Fischer-Klein and the attempted murder of Emersyn Allen, assuming she lives," Mel said.

Chief Rosen looked from Mel to Uncle Stan and shook her head. "If you ever get tired of baking cupcakes for a living . . ."

Mel felt her lips turn up. "Yeah, I'll call you."

As soon as they left, she returned to the emergency room to join the others, waiting for news about Emersyn.

Emersyn's parents, a lovely middle-aged couple, arrived and waited with them. When the doctor came out and told them that Emersyn's prognosis was good and that they'd be moving her to a private room soon, Mel took her first real breath in what felt like hours.

Hugs were exchanged, and watery smiles shared. Mel was so relieved, she even hugged Bernadette, who, to her surprise, hugged her back just as tight. While they watched Emersyn's parents go into her room to see her, Mel felt the pain in her chest ease. She realized the feeling had been with her since Rene had died. She had been too late to help Rene, but she had managed to save Emersyn. It wasn't the ideal outcome. She would have liked to save them both from Sunny, but at the moment it was all she had, and it had to be enough.

"Rene would have loved this," Peter said.

"Yes, she would," Mel agreed.

As planned, they'd closed Fairy Tale Cupcakes for Oz's send-off. The jukebox was cranking out tunes, and they'd decorated the place with a Hawaiian luau theme. All of their friends and family were there, and the party spilled out of the bakery and onto the patio in front, where Mel stood behind the punch bowl and the cupcake tower.

She glanced at Peter. Given the events of the past week, she was surprised Peter had joined them. He was even wearing the requisite loud Hawaiian shirt.

"It was nice of you to come," she said.

Peter held up a card, a gift for Oz, that he dropped into a decorated box. "Rene would have wanted me to," he said. "And I wanted to say good-bye."

Mel's eyes widened. "Good-bye?"

"Yes," he said. "Now that Emersyn is going to be okay and Sunny is in jail, thanks to you for grabbing that damning bit of evidence, I feel as if it's time for me to go. I'm packing up some of Rene's best pieces and going on a European tour. It kicks off in Prague in three weeks and hits another ten cities after that."

"Wow, that's incredible," Mel said. "Will you come back when it's over?"

"Yes, just in time to pack up *Seasons* and take it on a world tour," he said. When he glanced at her, his face was broken. "She should have been world famous. Sunny stole that from her, but I am going to do everything I can to make up for it."

Mel knew he wasn't just talking about Sunny murdering Rene. He was talking about his own faithlessness. She nodded. "What's going to happen to the gallery?"

"Bernadette and Byron are hoping to buy it," he said. He pointed to the two artists who were across the patio, talking to Mick, the tattoo artist. "They want to open the space up to more artists and make it a cooperative."

"Good, that's good," Mel said. "The world needs more art."

He nodded in agreement, then gave her a small smile. "That's something Rene would have said."

"Yeah." Mel felt her throat get tight. "I miss her. I wish I had known. I wish I could have stopped Sunny. Ugh, I have so many regrets."

"I know exactly how you feel," he said. His voice was gruff, and Mel knew that he had so many more than she did.

She stepped around the table and gave him a hug. She leaned back and looked him in the eye and said, "Rene would be the first to tell us to get over ourselves."

"True, but will we ever get over her?" he asked.

"No." Mel shook her head. She patted her chest and said, "But she'll be here, always."

Peter nodded. He squeezed her hand and then tipped his head and said, "Good-bye, Mel."

"Good-bye, Peter."

She watched him wend his way through the party and out the patio gate. His shoulders were drooped, and his head looked as if it hung heavily on his neck. Mel knew with a certainty that she would likely never see him again. The realization hurt. Despite all of the bad revelations over the past few weeks, she still remembered the good times. She remembered that he and Rene were once relationship goals to her and Angie, and she promised herself that when she thought of them, that's what she'd remember.

"Well, I'd say as far as send-offs go, this one is a doozy," Marty said, popping up at her side as if he suspected she needed a friend.

He was holding a coconut shell stuffed with fruit, a snazzy umbrella, and way too much rum. His grass skirt was sagging, his Hawaiian shirt was unbuttoned to display an impressive tuft of white chest hair, and his crown of plastic flowers was drooping low on his bald head. Even his grin was lopsided, but Mel suspected that had more to do with the rum than anything else.

Mel smiled at him. "So long as Oz is having a good time, it's a win with me."

She watched Tate and Angie dancing, while Joyce and Uncle Stan were talking to Joe, who toasted her with his own coconut when their eyes met. She smiled. In a few months, she'd be Mrs. Joe DeLaura, so that was something.

Her gaze moved over to a few of their favorite regular customers; the rest of the DeLauras; Oz's family and his girlfriend, Lupe, who still dressed more like a skateboarder than a medical student. She was laughing at something Oz said, and she looked at him with such pride that Mel knew the change Oz was making wasn't just for himself but to prove to Lupe that he was a mature and responsible adult. A grown-up. He certainly looked the part with his short hair. When had he become a man? She sighed.

Marty narrowed his gaze at her. "You're not having a good time."

"I'm having a fine time," she protested. Marty continued to stare at her. "I'm just going to miss him, that's all."

Marty threw an arm around her and said, "The only

constant in life is change, and this is one the boy needs to make. He can't be tied to your apron strings forever."

"I don't want him tied . . . okay, that's a lie," she conceded. "I just don't see why he has to leave us . . . me."

"If you love someone, you have to set them free. If it's meant to be, he'll come back to you," Marty said.

"What did you do, memorize every sorry high school yearbook cliché?" Mel asked.

Marty grinned. "Just because they're corny doesn't mean they're not true. Buck up, kid. Everything is going to be all right, I promise."

With that, he gave her quick hug, kissed her on the forehead, and darted back into the party, where the DeLaura brothers were clearing out the patio to fire up an impromptu limbo competition.

"If he throws his back out, I am not carrying him into the emergency room," Oz said as he took the spot beside Mel vacated by Marty.

Mel turned to him and laughed, "Yes, you will, and you'll lecture him the whole time."

Oz grinned. "Yeah, I will."

They leaned against the half wall that enclosed the patio. Mel glanced up at their pink and aqua Fairy Tale Cupcake sign, done with mid-century modern atomic flair. What was going to happen to this place without Oz? She hadn't been able to even think about hiring a replacement, hoping that maybe he'd change his mind. As she glanced at him now, she knew there was no going back.

"So, are you ready for your first day at the Sun Dial Resort?" she asked.

"Absolutely," he said. "I've got my kitchen prepped just the way I like it and my crew is first rate."

"Good, that's good," Mel said.

They were quiet, watching Ray DeLaura try to go under the limbo stick lower than Dwight Pickard had under the amused and watchful eye of detective Tara Martinez, who had stunned Mel by hugging her today in a grip that almost felt sincere. Things really were changing.

"I'm really going to miss these idiots," Oz said.

Mel burst out laughing. It was true. Their people were idiots, but that was mostly what she loved about them. She glanced at Oz to see his return smile, but instead, he looked worried, terrified even.

"What if I fail? What if I hate it? What if I can't handle it? What if I'm not ready?" he asked. His voice was low and intense, and the words came out in rapid fire, as if the lid to his internal pressure cooker had just blown off.

Mel's eyes went wide. This. Right here. This was her Oz. The kid who had started working at the bakery while in high school and had begun skipping school just to be in the kitchen. She'd had to tough love him back to school, but he'd stayed employed at the bakery, graduated from culinary school, and continued on as her right-hand man, her sous chef, the best pastry chef she'd seen since her own days at culinary school.

"Dude," she said, keeping her voice light but firm. "You're not going to fail. That's an impossibility."

"You don't know that," he said. He turned to look at her, and Mel locked her gaze on his.

"Actually, yes, I do," she said. "You're one of the best and brightest, second to none except maybe me." She grinned and was relieved when he did, too. "Oz, you can go anywhere, work for anyone, and you will be a rock star."

He gave her the side eye.

"I'm not blowing sunshine up your cupcake, I swear," she said. She grabbed his upper arms and gave him a little shake. "You've got this."

His smile, when it came, was as divine as a perfect chocolate ganache. "Thanks, boss."

Mel hugged him close. She felt her throat get tight, but she pushed through it enough to say, "Just remember, no matter how far you roam, you can always come home."

Oz squeezed her. When he stepped back and walked away, he kept his head down, and she suspected he was trying to hide his own emotions, a much bigger challenge without the fringe of bangs he used to hide behind. Mel sniffed and dabbed her nose with a garish hibiscus party napkin.

"You okay, cupcake?"

She turned to find Joe closing in on her. When he slid his arm around her and pulled her close, she took comfort in his solid warmth. She glanced at Oz, who had somehow gotten muscled into the limbo contest. As he tried to maneuver his big body under the broomstick, she laughed. She glanced at the faces, near and dear, that surrounded them on the patio. The seasons of her life were filled with these faces.

And just like that, she remembered Rene's piece, the colors, the vibrancy, how it pulsed with life as it spun in its never-ending circle. The brilliance of her friend struck her anew.

She hugged Joe close and said, "I'm all right. It's just a new season, not a beginning or an ending. Just another season in the circle of life."

Joe smiled down at her. "In that case, you know what you have to do."

Jenn McKinlay

Mel stilled. "No, what?"

"Limbo!" Joe cried, and without giving her a chance to think about it, or refuse, he took her hand and dragged her out onto the dance floor, and Mel went gladly, because as losing Rene had taught her, life was meant to be lived.

Recipes

Pumpkin Spice Cupcakes

A pumpkin spice cupcake with a cinnamon
cream cheese frosting.

2 cups all-purpose flour
1 teaspoon baking soda
1 teaspoon baking powder
1 teaspoon coarse salt
1 teaspoon ground cinnamon
1 teaspoon ground ginger
¼ teaspoon ground nutmeg
1 cup packed light-brown sugar

1 cup granulated sugar
2 sticks unsalted butter, melted
4 large eggs, lightly beaten
1 can (15 ounces) pumpkin puree

Preheat the oven to 350 degrees. Line a cupcake pan with paper liners. In a medium bowl, whisk together the flour, baking soda, baking powder, salt, cinnamon, ginger, and nutmeg. In a large bowl, mix together the sugars, the butter, and the eggs. Add the dry ingredients, and mix until smooth. Lastly, mix in the pumpkin until thoroughly blended. Scoop the batter evenly into the cupcake liners. Bake 20 to 25 minutes, until a toothpick inserted in the center comes out clean. Let cool before frosting. Makes 24.

Cinnamon Cream Cheese Frosting

8 ounces cream cheese, softened
1 stick unsalted butter, softened
½ teaspoon vanilla extract
½ teaspoon cinnamon
3½ cups powdered sugar

Beat the cream cheese, butter, vanilla, and cinnamon in a large bowl until well blended. Gradually add the powdered sugar and beat until the frosting is smooth. Put the frosting in a pastry bag and pipe onto the cupcakes in thick swirls, using an open tip.

Coffee Mocha Cupcakes

A rich coffee cupcake with a mocha-flavored
buttercream.

2½ cups all-purpose flour
2 teaspoons baking soda
1 teaspoon baking powder
1 teaspoon salt
½ teaspoon cinnamon
¼ teaspoon nutmeg
3 tablespoons instant espresso powder
1½ cups granulated sugar
½ cup vegetable oil
¾ cup milk, room temperature
1 cup strong black coffee, room temperature
2 large eggs, room temperature
2 teaspoons vanilla extract

Preheat the oven to 350 degrees. Line a cupcake pan with
paper liners. In a medium bowl, whisk together the flour,
baking soda, baking powder, salt, cinnamon, nutmeg, espresso
powder, and sugar. In a large bowl, mix the oil, milk, coffee,
eggs, and vanilla. Slowly add the flour mixture to the coffee
mixture and beat on medium speed until smooth. Do not
overmix. Scoop the batter evenly into the cupcake liners.
Bake 25 to 30 minutes, until a toothpick inserted in the
center comes out clean. Let cool before frosting. Makes 24.

Mocha Buttercream Frosting

1 stick salted butter, softened
½ cup cream cheese, softened
1½ tablespoons instant espresso (powdered)
1 tablespoon unsweetened cocoa powder
2 teaspoons vanilla extract
4 cups powdered sugar
3 tablespoons milk
Chocolate-covered espresso beans, optional

In a medium-sized mixing bowl, beat the butter and cream cheese on high speed for three minutes, until light and fluffy. Mix in the instant espresso, cocoa, vanilla extract, powdered sugar, and milk until it reaches the desired consistency. Spread or pipe on the cooled cupcakes. Garnish with chocolate-covered espresso beans, if desired.

Root Beer Float Cupcakes

A root-beer-flavored cupcake with a vanilla buttercream.

2½ cups flour
2½ teaspoons baking powder
¼ teaspoon salt
¾ cup butter, softened
1½ cups sugar

3 large eggs
1½ teaspoons root beer extract
½ teaspoon vanilla extract
1 cup root beer

Preheat oven to 350 degrees. Line muffin tins with 24 paper liners. In a medium bowl, sift together the flour, baking powder, and salt. Set aside. In a large bowl, cream the butter and sugar at medium speed, add the eggs, and beat until smooth. Beat in the extracts. Alternately add the dry ingredients and the root beer, until just combined. Fill cupcake liners two-thirds full. Bake 25 to 30 minutes, until a toothpick inserted in the center comes out clean. Let cool before frosting. Makes 24.

Vanilla Buttercream Frosting

1 stick salted butter, softened
1 stick unsalted butter, softened
1½ teaspoons clear vanilla extract
4 cups sifted confectioners' sugar
2–3 tablespoons milk
Maraschino cherries, optional
Straws, optional

In a large bowl, cream the butter. Add the vanilla. Gradually add the sugar, one cup at a time, beating well on medium speed, and adding milk as needed. Scrape the sides of the bowl often. Beat at medium speed until light and fluffy. Keep the bowl covered with a damp cloth until the frosting is ready to use. Pipe onto the cooled cupcakes. Garnish with cherries and straws, if desired. Makes 3 cups of frosting.

Passion Fruit Cupcakes

A coconut cake filled with passion fruit mousse and
frosted with vanilla buttercream, drizzled with a
passion fruit puree.

3 cups flour
1 teaspoon baking powder
½ teaspoon baking soda
½ teaspoon salt
¾ pound (3 sticks) unsalted butter, room temperature
2 cups sugar
5 extra-large eggs, room temperature
1½ teaspoons vanilla extract
1½ teaspoons coconut extract
1 cup buttermilk
14 ounces sweetened, shredded coconut

Preheat the oven to 325 degrees. Line muffin tins with 24
paper liners. In a medium bowl, sift together the flour, baking powder, baking soda, and salt. In a larger bowl, cream
together the butter and sugar, adding the eggs one at a time.
Add the extracts. Alternately mix in the buttermilk and the
flour mixture, adding the coconut last. Fill the cupcake liners two-thirds full. Bake 25 to 35 minutes, until a toothpick
inserted in the center comes out clean. Let cool before frosting. Makes 24.

Passion Fruit Mousse

½ cup sweetened condensed milk
¼ cup passion fruit juice concentrate, room temperature
2 tablespoons heavy whipping cream

Whisk the liquid ingredients until they form a solid consistency. Use a melon baller to scoop out the middle of the cooled cupcakes, about halfway down. Pipe the mousse into the hole, and cover with just the top of the removed segment of the cupcake. Refrigerate the filled cupcakes to help the mousse set.

Vanilla Buttercream Frosting

1 stick salted butter, softened
1 stick unsalted butter, softened
1½ teaspoons clear vanilla extract
4 cups sifted confectioners' sugar
2–3 tablespoons milk
Passion fruit puree, optional; can be purchased or made at home

In a large bowl, cream the butter. Add the vanilla. Gradually add the sugar, one cup at a time, beating well on medium speed and adding milk as needed. Scrape the sides of the bowl often. Continue beating until light and fluffy. Keep the bowl covered with a damp cloth until ready to use. Pipe the frosting onto the cooled cupcakes. Drizzle the passion fruit puree on top, if desired. Store the cupcakes in an airtight container in the refrigerator, and take out 15–20 minutes before serving. Makes 3 cups of frosting.

Turn the page to read the first chapter of

ONE FOR THE BOOKS

Jenn McKinlay's new Library Lover's Mystery
coming in Fall 2020.

"Why is everyone staring at us?" Lindsey Norris asked her fiancé, Mike Sullivan, known to everyone in their small Connecticut shoreline town as Sully.

"Are they staring at us?" He looked up from his phone where he was scanning the news, which for him meant the current sports scores, and glanced around the shop.

"Yes," she confirmed. "And it's kind of creepy."

Having slept late that morning, they were in line at the bakery, which was tucked into the back corner of the town's lone grocery store. Their dog, Heathcliff, was sitting between their feet and behaving like a perfect gentleman, so Lindsey was certain he wasn't the one drawing the attention of every other customer in the bakery their way.

"You're right," he said. "They are staring."

"But why?" she asked. She gave each of their persons a quick visual scan. They were both dressed with buttons aligned and zippers up and clothes right side out. There were no spectacular bedhead or egregious stains to be seen. Having been the focus of unwanted attention a few months before, Lindsey still felt the odd twinge of anxiety when stared at.

Sully put his arm around her in a comforting gesture and pulled her close, kissing the top of her head. "Wild guess here, but I imagine it's because we're getting married in a couple of weeks."

"Yes, but it's a tiny ceremony on Bell Island," she pointed out. "Just family and close friends, hardly an event worth noting."

"People like weddings." He shrugged.

"Sully, Lindsey, yoo-hoo!" a voice called, and Lindsey glanced past Sully to see Mrs. Housel, coming at them as fast as her short legs could carry her. Heathcliff hopped to his feet and began wagging his bushy black tail, looking for love from anyone willing to give it.

"Morning, Mrs. H," Sully said. "What can we do for you?"

"I just need to know where you're registered," she said. She was breathless but still bent over to pat Heathcliff on the head before rising back up to smile at them.

"Registered?" Lindsey asked.

"Yes, you know, for a wedding gift," she explained. "I can't possibly show up at your wedding without a gift. It would be bad form."

"Uh." Lindsey glanced at Sully in a mild state of panic.

Mrs. Housel was one of Lindsey's favorite patrons. They had bonded over a deep and abiding love of all things Agatha

Christie. A tiny little bird of a thing, Mrs. Housel was the sweetest of the sweet. She lived on a fixed income in a modest cottage in the old part of town. Telling her the wedding was private and that she wasn't invited would be like punting a puppy into oncoming traffic. Everything inside of Lindsey rebelled at the mere idea. Judging by the flicker of alarm in Sully's eyes, he was thinking the same thing.

"Mrs. H, Lindsey and I really appreciate the thought," he began, and then he stalled out. Sully's heart was as big as one of the tour boats he captained around the Thumb Islands in the bay, and Lindsey knew he was struggling to find the right words. She immediately decided having one more guest wasn't going to be a problem, especially one as tiny as Mrs. Housel.

"We haven't registered anywhere," Lindsey said. "In fact, we're asking anyone who attends our wedding to donate a book to the library instead of giving us gifts." This much was true, at least.

Mrs. Housel clasped her hands over her heart. "How wonderful. I just love you two. You're like family to me."

"And we love you, Mrs. H," Sully said. He looked oh so relieved.

Mrs. Housel reached forward and squeezed their hands with hers. Then, with a wave, she fluttered out of the bakery as quickly as she'd arrived.

"That was nice of you, darlin'," Sully said.

Lindsey shrugged. "What's one more guest when it clearly means a lot to her? Besides, she's so tiny. How much could she possibly eat?"

"Yeah, it's like inviting a hummingbird to the wedding," he agreed.

Lindsey smiled, then tipped her head back to meet his

gaze. He was wearing his thick wool peacoat, a knit hat over his reddish brown curls, and a blue scarf Lindsey had knit him last winter that matched his eyes perfectly. His cheeks were ruddy from the cold, making his bright blue eyes even more so. Lindsey felt her heart squeeze. He was going to be her husband in just a matter of weeks.

The thought never ceased to make her dizzy. She knew it was silly, that some would say marriage was just a piece of paper, but it felt like more to her. Much more. She was committing to spending her life with this man, a commitment she didn't take lightly, and she found the thought positively thrilling.

"What are you grinning at?" he asked. A smile played on his lips, bracketed by deep dimples in each cheek.

"We're getting married," she whispered, as if she was giving him brand new information.

"Well, I, for one, can't wait," he said. "Mrs. Mike Sullivan has a nice ring to it."

"As does Mr. Lindsey Norris," she retorted.

"It does at that." He grinned and kissed her quick before gently moving her up the line.

Brendan Taggert was working the counter. He grinned at the sight of them. "There's the bride and groom! Not much longer now, eh?"

Brendan was a big man in his midthirties. He was the chief baker who occasionally came out of the kitchen to lend a hand when the bakery was especially busy. He gave them each a large coffee in a thick paper to-go cup and pushed a bag of muffins at Lindsey while Sully paid. She glanced inside to find their usual, a lemon poppy seed for Sully and a cranberry walnut for her. The morning was looking up.

"Your wedding cake is going to be a thing of beauty," Brendan declared.

"Since you're baking it, I have no doubt," she said.

"I'm just a little worried though." Brendan rubbed his jaw with the back of his hand.

"Oh?" Lindsey tried to keep the panic out of her voice, but two weeks before a wedding a woman did not want to hear her cake baker expressing doubts. She knew she'd failed when Sully gave her shoulder a reassuring squeeze.

"Yeah, I don't think you ordered a big enough cake," Brendan said. "I hear people talking in the bakery all day long, and it sounds as if a lot of folks are planning to attend your big day."

Lindsey and Sully exchanged confused looks. Was Mrs. Housel not the only one planning to crash the wedding?

"But we're keeping it small," Sully said. "Just family and close friends." He frowned, clearly not understanding how it could be spiraling out of their control.

"I don't know what to tell you." Brendan shrugged. "You're the town boat captain, a native son no less, and she's the library director. Everyone knows you two, and they're very invested in your romance. Whether you invited them or not, people are planning to attend. You're going to want a bigger cake. I'm just sayin'." Brendan raised his hands as if to signal that he'd done his part in warning them.

Lindsey felt her heart pound hard in her chest. Surely he was overstating it. People didn't crash weddings en masse, did they? Then she thought of Mrs. Housel and her determination to be at their wedding, declaring that they were like family to her. How many other Briar Creek and Thumb Island residents felt that way? Oh, no.

*　　*　　*

A puppy—not Heathcliff, who'd gone to work with Sully—romped past the circulation desk where Lindsey Norris stood. White with floppy ears and a stubby tail, it had a coat covered in bright colored spots of purple, green, yellow and all the other colors in the rainbow.

It was a big puppy, more like the size of a small horse. Lindsey squinted at it. Sure enough, a closer look identified the canine as being the Briar Creek Public Library's children's librarian, Beth Barker, wearing what looked like adult-sized footed pajamas that she'd tailored to look like a dog by adding ears to the hood, a tail to the bottom, and spots all over.

"Reading *Dog's Colorful Day* today?" Lindsey asked.

"Woof!" Beth barked. "Colors and counting, does it get any more fun?"

"It does not," Lindsey agreed. "Unless it's crafternoon Thursday and we're discussing *A Christmas Carol* by Dickens."

Beth stopped romping and her eyes sparkled. A thick thatch of black bangs stuck out from under her hood, giving her delicate features a mischievous air.

"Do you think Nancy made cookies?" she asked. She hugged her belly, where her new status as a mom-to-be was just beginning to show. "She's in charge of food this week, and baby and I are craving some of her Scottish shortbread."

"No." Lindsey shook her head, knowing full well that Nancy, who was her former landlord and a good friend, had surely made some. Then she teased, "But I'll bet she made you some dog biscuits."

"Woof woof, so funny," Beth retorted. Then she looked thoughtful and scratched one of her dog ears. "Actually, if Nancy made them, they're probably pretty good."

"Fair point." Nancy was their local amateur baker extraordinaire and was known all over Briar Creek for her magical cookies.

"Whatever she brings, save some for me. I'm eating for two!" Beth cried as she scampered off to the story time room in anticipation of the toddlers who would begin arriving in the next thirty minutes.

Petite in build and swallowed up by her slouchy dog outfit, Beth looked like a kid herself. Lindsey smiled. The town was very fortunate to have such dedicated librarian. Beth's programs packed the house, making a delightful connection with the next generation of enthusiastic readers.

"Well, that should be quite a fun story time."

Lindsey turned to find Ms. Cole, nicknamed "the lemon" for her frequently sour disposition and old-school librarian ways, standing beside her.

Lindsey blinked. "Are you feeling all right, Ms. Cole?"

Today Ms. Cole was in her purple outfit. Purple tights with a dark purple wool skirt matched, sort of, with a twilight-hued purple cardigan and a lavender silk top. It gave her an overall ombré effect that was actually rather appealing. Ms. Cole favored outfits that fell distinctly into one category on the color spectrum, so apple green was worn with chartreuse and forest green as if they all matched. They didn't. In fact, none of her outfits really matched, but neither Lindsey nor any of the other staff had the heart or nerve to tell her so.

"Yes, I'm fine. I'm trying to be less rigid," Ms. Cole said. She glanced at Lindsey over the tops of her reading glasses. "How am I doing?"

"Well, you didn't shush her," Lindsey said. "I'd call that a big improvement."

"I haven't shushed anyone in months," Ms. Cole said. She sounded forlorn. "My shusher has probably atrophied, but Milton told me that if I'm serious about running for mayor, I might want to be friendlier to my constituents."

Milton Duffy, town historian and president of the library board, was Ms. Cole's significant other. Ms. Cole had squashed any use of the word boyfriend, saying it sounded ridiculous to call a man in his eighties a boy, and she wouldn't tolerate being called his girlfriend either.

"He didn't tell you to smile more often, did he?" Lindsey teased. "Because that would be annoying."

Ms. Cole laughed, which was a rare occurrence, and it made Lindsey smile. "No, he didn't. He did say I need to start attending all of the town events so that I become more well known. I'm even going to the Briggs's Annual Christmas Bash this weekend."

"You are?" Lindsey could not have been more surprised if Ms. Cole had said she'd taken up exotic dancing for fitness.

"Yes." Ms. Cole sighed. "I've lived in Briar Creek my entire life and I have never attended one of the famed Briggs Bashes. I thought I'd be shuffling off this mortal coil with my streak intact, but politics make strange bedfellows, as they say."

It was a wise political move. Steve Briggs was a corporate attorney and one of the wealthier residents of Briar Creek, and he was also the local justice of the peace. Ms. Cole needed to have his endorsement if she was to stand a chance against the incumbent Mayor Hensen.

"Steve's not so bad," Lindsey said. "A little over the top in his enthusiasm for his parties, but during the holidays that's not such a bad thing."

The Briggses threw a holiday extravaganza every year. Lindsey and Sully always made an appearance because Sully and Steve had grown up together in Briar Creek and were, if not quite friends, then very warm acquaintances. While the parties were fun, Lindsey and Sully never lingered. Being an introvert at heart, Lindsey had a two-hour window for the overcrowded, loud, sensory overload that was a Briggs party, and Sully was right there with her. If ever she needed proof that they were soul mates, that was it.

"Isn't he officiating your wedding ceremony in a few weeks?" Paula Turner, the library clerk, asked. She was working at the station on the other side of Ms. Cole, checking in the books from the book drop.

"Yes," Lindsey said. "Since we're getting married on Bell Island where Sully grew up and not in a church, we thought he'd be the perfect choice."

The coastal town of Briar Creek overlooked an archipelago of islands called the Thumb Islands, which had sported the summer homes of some of America's richest families during the height of the Gilded Age. A hurricane in nineteen-thirty-eight had all but wiped out the old Victorian mansions that had once dominated the islands, and now the residences were smaller and more sustainable, mostly used as summer cottages, with only a few islands—like Sully's parents' Bell Island—equipped with electricity to make them habitable year round.

Paula glanced at the calendar on the desk. "The wedding is in two weeks. Are you ready, Lindsey?"

Lindsey blinked at her. Why was it so jarring when someone else told her the wedding was two weeks away? It wasn't as if she wasn't aware. It just felt more significant when someone else said it. Her heart thumped hard in her chest but she refused to freak out. This was why she and Sully had decided on the island. They wanted to keep their wedding small and simple for friends and family only, in a lovely ceremony in a heated tent on the communal lawn in the center of the island.

"You look odd," Ms. Cole said. "Maybe you should sit down."

"Oh, no, I'm fine," Lindsey reassured them. She went to wave Ms. Cole's concern away and noticed that her hand was shaking.

"Uh-huh." Ms. Cole glanced from Lindsey's hand to her face and frowned. "Sit."

"I'll get you a glass of water," Paula said. She slipped off her stool, moving it close so Lindsey could sit, before going into the workroom, where there was a water cooler.

"You're not getting cold feet, are you?" Ms. Cole asked.

"Uh . . . I . . ." Lindsey stammered.

"Cold feet? Who's getting cold feet?" Nancy Peyton and Violet LaRue appeared at the circulation counter.

They were carrying bags of food for the lunchtime crafternoon that met every Thursday at midday. Both women were wearing winter coats, hats, and scarves, as the weather had turned decidedly wintery over the past few days, and the temperature had plummeted.

"With this freeze snap, it's small wonder your feet are cold," Violet said.

"I think that was a metaphor," Nancy returned. Her bright blue eyes were filled with concern.

"Oh," Violet said. A former Broadway actress, she could convey more in one word than most people could in a whole sentence. She studied Lindsey. "You don't look well, dear."

"I'm fine," Lindsey protested.

"No, she isn't. She's freaking out," Paula said. She handed Lindsey the water. They all stared at her as she took a sip.

"I'm not, really," Lindsey said on a swallow. The water went down hard. "It's just that the wedding is coming up so fast—"

"Isn't it thrilling?" Mrs. Cleeves, a patron, paused beside the desk on her way out. "Well, speaking for me and my quilting circle, we can't wait. Our group has made you a special surprise. Goodness knows, you've given us plenty of time. It feels as if I've been waiting for you and Sully to tie the knot for years. And is there anything more romantic than a winter wedding? Maybe we'll get lucky and it will snow."

"Uh . . ." Lindsey's eyes went wide as Mrs. Cleeves waved the Nova Scotia quilting pattern book she'd just checked out as she strode to the door.

"I thought you said this was going to be a small friends-and-family-only wedding," Nancy said.

"It is," Lindsey said.

"Really?" Violet asked. "I didn't think you were that close to Mrs. Cleeves and her quilting circle."

"I'm not," she said. "I mean, I enjoy them all, but we're not best pals or anything."

"Well, you'd better make room for a few more at your wedding reception, because it sounds like they're planning on being there," Ms. Cole said.

"Oh, man." Lindsey rubbed her temples with her fingers.

"Look on the bright side, maybe they made you a nice quilt," Paula said.

Lindsey tried to smile, but given Brendan's warning about her cake being too small, Mrs. Housel's inquiry as to their registry, and now Mrs. Cleeves's announcement that her quilting circle was coming, she couldn't help but think that something had gone horribly wrong.

"You all received invitations, correct?" she asked.

They all glanced at each other and then nodded.

"They were really beautiful, too," Paula said. "I especially liked the calligraphy."

"The woman at the stationary store specialized in that," Lindsey said. "And I had her mail the invitations for us."

Ms. Cole frowned. "There was no RSVP card included."

"Since we invited so few people," Lindsey said. "We knew we'd get verbal confirmations from everyone and we have."

They were all silent, trying to puzzle out what could have happened to cause Lindsey's guest list to expand without her knowing.

"When you made your guest list, did you start with a big number and then cut it down?" Nancy asked.

"Yes," Lindsey said. "We originally had over a hundred people on the list, but the island is so small, we decided to keep it just family and close friends."

Violet gave her a shrewd glance. "Is there any chance you gave the stationer the wrong list?"

A cold knot of dread tightened inside Lindsey's chest. She stood and swayed on her feet. Given how crazy things had been at the time she'd hired the stationer, it was more than likely that she had given her the wrong list.

Suddenly her intimate wedding for thirty-five was now

looking like it would be for three times that many. She thought she might be sick. She didn't even know if they could fit that many people on Bell Island. She glanced around at her friends in panic.

"What am I going to do?" she asked.